THE

Last Knight
of Albion

THE

Last Knight
of Albion

Peter Hanratty

BLUEJAY BOOKS
NEW YORK

This book is printed on acid-free paper. The paper in this book meets the guidelines for permanence and durability of the Committee on Production Guidelines for Book Longevity of the Council on Library Resources.

ISBN: 0-312-94210-9

1

It had been raining continuously since early morning. Now it was late afternoon, but the steady unremitting downpour showed no sign of abating. The knight was not greatly concerned for himself, but he was worried for the damosel who, sitting before him silent and uncomplaining, was almost certainly soaking wet beneath her thin garments.

"I hope we may reach there before dark," he ventured.

She did not turn her head. "We are almost there."

It had been a dismal enough journey, even without the rain. In the time they had spent together since her rescue from the ogre, she had volunteered little and had responded to his own attempts at conversation with ill-concealed reluctance.

He understood her reticence well enough. She had already undergone a trying experience. Now she must make the long journey home in the company of a dubious stranger, a disheveled and aging knight whose speech was no fairer than his appearance.

He understood, but it was disappointing nonetheless. Over the years he had succored many in the bleak and forsaken place they had left behind them:

1

traveling merchants who had strayed from their path, the occasional peasant whose curiosity about the region and its fabled denizens had overcome his good sense. But he had never rescued a damosel.

As he had led her from the place where the ogre and he had fought their short, desperate battle, he had introduced himself.

"My name is Percevale, knight of the Round Table of King Arthur."

She had expressed no surprise. Then, as if sensing an obligation to reply, she said, "I am Elaine, daughter of Robert the Physician and his wife, Anne. I am much beholden to you, for he would most certainly have raped and afterward killed me had you not arrived."

Now, there was a word that in his day few decent ladies would have dared utter in mixed company. But recent times had seen stranger things and he gave the matter little thought. As he lifted her onto his horse he noticed her glance back at the pathetic creature lying on its crooked back, a gaping hole in its throat where the lance had pierced, true and quick. She had shuddered briefly and turned away. If her words had jarred his expectancies a little, her gratitude, at least, was sincere.

And that, he reflected, was what he was in it for.

In every other respect she seemed all that a damosel should be. She was comely, with fine dark hair flowing evenly over her shoulders, and young—but a little over twenty, he guessed, though he was an unpracticed judge of such matters. She was also light, and as the destrier would have to bear them both, this was indeed important.

Her home, she had told him, lay some two days' ride to the southwest.

"How came you to be so far away?" he inquired gently. "This is no place for gentlefolk."

There was a pause before she replied. "I was with my betrothed."

"And where is he?"

"He is dead. At the hands of the ogre. Long ere you arrived."

Whether this was intended as a reproach or an exoneration he could not tell. He wondered what the ogre had done with the young man's body. Whatever had happened, she had undoubtedly seen it and he was thankful that her father was a physician.

Several times he had tried to make conversation, for he wished to lighten her spirits, and pleasant discourse was a diversion sorely lacking in this bleak and inhospitable region.

"Are you quite comfortable?"

"Thank you, yes."

"Do not worry about the destrier. He is a strong horse and will bear the two of us easily."

"Good."

"The weather has been poor of late for June. Perhaps it will improve now."

"Perhaps."

That first evening, after the knight had erected his faded pavilion, they had sat outside and supped biscuits and honey, watching the sun go down on the silent, unchanging landscape.

"I cannot risk a fire," he said.

Afterward she had retired within the pavilion and he had found a nearby rock, and after carefully checking that nothing unwholesome or dangerous resided there, he made himself as comfortable as he could in one of its narrow clefts.

When morning came, he had awoken cold and stiff-limbed, for he was no longer of an age where he could treat discomfort lightly. When the damosel was risen and dressed, he entered the pavilion and prepared a simple breakfast.

Then it had started to rain.

For most of the morning they had sheltered in the cramped and dark pavilion and he had gazed out upon the discouraging view, searching hopefully for signs of a break in the sweep of gray.

"We may not stay here," he had said eventually. "News of our presence and of our doings here will surely spread. It would be folly to remain."

She had nodded pliantly, rising from the bed. Removing his wolfskin cloak from the sack which held his helm and his spare suit of mail, he made to put it around her shoulders. She stepped back quickly, saying, "Thank you, but that is your cloak. My own garments will be protection enough."

"Nonsense," he replied. "You will be soaked through in minutes. You'll catch your death out there."

She shook her head and for a moment he was nonplussed, quite taken aback by her unmaidenlike refusal. "Please," he had entreated.

"It is your cloak," she said. "You need it to protect your armor."

"I cannot in honor wear it," he replied, quite confused, "in the circumstances."

"No more can I." Her dark eyes had flashed briefly then, as if daring him to remonstrate further. Some rain had penetrated the thin canvas of the pavilion, plastering her hair to the sides of her face, lending it a harsh and angular appearance. He did not argue further.

Nor would she permit them to stay until the rain abated, and so together and in silence they had dismantled the pavilion and secured the knight's equipment to the back of the sumpter horse.

Several times during that day he had repeated his entreaty, but she had been resolute.

"I do not need your cloak. My garments are quite adequate."

"This is silly," he said. "That we should both suffer thus, it is absurd."

She shook her head and for a moment he had thought of wearing the cloak anyway. If he did not, his mail would surely rust. But he left it where it was.

Damn Chivalry, he thought.

But at last the worst of their journey was over. They had left the wasteland and were riding through a healthy green wood with an extensive clearing on either side of the narrow track—a reliable indicator that civilization was not very far away. He was pleased, too, for the overhanging branches would afford at least some protection from the rain.

"Is it far now?" He did not wish to spend another night in the open.

"This pathway will lead us home," she replied.

Even so, many hours passed during which they met no other travelers, the silence between them attended by the sound of the horses' hooves plodding thickly through the mire and the steady dropping of the rain as it filtered through the sodden branches above.

Dusk was beginning to fall when they finally reached the edge of the wood. Here their own road joined a wider, busier one.

"Turn right here," she said.

The road dipped gently downward. Below, in a large valley, were fields, arranged not in the familiar medley of open strips but in regular patterns of squares and rectangles and each separated from its neighbor by hedges or rows of trees. By the side of the road was a scattering of peasants' huts wreathed in a haze of smoke.

And there was a town. It was of some considerable size and surrounded by a wooden palisade.

"You live here?" he asked.

"Yes."

Percevale was surprised. He had traveled much throughout the country and passed through many settlements that called themselves towns. Most were

mere collections of clay and wattle huts. Here below
him were cobbled streets, a market square with a
patchwork of colored awnings. He could see timber-
framed buildings, solidly built and pleasingly proportioned. Each had several windows and a roof of gray
thatch and many were at least two stories high.

He was impressed; also a little disturbed. "I have
not seen the like of this before," he muttered to himself.

This was not wholly true. Many years before, as a
young squire with the Italian expedition he had marveled at the beautiful towns that dotted the Lom-
bardy plain. These buildings were far simpler in
conception with nothing of the studied elegance of
the Latins. Nevertheless they were far superior to
anything he had seen in Albion since the war.

It was a busy road they had joined. They passed
carts and wagons whose occupants stared at them
with a frank and surly curiosity, making no sign in
reply to Percevale's polite nods, so that eventually he
stopped bothering.

They passed close by some of the huts. At last it
had stopped raining, but there was a heaviness in the
air still, and the smoke from the feeble fires within
would not rise but lay like a dismal shroud, stinging
his nostrils and irritating the horses.

From one of the huts a woman emerged. She was
dressed in faded garments of indeterminate shades of
brown on which she was carefully wiping her hands.
On seeing the knight and his passenger she put her
hand to her mouth to stifle a little scream, then ran
back inside.

Some of us, I know, were a bad lot in those days,
thought Percevale dejectedly, but it is a sad thing
when even a middle-aged peasant woman must take
to her heels on seeing an armored knight.

He came to the gateway and halted.

Closer, it was not such a grand place. The palisade,
though tall, was flimsy and much of the wood was

rotten. The gate was open and unattended—there would have been little point in closing it, for its hinges were rusted and there were holes which had been indifferently patched. Before him there stretched a wide cobbled street with fine elegant buildings on either side. But the streets that led off from it were narrow and dark, their cramped buildings hidden from the sun.

He turned his attention to the girl. She sat before him in stiff silent profile, her eyes turned steadfastly to the ground. In the brief glance she returned he thought he discerned some faint trace of apprehension, even importunacy. It had already occurred to him that her story might not be wholly true, that her parents' pleasure at her safe return might not be unalloyed.

He hastily formulated some words of comfort.

"It is rarely that I come thus much into your world. My anxiety is possibly as great as yours though it be of a different kind."

There was no reply. The look he had seen or fancied had vanished, and what, if anything, that slight shifting movement behind him betokened he could not tell. Gently he urged the horse through the gateway.

2

Faces peered at them from windows and people in the street slowed their progress and watched. Percevale tried to compose his features into an expression of polite regard but could discern little sign of welcome in the glances, often furtive, that were directed at him.

It was different with the children, he noticed. For them this was a magical sight, the knight on his tall gray warhorse emerging out of the fading light. With bemused awe, their boisterous street games quite forgotten, they gaped and pointed at the damosel, her face downcast and shrouded by a curtain of hair, at the knight's mail coat, glistening palely, at his green surcoat and the white gryphon segreant that stood fiercely at its center with long curling tongue and claws poised to strike. And when Percevale had passed, they followed at a respectful distance, whispering and passing comment among themselves.

They came to the house she had indicated and halted.

Someone must have already told the parents of her arrival, for they were standing in the doorway, the woman tall and erect, the man small and round-shouldered and wearing the absurd felt cap of his profession. Like the crowd that had gathered, they watched in silence as Percevale first dismounted, then lifted down the girl. Some of the bolder children, eager to confirm that this was indeed no illusion, moved cautiously nearer, and Percevale, in an effort to be friendly, attempted to pat the nearest on the head. But the years of isolation had tended to blur within him the distinction between a friendly gesture, for which he had little use these days, and a menacing one. At the sight of the descending gloved hand and the caricature of a smile, the children scurried back to the safety of the crowd.

The parents came forward and Elaine went to meet them. Sensing immediately the coldness in her mother's bearing, she clasped her father's hands and lowered her head in a simple gesture of penitence.

"Father, Mother, I am sincerely contrite."

"Not here, my love," said her father. He looked about him. "Not that the neighbors haven't enough to talk about." Gently he squeezed her hand in his. "Go indoors with your mother. We can talk when you have rested." Turning to Percevale, he said, "You are welcome, sir. My name is Robert and this is my wife, Anne."

The woman picked up a corner of her daughter's clothing. "You're soaking wet, child!" she exclaimed, and darted a brief look at Percevale before sweeping the girl indoors.

"I am Sir Percevale, late of the Round Table."

The physician raised his eyebrows. "*The* Round Table? King Arthur's Round Table?"

"I have heard of no others."

"Well," said Robert, visibly impressed, "I am bounden to you for bringing back my daughter. We had almost given up hope of seeing her again."

There was a further, overriding reason for Percevale's

presence, but explanation of it, he decided, could wait.

The crowd, deprived of the scandal it had expected, was gradually dispersing. Only a few stubborn children remained, gazing with frank admiration at the great shield that hung from one side of the sumpter horse. It was so battered and dented that its device was barely recognizable. The knight's thick lance of ash was bound vertically to the horse's other flank, and this, too, they admired.

"We have no lad at present, but I will gladly stable your horses for you if you would care to wait inside the house."

Percevale thanked him and entered. To the right of the hallway a partly curtained doorway led into the surgery, a remarkably well-equipped one, he observed. Turning left, he entered a larger room, elegantly furnished and with a sizable hearth. Percevale, standing in its center in his knightly raiment, felt uncomfortable and out of place.

At length his host returned. "I am sorry about the less than fulsome welcome," he said. "We are untrustworthy folk hereabouts."

"I think I frightened some of them. I did not mean to."

"The children? Not to worry. They think that you are something out of a fairy tale, I suppose. We have not seen one of your kind for I don't know how long."

"There aren't many of us left," said Percevale.

"That is a fine charger," said Robert. "Strong yet docile. Has it a name?"

"The destrier? He is called Fleet. He has been with me these last two years."

"Ah." Robert paused. Although usually he had little time for matters of etiquette, preferring to be uniformly courteous to all, he found himself wishing that he knew of the correct way to address a knight. The man's stature and bearing seemed to demand something more dignified than the usual trite conventionalities. "There was a young man with my daughter? . . ."

"He is dead, I am afraid. Killed and presumably eaten by an ogre."

"You mean a mutant? How horrible. They went as far as that?"

"I found your daughter some two days' ride from here. The young man, has he kinfolk who should be informed?"

"No, no," said Robert. "He was just our stable lad and my daughter is at an awkward age. You know the sort of thing."

Percevale did not and frowned slightly. Reading the look, Robert hurried to dispel the suspicions that lay behind it.

"I am simply glad that she is back. That is all I care about, frankly. I have had little cause to think well of Ralph these last few days. No," he added, "that is wrong, isn't it, to malign the dead simply through fear of scandal." He shook his head and sighed. "The gods know he was a wayward lad and a malcontent, but then, Elaine is a headstrong girl. I should not like to say who was leading whom in this foolish venture of theirs. I don't suppose she said anything to you of her reasons for running away?"

"They were not betrothed?"

"Certainly not. Did she tell you that? Now I wonder why she should say that."

"I do not know."

"And you say she fell into the hands of one of those poor creatures out there. I always thought they were harmless."

"Some are more vicious than others," Percevale said. "At any rate, she was quite unharmed, though the experience does seem to have affected her somewhat. Her manner these last few days has been vague and distracted."

"Shock, I expect. She'll get over it. She's tough, that one. Like her mother. How remiss of me," he suddenly exclaimed. "I rarely drink myself before dinner, but I should nevertheless have offered you some refreshment. Will you take some mead?"

"Thank you. It has been a long and thirsty journey. How is your daughter?" This last remark was addressed to the mother, who had just entered the room.

She was a tall woman. Taller and years younger, it seemed, than her husband. He knew it to be an ungenerous thought and none of his business anyway, but they seemed an ill-matched pair. The typically bourgeois physician with balding head and myopic-looking eyes which seemed capable of encompassing only passing concerns, and the wife, straight-backed and strong-featured. Her chin firm and assertive, her mouth set. She looked like one who cared little for the world or its opinions. I do not think, thought Percevale, that a scandal in the household would greatly concern her. He should, he knew, feel some affinity toward such a woman. Strangely, he felt only a dawning unease.

Eventually she answered him. "Well enough considering, though tired. Robert, I think you should examine her."

"I will, my dear, but let her sleep first."

"How long is it since you found her, Sir Knight?"

"Two days, lady."

"I see," she said, and, turning, returned soundlessly from whence she came.

Percevale took the proffered cup and drained it with almost impolite haste. He took a more leisurely look about the room. On the wall opposite the street there hung a large and beautifully wrought tapestry. He gazed in admiration at it for a few moments. It depicted the hunting and killing of a stag by brachets. Around the scene of the kill were several horsemen. They rode mounts much smaller than themselves and were seated in stiff, self-congratulatory poses, some with weapons still poised. Many of them wore insignia, but the tapestry was old and faded and such details were no longer discernible. Such tapestries, he reflected, had graced the old court, though only the best were as rich and fine as this. For old though it was, and commonplace the theme, it still excited his admiration and it puzzled him how such a work came to be in the house of a leech.

With a start he realized that his host was talking to him. "I'm sorry?"

"I was saying that the least I can do to repay your services is to offer you food and shelter until such time as you wish to resume your travels. You will accept this, I hope?"

Percevale smiled. "Most people offer me money," he began.

"I'm sorry, I did not think you'd accept. After all—"

"You mistake me. I am pleased that you do not offer money. There are few opportunities for spending it out there."

The physician nodded. "But there are times, surely, when you need money. Your equipment, for instance."

"I have learned to look after it myself. My shield, for example—" He checked himself. This man did not want to know all the details. "Then again, there are others who likewise have no need of money and are pleased to do or return a favor. However, as you say, there are times"—again the wry smile—"when it is advisable to temper principles with pragmatism."

Robert's face visibly relaxed. He suddenly felt more easy in his own home as his guest diminished in stature to something more approaching human proportions.

"Have some more," he said, "and stay tonight and eat with us."

Percevale gladly accepted both offers. Though he had grown unused to the comforts of human society, he was not above enjoying them and the last few days had been uncomfortable ones indeed.

He turned again to the faded tapestry. "Here is fine workmanship indeed," he said.

"Yes," replied Robert. "It is from the old court of Cornwall, or so I was told by the fellow who sold it to me. In the years immediately after the war such things were cheap and easy to come by. It is only of late that their true value has once again been appreciated. I have other pieces," he added a little hesitantly, as if fearful lest his guest mistake his harmless interest for ghoulish curiosity, "which you might like to see sometime."

Percevale nodded politely.

"I have always been interested in that sort of thing. We named Elaine after Galahad's mother, you know."

"Lancelot's first wife, yes." Percevale could not help the brief frown.

"I don't suppose you ever—?"

"It was before my time."

"Ah." The physician gazed thoughtfully into his cup before looking up again. "My wife was against it but I like the name. People had such good names then—they carried resonance."

There were some good people too, thought Percevale.

"And what about now; do you serve one of the new courts?" The phrasing was deliberate. In the first place, it was unlikely—the knight was too far south to belong to one of the quarrelsome and constantly shifting kingdoms of the north. In the second place, if he did, then it promised danger for the whole locality. The bands of venal, swaggering robbers who styled themselves knights and their hapless territories kingdoms were but shadows of their namesakes of old. Nevertheless, as the only armed and organized groups of significant size at that time, their existence posed a formidable threat to the scattered and fiercely insular communities of the south. Should one such group choose to move in their direction, the consequences would be disastrous.

"I am a knight of the Round Table," Percevale said stiffly.

The mead had made Robert bold. "Yes," he persisted warily, "so you have said. But that must be a lonely occupation these days. I thought that perhaps—"

"There are no courts worthy of the name. I travel alone."

His host seemed pleased with the reply. "I am sorry, I did not wish to cause offense." He turned to the open window which looked out onto the street. "Go away, Walter." He gestured impatiently at the anxious face that had thought itself hidden there. The face remained for a second longer, until Percevale turned his head, then it vanished.

"Who was that?"

"One of our town councillors. You must pardon his rustic's lack of decorum. He's a good enough fellow. I think he was worried about what your presence might signify."

Percevale was about to tell him, when a servant appeared and announced that the table was prepared. He found himself ushered into an adjoining room as large as the first and dominated by an oak table, which stood at the center.

Percevale was introduced to the rest of the family, who were standing around the table while the servant laid out the last of the trays. To each in turn he nodded: the mother, the son, and a younger daughter whose pleasant features bore little resemblance to those of the still-sleeping Elaine. She appraised him with an affected modesty. Strangers were uncommon in her father's house, and she wished to make a good impression. The son, a pale young man whose face was liberally sprinkled with freckles and whose name Percevale had already forgotten, was more frankly curious.

"I have read much about King Arthur and his times," he said as they sat down, "though the accounts differ greatly."

"You have books here?" Percevale asked.

"Only what I am able to pick up on my small wanderings," Robert interrupted. "Nonetheless, it is quite a respectable library you have now, is it not?"

"Father thinks I read too much," the young man confided. As he leaned forward, his thin, wispy beard lightly skimmed the top of his soup bowl. "Tell me," he said earnestly, "was it a golden age, as some men say, or a time of misery and oppression for the majority?"

"Simon," his father interposed irritably, "this is not the time."

"People here," the young man continued, "do not care about such things. They try to forget the past, or worse still, misprize what it may teach us. But I think it is important, do you not agree?"

Percevale did.

"But there are things which puzzle me. One writer tells me how Arthur loved his subjects and cared for them. Another will censure him for his callous disregard of the needs of the poor and helpless."

"It all rather depends upon whose side the author was on, does it not?" Percevale replied. He knew he should feel grateful for the youth's eager, almost desperate curiosity. Few people these days were interested, and of course he was proud to have been a part of that stirring epoch. Why then did these questions leave him with a vague feeling of discomfort?

"Ah." His interrogator sat back and stroked his beard energetically for a few moments before he resumed eating. He was clearly less than satisfied.

"That's enough, Simon," said the physician firmly. "If you wish to question our guest on matters of ancient history, then perhaps you can do so later, when he has rested."

Percevale smiled. "Of course," he said without enthusiasm.

The conversation moved on to brighter if more commonplace matters. Robert launched into a series of anecdotes concerning the cases he had handled that day. Percevale noticed that most of the family seemed to approve of this rather one-sided form of conversation—perhaps for that very reason. He noticed, too, that his host took pains to include him among the audience. Percevale had thought him a slight and inconsequent figure. Now it gave him pleasure to watch his animated face in conversation and his domed forehead glowing in the ceiling's reflected light as he entertained his attentive and appreciative audience.

As for the meal, it was nourishing if unmemorable, consisting of a thin, watery but refreshingly hot soup followed by a savory wheatmeal porridge which was supplemented by white bread. There were compensations, however. Eating indoors was one; a very fine Gallic wine another.

"I apologize if this seems to you rather plain fare," remarked his host at one point.

Percevale shook his head and quickly swallowed a mouthful of porridge. "It is better than I have eaten for a long time," he eventually replied, "and the wine is truly excellent."

"Ah, yes, now, that is special. It is a prewar vintage, you know." This caused Percevale to raise his eyebrows, a gesture which clearly pleased his host. "There aren't many of those about."

The meal ended and the servant once more entered to clear the table. Percevale remembered the purpose of his errand. Reluctant as he was, he could hardly delay it further.

"The fact is," he began, wiping his lips carefully, "I was riding this way even ere I found your daughter." Again he fancied he caught the mother's piercing gaze. "Some of the kingdoms in the north, if they can be so called, have made temporary alliance and mean to move southward. They may already be on their way."

His news had much the sort of effect he had expected, quickly dispelling the atmosphere of pleasant, if rather strained—in the presence of so suspicious a guest—conviviality which had hitherto prevailed. It was the wife who eventually broke the silence. "How do you know this?" she asked.

"I learned it from a traveling weapons dealer some weeks ago. And the news was old then."

"Then it may not be true," observed Simon quickly, "for surely such a man might have much to gain from spreading a rumor like that."

"I wish I could agree with you," said Percevale. "But I know the fellow well and he believed his own story, for he has since left the district in fear of his life."

There was a silence again for a while. Everyone looked at their plates, and, when these were gone, at the bare table. At length the physician pulled himself up and said, "I had better call the council together. They should hear of this." His manner was subdued now, his forehead creased with anxiety.

"I should have told you earlier," Percevale began guiltily, "but I thought—"

"One blow at a time was quite enough. You were quite right, Sir Percevale, and I thank you for your consideration." Reaching for his jerkin, he turned to his wife. "Please see to our guest's needs, my dear." And to Percevale, "I hope you will excuse me."

Percevale nodded and Robert hurried out of the room. His wife passed him the bowl of fruit, but as everyone else had declined it, Percevale felt obliged to do the same. Eventually those seated around the table began to get up and drift silently away. Before the room emptied entirely, the mother rose and spoke to him.

"Your room should be ready now. It is upstairs, if you will follow me."

She took a candle from the table. Percevale followed her up a narrow wooden staircase that led to a small but clean and airy room—the guest room, she called it. He noticed, as he stepped inside, that the curtain across the window was not drawn, nor were there shutters, yet there seemed to be no draft from outside. He went forward to investigate.

"Glass," said the lady coldly but informatively. "It is a distillation of sand, limestone, and soda ash. We have it in all the rooms."

He was none the wiser. Nor, he suspected, was he supposed to be. He had not noticed the windows downstairs. "It is truly remarkable, lady." His fingers explored the unfamiliar transparent hardness as he peered into the darkened street below. There seemed to be some activity down there. "I have never seen its like before." And yet something told him he had seen it before. Somewhere.

He turned toward the bed. Another marvel. Instead of a pile of partly cured animal skins, there were blankets. No innovation this time, but a treat nonetheless. He could not recall when he had last slept beneath blankets.

"I will leave you now." She stood in the doorway holding forth the lighted candle. Percevale took it.

"I bid you good night."

"Good night, lady."

She turned and slowly faded into the darkness beyond the candle glow. He closed the door and set the light upon a small table that stood beside the bed. He felt a sense of self-indulgence creep over him and felt guilty about it. Blankets! It came as something of a revelation to learn that all those years of hard living had not coarsened his appreciation of homely comforts. He shrugged off the guilt without too much difficulty, undressed, and climbed wearily and with an anticipatory relish into the bed. The coarse material enfolded his body as he pulled the blankets tight about him, relishing their harsh warmth. For a while he lay there, savoring these pleasurable sensations, while outside he sensed the hushed and urgent activities of the worried burghers. He listened to the barely audible and quite incomprehensible conversations that passed by beneath his window and watched the shifting geometry of light and dark as the doors of the shuttered buildings opposite opened briefly to admit or disgorge their anxious, frightened visitors.

I really do seem to have stirred something in this strange place, he thought without satisfaction before he fell asleep.

3

The first thing he noticed when he awoke was the dirt on the window. A few shafts of daylight had managed to pierce the thick film of exterior grime, and peering through this small clear area he was able to confirm that it was indeed morning, though still early, not yet five o'clock, he guessed.

Yet someone was tapping on the door.

He muttered a sleepy response and a figure slipped into the room and stood in the shadows by the doorway.

"Lady," he began in the most courtly manner he was capable of summoning at such an hour and in such a state of mind, "this is not seemly. It is not meet." Even as he uttered the words it struck him how affected and out of place they seemed.

Elaine smiled. It was a smile that scarcely concealed her hesitancy and discomposure, but seeing her in the half light, Percevale was aware only of the precocity and impudence that her presence seemed to betoken.

"It is daylight," she said. "And if you should leave soon, I may not have the opportunity to speak with you of matters which trouble me."

"Then speak." His manner was more brusque than

courtly. Sitting up, he reached for his cloak. If the girl was not leaving, then he might as well be comfortable.

"I owe you my thanks," she said, her small body still pressed against the wall. Percevale raised his hand in a gesture of mild protest. She continued. "Also an apology. I was poor company on the road."

"Of course—" Percevale began.

"The experience was not a pleasant one for me. I think I am recovered now."

He recalled how he had found her, crouching in a corner of the ogre's cave, her eyes wild and watchful, a small heap of anonymous bones at her feet. It had taken him a little while to convince her that her ordeal was over, her captor dead.

He did not reply immediately but gazed at her reflectively across the room. Her face, clearer now as she moved with hesitant grace a few steps nearer, showed a seriousness and uncertainty that he found rather becoming. He recognized belatedly the diffidence of her earlier smile and repented of his harsh judgment.

There was something about her, about the dark hair and the wide brown eyes, the delicately formed yet strong features, that caused him to search his memory. But important though he felt it to be, it eluded his grasp for the moment.

He recalled the warning his mentor Gawaine had delivered many years before: "There are three diversions which if pursued will strip a knight of all his manliness. They are dancing, poetry, and women, and of these three women are the most dangerous, for without them there would be no dancing and certainly no poetry."

"All women?" the young Percevale had ingenuously inquired.

For a moment the old knight had looked thoughtful. Then in his thick laird's accent he had said, "Aye, well, mebee not all women. Not the old and certainly not my mother. But"—and he had fixed Percevale with stern admonitory eyes—"there are many lasses who would eagerly welcome a wee bairn fathered by one of our company. Ye ken my meaning?"

Percevale had. "Please be seated," he said to the girl with nervous haste. He indicated the rush-seated chair that stood at the end of the bed. "I am sorry that I could not have arrived earlier. I might have been able to save your friend."

She nodded quickly and Percevale wondered if he should, perhaps, have avoided reawakening painful memories.

"I suppose you realize they have been talking about you down there." She gestured in the direction of the building opposite. "That is the Moot Hall. They have been in session all night."

"You know then?"

"Blancheflor told me."

"Your sister?"

"She made me promise not to tell, but she is smitten by you."

Percevale raised an eyebrow. "Then you have broken a promise" was all he said.

"The council will be loth to let you go," said Elaine, serious again. "Perhaps you had guessed as much?"

"The thought had occurred to me."

"This town has not seen any fighting since the war," she said gravely. "Real fighting, that is. We have a ritualistic substitute on occasional Saturday afternoons, when the apprentices assemble on the common beyond the walls and bash each other's heads in with their wooden clubs. Such skills will prove of little avail against armed warriors even if they are barbarians."

"That is curious behavior," Percevale remarked. He watched her hands as they absently plucked at the shining hair that lay about her shoulders. "Why do they do it?"

"Oh, there are several theories. They say it is because of boredom and they call it sport. Father says it is their residual tribalism."

"He does not take part?"

"Goodness, no." She laughed. "We are far above such things." Percevale found a certain charm in her self-mocking tone and he could not help but return her smile of irony.

"Simon, my brother, on the other hand, claims it is a device conceived by the ruling class to distract the people from dangerous speculation about their economic servitude. A diversionary tactic, he calls it."

The knight was genuinely perplexed. "To fight in order to improve one's skills, that I understand. But this: I cannot comprehend this."

"No more can I," the girl said, "though it is good for business. Father does his most lucrative trade in mending broken heads." Then she added, more earnestly, "These people are not cut out for war, Sir Knight, but they know that they need your help and if you will not offer it freely, then they will find means of forcing you to stay."

Percevale shrugged. He was not entirely unprepared for such an eventuality.

"I did not intend staying above a day; I have pressing business of my own to attend to. However, I fear it will be as you say: I shall remain here whether I will or no."

"They will prize you and regard you with honor and respect."

"I do not think so. Those values died out long ago."

"That's rather a pessimistic view."

"I'm supposed to be an expert in the field, remember? I should know about such matters."

"Well," she said, trying another tack, "if you care

not for the esteem in which you would be held, you would at least enjoy a comfortable life here."

"That is true. It is many years since I have slept so well."

"And I am keeping you from the rest which you have richly earned." She rose to go. "You are right, of course. It is early and I should not be here."

Percevale knew that at this point he should encourage her to leave. Not to do so was surely to violate the letter, if not the spirit, of his code. But he wanted to learn more and he wanted her to stay.

"And yet you would gladly spurn all these inducements and go your way?" she asked as she resumed her seat.

"I would rather go, though not gladly, yes. It is no matter, it will wait."

"What will wait?" She had not intended to drop her guard, but the knight's tone of submissive world-weariness vexed and irritated her. Her voice rose, echoing her frustration. "What is so important that you will leave these people to their uncertain fate at the hands of brigands and murderers? I thought you people were supposed to succor the weak and helpless."

"There is nothing uncertain about the fate of your people if they stay here," said Percevale. "As for my knightly obligations, they do not require me to throw my life needlessly away against hopeless odds. I have brought good warning and that is more than many others have had. To the north are the mountains of Wales. They may find refuge there."

"Had you simply brought your news and left," said the girl, glad that he had not, "then I daresay they would follow some such course. But your presence has stiffened their resolve."

"You are right," Percevale agreed. Throwing off the comfortable blanket, he reached for his leather jerkin. "There is still time. I may yet leave unnoticed."

"I fear not." For a moment she was taken aback by

the knight's sudden show of decision. "They have already taken your horses. And your weapons." Seeing his face darken, she added quickly, "I should have warned you earlier, I know. I came here partly with that purpose in mind. But I feared there would be bloodshed. I'm sorry."

Percevale laid down the jerkin and sat resignedly upon the bed. Whose blood, he wondered, was she concerned about? He had been expecting something of the sort; in a way it was a relief to know that the burden of choice was no longer his. In a tone more of disappointment than of vexation, he said, "That is a poor reward for the service I have rendered your father."

"I know," she said. "Do not censure them too harshly. They are afraid. They look to you for help."

"Well," said Percevale, "if they can show such initiative, perhaps they can show some fighting spirit as well."

"Then you will help them?" Despite her earlier uncomplimentary remarks about her fellow townsfolk, and the way she attempted to distance herself by referring to them in the third person, she clearly was concerned.

"It seems I will have little choice. Though whether my help will be of any use against the barbarians— but I will try."

She appeared to find this acceptable. At any rate, she spoke no further on the subject.

"And what is it that will have to wait?" she asked at length.

"Ah," he replied, and looked at her with evident seriousness. "It is my quest."

A brief silence followed. Percevale became acutely conscious of the curious spectacle he presented. It was all very well to talk in such lofty terms when accoutred in splendid raiment and mounted upon a fine warlike horse. But in a cold room, voiced by a tired, middle-aged man in a frayed nightgown, such utterances, he thought, must seem more a sign of doubtful sanity. Well, it was said now.

And whatever she thought, she controlled her response. "Your quest," she replied evenly. "Is not that just a little old-fashioned?"

"This is no ordinary quest," Percevale replied stiffly. "I am not seeking the favor of a fair damosel or the regard of a king. There are few damosels to be found out there"—she blushed a little here—"and certainly no king whose regard is worth the seeking. My quest deals with weightier matters. I seek Mordred."

"*The* Mordred?"

"The Mordred. Murderer—"

"—of his father and defiler of his land," she intoned, completing the anathema.

"You know your history well," he said, impressed.

"History is not taught in the school here," she said. "It is considered too depressing a subject. However, I know enough and I know that Mordred is dead. Everyone knows that."

"Everyone is wrong. Mordred did not die in the final battle, though it suits his purpose that people should believe that."

"How do you know this?"

"Because I saw him."

"Where?" She was incredulous.

"At Glastonbury."

There had been no survivors after that frightful holocaust, that was well known, but the knight's simple certainty caused her own to waver.

"Tell me about it," she said.

"It's a long story. And I do not know if you are quite ready to believe it."

"Look," she said, reasoning with herself as much as with him, "my father brought me up to believe that the so-called ogres were merely the harmless descendants of people crippled and deformed by the war

and that all knights worthy of the title perished in
that same war. Yet in the space of a day I am nearly
eaten by an ogre and rescued by a knight. I think
my natural skepticism may withstand a few more
surprises."

Percevale was both pleased and discomfited by the
girl's reply. There was a sharp and formidable intellect sheltering behind that comely brow. One that
could run rings around mine, he thought. All of a
sudden he was uncomfortably aware of his size, his
maladroitness, his stiff chivalric manner compared to
her modern informality. He was not accustomed to
women who were unafraid of displaying their intelli-
gence. Guinevere, he recalled, had been a bright one,
but she had been very discreet about it and few people had noticed.

"Please," she said, "I should like to hear your story."

"Now?"

"If you are not too tired."

"No, I am not too tired."

4

He sat astride Grimalkin, his body shaking with suppressed excitement. The mare could sense it, too, the rising scent of victory. Her nostrils quivered, her hooves scratched at the hard ground. Nearly an hour had passed since their last errand and she was growing impatient.

Below the narrow escarpment the plain stretched away for miles on every side. To his left he could see the River Brue; directly in front lay Glastonbury itself. From his vantage point above the field of battle he could follow with his eyes the river's slow, winding progress. Earlier in the day, when the sun had been high, he had fancied he had seen a distant glimmer where a small tributary branched off toward the Mendip Hills. But now the smoke obscured his view. Some of Arthur's men had raided Mordred's supply train; pallid columns of smoke drifted slowly across the plain, urged on by a slight westerly breeze. It lent a suitably gloomy aspect to the dismal scene of carnage.

Apart from a few camp attendants, he was alone. Behind him Arthur's huge battle pavilion stood empty. Above it the royal standard hung limp, stirred only fitfully by the light air. The king and his bodyguard

had ridden off on yet another sally against the enemy's depleted and demoralized ranks. How he longed
to be with them! Not that he entertained any illusions about the glorious spectacle of war. If he had,
his frequent errands across the battlefield and the
horrors he had there witnessed would have soon dis-
pelled them. It was not a desire to share in the casual
slaughter proceeding on the plain below; rather, a
need to live up to his newly acquired status. That
morning, shortly before the commencement of battle,
he had been made knight. He had been dubbed by
Arthur himself. It had been a short and unceremoni-
ous affair—knighting in battle often is—but to him it
was the most significant event of his twenty-one years
and a memory he would cherish for many more. Thus
his thoughts ran as he knelt before the tall dark-haired
king, whose aging, careworn features and tired eyes
could still not hide the strength and nobility of his
gentle visage. The king was desperate for new knights;
the Round Table had lost more than a third of its
number in the campaign so far. Fourteen others, squires
like himself, whose masters had been killed or had
deserted to the enemy, had been knighted that morning. Faced with such a shortage of trained armor,
Arthur had been forced to lower the standards of
entry into his elite order. Percevale was not unaware
of this, but neither was he ashamed. He fully realized
his own disqualifications as well as those of his companions in arms. Like him, many of them had not
fully completed their training. Many of them also
were ill-suited in character or temperament to bear
the new titles they so grandly adopted for themselves.
None of this depressed Sir Percevale. He knew that
the king must have a fair sprinkling of knights among
his battle array. It lent strength of purpose to the rest
of the army. As for the enemy, well, the very name of
the Round Table still carried enough weight to compensate for the moral deficiencies of some of its mem-

bers. More important, he was going to be different. He was determined to prove himself worthy of the title that had been so liberally and unexpectedly bestowed upon him. He had several points in his favor. For one thing, he had been Gawaine's squire. Gawaine had had many faults, but inattentiveness to duty had not been one of them. He had made his squire work twice as hard and practice twice as long as the other apprentice knights. He had made Percevale fight with a sword weighted with lead; his training shield had had a double thickness of wood. The other knights had made their squires run once around the castle perimeter, in mail, every morning before breakfast. Percevale had been made to run three circuits every day, at midday. Under Gawaine there had been no time he could call his own. All through the days he had toiled and sweated and ached, stopping only to eat and rest briefly. The nights were spent in deep, exhausted sleep. Many times during this period he had cursed the Scottish knight and his harsh, unremitting regime. When hacking sluggishly at the thick oaken post he had been ordered to demolish with his leaden sword, which seemed as blunt as it was heavy, he would imagine that the post was Gawaine and assault it with redoubled vigor. Gawaine himself, who knew full well what was on the young man's mind, would smile with satisfaction as he watched his effigy being steadily reduced to small splinters of flying wood.

Often Percevale had inveighed against the old knight, wishing him dead or worse. Yet when Gawaine had died, he had wept bitterly for days afterward, for he knew he had lost the only father he had ever had and the only friend. Far from rejoicing in his newfound freedom, he had bewailed it, for it meant he would have to continue his training alone. He started to rise an hour earlier and go to bed an hour later. There had been many times when he had wondered if it was all worth it. Now he knew that it had been, and this knowledge made him all the more impatient and ill-tempered. If any of the new-made knights was capable of acquitting himself well in this battle, it was he. And yet the king had kept him behind when he had sent the other knights to their stations at the head of his battalions.

"Sir Percevale will stay by my pavilion as my courier," he had declared to one of his aides. Desperate as he was for high-born battle fodder, it had nevertheless pained Arthur to see so many bright and hopeful faces turned up toward him. They will all die, he had said to himself while intoning the words of knighthood above each eager squire. He knew they had little chance against Mordred's seasoned veterans. But they would buy time, and time was of the essence.

And so the fourteen new knights had galloped enthusiastically down the ridge and he had stayed behind to fret in bitter silence.

At various times during the day he had come across some of his fellow initiates. One of them he recognized only by the bloodstained device on his shield, for the head was gone. Another, whose injuries were so bad, had begged Percevale to dispatch him mercifully, and reluctantly he had done so, for it was clear that the fellow was beyond medical aid. It was the first occasion on which he had used his sword to kill. All day long he had traversed a field strewn with dead and dying. He had been near enough to the main battle to taste it, yet his orders forbade him to engage in combat; the messages he carried to and from the king's commanders in the field were too important to risk their loss. Many times had he passed isolated groups, stranded like animals on the foreshore by the ebb and flow of battle, yet still fighting even when fighting seemed futile. Each time he had passed by, unnoticed and unharmed.

Now he sat astride Grimalkin, watching the distant

maneuvers as Arthur's forces steadily pushed the enemy farther and farther back toward the river. There would be no more errands across the battlefield now, he reflected resignedly, no more opportunities to prove himself. Mordred's bid for supreme power had failed. Albion would be united once again, but under Arthur, not his traitor son. The day will long be remembered as glorious, he thought, and I must be thankful to have played some part in it, however insignificant.

His reverie was interrupted by a cry from among the small knot of camp attendants who had also gathered to watch the expected victory.

"Smoke! See!" In the distance, far behind the battling princes, it rose in a tall thin column, darker and thicker than the insubstantial and slowly dispersing haze from Mordred's by now burned-out supply train.

"It is Lancelot!" someone cried. They turned to Percevale, as if to an oracle, with inquiring faces.

"Indeed, it must be Sir Lancelot," he agreed. "Glastonbury is taken." Now the real slaughter would begin. The river where Mordred had so skillfully anchored his flanks now blocked his retreat. Soon Lancelot and his French would take him in the rear. There would be no surrender, he knew enough about Mordred to realize that.

Like many others, he had wondered mightily at the suddenness of the pact between the king and the renegade knight who had stolen the king's wife and foully murdered his most highly favored knight, Sir Gawaine. Like many others, he had doubted the wisdom as well as the ethics of such a move, especially now that victory seemed assured with or without Lancelot.

Another cry from the spectators made him look down. Three riders were approaching at speed toward the ridge. They galloped abreast. One carried the royal pennant while another was leading the horse of the middle rider, who was slumped forward on his saddle, one hand uneasily gripping the pommel, the other dangling uselessly at his side.

"It is the king," someone said, and an apprehensive and watchful silence descended upon them.

As the riders breasted the hill, some of the attendants ran forward to help them dismount, but the pennant bearer, whom Percevale recognized as Sir Lucan, forbore them. He rode closer.

"The king has been hurt," Lucan was saying. "His wound is not serious, but it must needs have immediate attention. We are taking His Majesty to Cadras."

Some of the crowd murmured disapprovingly, and Percevale well understood their anxiety. It could hardly presage well if the commander-in-chief was removed from the battlefield at the very moment of victory. The other rider he recognized as Bedivere, an old friend of Gawaine's. He pulled his horse up alongside.

"How bad is it?" he asked. The king looked pale, his grip unsteady. Percevale noticed that he had been lashed firmly to the horse by his waist.

"All this jogging about won't help," Bedivere replied, trying, for the servants' sake, to show less concern than he felt. His hair was matted where mud and sweat had mingled and dried together. His shield was badly dented and his helm had been so knocked about that he had discarded it altogether and had fought through half the battle without head protection. His leggings were caked with blood, none of it his own. He leaned over heavily and whispered in a voice loud enough for the closest attendants to hear, "We thought little of it at first, a mere scratch, an arrow at the extreme limit of its range. Then it turned bad, as you see."

The king was mumbling weak protests, which were drowned by Lucan's stern, assuring tones.

"Be not concerned. See." He pointed in the direction of the still-rising column of smoke, thicker and blacker now. "Glastonbury is ours once more. The fate of the traitor Mordred is sealed whether the king remain or no.''

"A poisoned arrow?" Percevale suggested.

"Possibly. Mordred is perfidious—but clever," Bedivere conceded reluctantly. "If we but possessed his disregard for common morality, this war might have ended sooner.''

"Will His Majesty survive the ride to Cadras? He looks not fit to me.''

"It is but ten or twelve miles distant and we can save him if we hurry. The wound was not deep enough to be mortal.''

"But the jarring of the ride, it will spread the poison.''

Bedivere shrugged. "Either way there are risks; this way there are fewer.''

"Let me come with you." He turned an importuning gaze in turn upon Bedivere, the king, and Lucan. "Please.''

There was a short silence. Then Arthur spoke.

"Let the boy come," he said in a low voice, as if he were conserving energy. "I have denied him the chance to win his spurs. Let him come. He may win them yet." Slowly and with effort he raised his injured right arm. The crowd of retainers cleared. Bedivere reached over and took the king's bridle once more. He spurred his mount and galloped off, following the stony pathway that led eventually to Arthur's summer residence. With one departing glance at the battle, Percevale followed them.

They rode for five miles through a countryside that had long suffered the ravages of civil war. It was high summer, yet there was little sign of it amid the desolation that greeted the riders on their journey. They passed deserted villages, untended orchards, and unsown fields. Come fall, the fruit would rot on the trees and such crops as had been sown would provide rich banquets for the birds and other creatures.

Percevale reflected grimly on the famine that would ensue when winter came. At one stage, they passed a column of refugees, dispossessed of everything save a few pathetic belongings which they carried on their backs or pushed before them in crudely fashioned handcarts. Where they were going he could not fathom; ahead of them the prospect was much the same as what they had left behind. Nor did they seem to know—or care—where their weary, plodding footsteps took them. They gazed for the most part without interest at the battle-scarred riders and seemed to care little for the dust that their progress raised. When they had passed the end of one such straggling column, he turned to see one of the peasants, his face disfigured by hunger and impotent rage, shout something after the departing horsemen. A small boy, sickly and poorly clothed, was clutching the man's hand as if it were his only means of survival. The man stood in the middle of the road, one hand holding the boy, the other a clenched fist that seemed to lend strength to his hoarse imprecations. For a long time, it seemed, he stood there, oblivious to the choking dust and the unresponsiveness of the riders, who heard nothing above the thunder of their horses' hooves. Percevale was thankful when his diminishing angry figure was finally engulfed by the clouds of dust, but the image remained with him for a long time after.

When they reached what Lucan judged to be a spot roughly halfway to Cadras, they dismounted and rested their horses for a few minutes. The king remained mounted. Percevale, leaving Grimalkin to drink from a small clear stream that ran beside the road, walked over to where the two other knights sat. They were talking about Lancelot.

"It much concerns me," Bedivere said. "With the king gone, it will seem as if the victory is his alone."

"Tush, man," said Lucan. "There is no helping it. We must save the king first."

Bedivere shook his head. "Nay, but I do not trust him."

Stepping forward, Percevale said impulsively, "Sir Lancelot is my mortal enemy and I am sworn to kill him."

Lucan turned on him with a brief scornful glance. "Hah!" was all he said.

Bedivere smiled. "Nay, lad," he said gently, "you cannot fight him."

"I have trained hard."

Bedivere nodded. "Gawaine always spoke well of you, Percevale. You are well fitted to bear his device and ride his destrier."

"Well, then—"

"But you may not touch Lancelot. It is part of the treaty. You have good cause to hate him. So have I, so have many others. We must all stay our hands."

"Politics!" Lucan spat out the word with bitterness.

"But if he breaks the pact?"

"Then you must wait your turn. I believe I am first in line to have a crack at the Frenchman, is that not so, Lucan?"

"And I am second. So there will be little for you, boy, but to pick up the pieces."

When it was time to resume their journey, Bedivere said to Percevale, "My arm is stiff from carrying the bridle, and Lucan insists on holding the pennant. Lead you on with the king and we will follow."

Deeply conscious of the honor, Percevale bowed. He mounted and took the king's reins in his left hand, gripping his own more tightly in his right. Arthur looked at him and gave a faint smile of recognition. Percevale steeled himself to say something, but his awe and dread of the great monarch failed him at the vital moment.

"I hope Your Majesty is not too greatly fatigued," he ventured to say. But all that emerged was a strangled cry which he then attempted to still by bursting into a sudden fit of coughing. A puzzled frown momentarily crossed King Arthur's face. Had he, perhaps, lowered the qualifications for knighthood too far? he wondered.

"Lead on, Sir Percevale," he said wearily. "We have a good way to go yet."

A further mile passed without incident, and soon they came to the temple. It was deserted now, for the war had driven the Druids to seek refuge, either with Arthur or with his son. Nevertheless, it was a welcome sign, for it meant that Cadras was not far away.

Still leading the king's horse, Percevale followed the road as it rounded the side of the temple. Lucan and Bedivere were following about fifty paces behind. He was still in the shelter of the high stone wall when the horror struck. He was blind. Or so, for a moment, it seemed. A radiant whiteness seared his eyes, blotting out everything before him. The roadway, the trees, everything disappeared, merged into brilliance. He turned his head, shielding his eyes from the merciless glare. He felt Grimalkin rear in panic and, looking down, saw to his relief that he was not blind. Dimly, as if through a silver mist, he saw his own right leg and the mare's twisting flank. Turning, he saw the king, his slumped figure bathed in the same brilliant light. His mouth was open and he was shouting something, but Percevale could not hear, for as the light became less fierce, so worse horrors followed. He heard, not just heard but felt, a heavy rumbling. It seemed to approach from the earth, from the sky, indeed from every side. To Percevale, desperately trying to control his own panic-stricken mount and the king's, it sounded like the relentless approach of some terrible and nameless doom.

The heat engulfed him before the noise. That, too, seemed to strike invisibly. From nowhere and yet from everywhere. His nostrils were on fire, his whole face was ablaze, though there were no flames. Choking from the intense heat and unable to control the horses any further, he fell heavily to the ground and, oblivious to his bruises, began rolling frantically in every direction, trying to shield his body from the invisible flames. Dimly, as if on the edge of perception, he became aware that the heavy rumbling had ceased. In its place he could hear a rush of air. A small part of his pain-racked mind wondered at the power that could command such phenomena; a blinding light, a thunder in the ground, and a wind that blew invisible fire. It is the wrath of heaven, he concluded, as he blindly tugged at the suit of mail. Far from affording protection, the metal covering was effectively incinerating him. Somehow in this battle we have displeased the gods, he thought, flinging the armor away from him. Still there was no escape from the pain, and the bruises he had incurred from his fall also made movement difficult. He lay still, eyes closed, enduring as best he could the divine anger.

The howling in his ears continued to rise in volume and then, steadily, mercifully, it began to diminish. The temperature, too, began to drop. The flames which had licked, unseen, at his body had, it seemed, been extinguished.

Carefully he pulled himself to his feet. For a few moments he stood, unsteadily, gazing in uncomprehending awe at the scene before him. From nowhere a huge dark cloud had appeared. It blotted out the sky and darkened the earth below. Against this grim backcloth a strange vision arose. Two figures on horseback, each surrounded by a golden aura, a halo of fire, flickered and danced before him through the smoke and the flames, writhing in a slow silent ecstasy. Then the flames died and the horses collapsed, bringing down with them the charred and lifeless remains of Lucan and Bedivere. Appalled, Percevale ran forward only to be driven back by the smell of burning flesh and the sight of the dead figures as the smoke cleared and wafted away. Stumbling backward and choking for want of fresh air, he looked around for the king.

Arthur lay in the shelter of the temple wall, now reduced to rubble. His horse had thrown him earlier, and he lay still, unable to move. As Percevale approached, he looked up. He was covered in a fine gray dust and his face was marked by livid red scars where the heat had sought out the most sensitive parts. Percevale wondered if he, too, had been so affected. Arthur's mouth opened to speak, but no words came.

"Soft, my lord," said Percevale. He reached down and helped the king to a sitting position, his back resting against the remains of the wall. Their horses, he noticed, were still alive. After throwing their riders, they had both bolted, but on finding the torment even greater outside the shelter of the wall, they had returned and were now treading anxiously the still-warm ground. Slowly he went toward them, making assuring noises as he approached. Within his confused mind a plan was beginning to take shape. After securing the horses he would look in the ruins of the temple. If the underground chambers were still accessible, he would move the king down there. It would be cooler below ground, he reasoned. It might even be that the Druids had left some useful supplies behind in their flight, some ointments for the king's sores, perhaps. Later, when he judged it safe, they would move on to Cadras. Then it occurred to him to wonder whether indeed there still was a Cadras. If this was, as he suspected, the Last Day, then there would soon be no world at all and certainly little point in making short-term plans.

These depressing reflections were interrupted by a new phenomenon, an earthly one this time: the rhythmic hoofbeats of a galloping horse. Percevale turned as the rider rounded the corner of the temple. His head was uncovered, but even if it had not been so, he would have recognized immediately the lion passant on the rider's shield. Arthur, too, recognized his son, but, unable to speak, he sat there, eyeing Mordred with a tired gaze.

So this cannot be the end of the world, thought Percevale. For Mordred surely would be damned before so many other goodly knights.

The king of the Eastern Kingdom pulled up his horse with a sharp tug on the reins and approached them at a slow walk, his eyes narrowing with caution. He looked worn and haggard; his eyes were bloodshot and his face pale. Somehow he had escaped injury. He has the luck of the accursed, thought Percevale. Nonetheless, his appearance was startling. Percevale had seen him once before: at Arthur's court when he had still been heir to the throne and the king's honored son. Even then, peevish, middle-aged, his impatience already waxing dangerously strong, he had possessed the bearing of a king. Now, amid the blasted empty landscape he seemed much diminished in stature, a frightened man in a hurry.

Ah, a small voice warned him, but Mordred is a clever one. Be careful.

Mordred stiffened as he recognized the broken figure that lay in the shadow of the wall. He edged his mount closer to confirm this improbable sight. For his part, Arthur did not attempt to speak; his eyes remained expressionless. They were inadequate to convey his feelings, so he judged it better to show nothing at all.

Mordred looked down at his helpless father, and for a moment his features were softened by the look of pity that crept into them. Fear, remorse, and the remnants of filial affection struggled for a moment in his face. To Percevale, who was holding the horses' bridles while at the same time casting about wildly in his mind for some means of unhorsing the traitor and thus shortening the odds between them, the resulting expression was something like an uncertain sneer. Forgetting for a moment his vulnerable position, he spoke out angrily.

"Do you even now dare to gloat after a triumph so hideous and so dearly bought?" For he was now certain that it was Mordred who was responsible for this disaster.

Mordred turned slowly. The expression had vanished from his face, but the struggle it had signified continued behind. Ignoring the young man's reproach, he said simply, "Look you unto his wounds, for he is a true and valiant knight and I much fear that he is hurt unto death."

For a moment Percevale was disarmed by the unexpected softness of the reply. Then he reminded himself of Mordred's reputation for cunning and dissembling. "What foul sorcery is this?" he demanded, his arm sweeping the black and smoldering horizon.

"I did not mean it to be so," replied the traitor. There was a hint of pleading in his voice which Percevale noted with grim satisfaction. If he is about to excuse his guilt, he thought, he has chosen a poor audience—a dying king and a knight of no proven worth. There was no sign now of the vaunted cunning or inscrutability behind which Mordred concealed his ambitious designs. "I did not think it would be like this," he muttered feebly. "They did not tell me it would be like this." He looked again, more closely this time, at the curious pile of debris on the roadside, realized what it signified, and turned away quickly, sickened and horrified. He had passed similar sights during his flight from the battlefield, but it would be a long time before he could accustom himself to so unnatural and undignified an aspect of death. Seeing the scorn on the young man's face, he rapidly composed himself. Without another word he nudged his horse gently forward. As he passed, Percevale reached out and gripped his bridle. With a suddenness that took the younger man by surprise, Mordred swept the restraining hand away.

"Look you unto your king and leave me to go my way."

He glared angrily at Percevale, and for a fleeting moment he became, once more, king of half Albion, with a capacity to awe that almost matched his father's. Caught off guard, Percevale involuntarily stepped back and let the rider pass.

As soon as he had done so, he regretted his sudden weakness. Now he had an added reason to kill the traitor. Mordred had a lance, so his sword would be of no avail. His own lance he had left behind in the haste of their departure. He remembered the pennant which Lucan had carried with such proud aloofness. Had it been consumed by flames like its bearer? Mordred was riding away slowly, as if scorning any attempt to stop him. There was yet time if he hurried. Ignoring with some difficulty the bruises that pained his every movement and the smell that still rose from the heaped bodies, he willed himself forward. Black and scorched, the spear-tipped pole lay where Lucan, in his death agony, had dropped it. Percevale bent down and picked it up. Fragments of burned silk fell away and drifted to the ground. He ran his hand gingerly along the wood. It was scarred but solid enough. It was not a proper lance and the spear tip was blunt, being intended for ceremony and not for use, but it was the correct length and it would serve.

Carrying the makeshift lance over his shoulder, he hurried back to where Grimalkin stood. Painfully, he lifted himself into the saddle. Mordred was a good way along the road now but not yet beyond shouting distance.

First, however, he had to get the words right. He had never before uttered them in anger and in his present state of nervous excitement it would be easy to misplace a syllable and make a complete fool of himself. He hurriedly composed a fitting sentence, then shouted at the top of his voice, "Mordred, thou art base, false, and treacherous. Turn and defend thee that I may destroy thee in the name of King Arthur, Lord of Albion!"

Like rolling thunder his words reverberated amid the stillness of their surroundings, thrilling the young knight with their magnificence and stirring Arthur into sudden wakefulness, disturbing the welcome sleep that had been stealing over him. Percevale saw Mordred stiffen for a moment, then ride on. Out of the corner of his eye he saw Arthur lift a weary hand and let it fall. He is bidding me good fortune, Percevale thought with a sudden exulting pride. He called again to his seemingly reluctant adversary.

"Mordred, turn ye and defend ye or be forever remembered as a recreant and no knight!"

Not even Mordred could resist such a taunt. With the resigned air of someone who has better things to do, he stopped and turned. Though he did not welcome it, the impending combat did seem to revive his spirits. He felt suddenly sharper, more alive.

"Ye are tired of life, Sir Knight. Very well then."

Both knights fastened their helms and dressed their shields. Percevale's view narrowed to a thin oblong of light. Save for this, all was darkness inside his helm. He edged Grimalkin until the opposing rider was in the center of his greatly restricted field of vision. Obeying a discipline born of many months of rigorous training, he forced himself to forget his impassioned anger. Now his fury quickly cooled, crystallizing into a series of meticulous calculations concerning his opponent's probable weight, the speed of his approach, and the likely angle of his body at the moment of impact. The issue of the contest, he knew, would

depend upon such technical judgments as these and
not on some fancied moral superiority. The only emotion he did allow himself, and this only momentarily,
was the thrill of pleasure that ran through his body at
the anticipation of this, his first real combat.

Slowly the two figures aligned themselves across
the silent plain. Mordred had backed his horse a little
way. The longer the field, the faster the combined
speed of the horses at the moment of impact. The
rider who was traveling fastest at this particular point
possessed a definite advantage.

He's taking no chances, Percevale thought. He thinks
I'm an unpracticed novice but he takes no chances.
He brought down his spear and set it in rest.

For a moment the two figures remained still, each
waiting for the other to make the first move. Percevale
could control his impatience no longer. Concentrating
the whole of his mind and body in the direction of the
tiny figure before him, he dug his spurs into Grimalkin's flanks. Speed was of the essence now. He had to
reach a gallop before Mordred did.

The gray mare responded swiftly. She, too, had
sensed with a growing expectation the significance of
the approaching combat. She, too, had been trained to
respond with absolute precision at just such a moment as this. Heeding rather the unspoken command
of her rider than his cruel spurs, she sprang forward,
increasing her speed at every step. Mordred had
spurred his own horse only a split second later. Like
ungainly tanks, the two armored figures thundered
toward each other, rapidly closing the distance between them.

Through Percevale's visor the dark figure of his
enemy loomed steadily larger. He seemed to detach
himself from the surrounding landscape with its
cindered fields and blackened sky and rushed forward,
a seemingly irresistible figure, full of evil and head-
ing straight for him.

The constant roar of hoofbeats reverberating inside his helm, the vision of impending doom advancing rapidly upon him—these he pushed to a far corner of his mind. He shifted his body in readiness for the inevitable clash of wood upon metal, the thud of metal upon flesh. With a surge of delight such as a mathematician feels when hours of labor are finally rewarded by the predicted and hoped-for result, he knew, with an unshakable inner conviction, that his own calculations had been right. His own crude lance would pass around the inner edge of Mordred's shield and pierce him through the chest. Speed would more than compensate for the bluntness of the spear. No armor could withstand such an impact as Mordred's would receive. At the same time, Mordred's own lance would glance harmlessly off Percevale's shield. In that fraction of a moment, with the figure of his enemy filling his own vision, he knew he had won.

And then Mordred was no longer there.

In that same fraction of a moment during which Percevale had not even time to blink in surprise, he had rolled sideways in the saddle. Percevale's lance passed harmlessly over Mordred's left shoulder. His own struck true just where he had planned it all along.

To Percevale it felt as if Grimalkin had slammed into an invisible wall. As his astonished body shot forward, clutching vainly at the air, he heard a scream of pain which then merged with his own as he hit the ground, rediscovering the bruises which, for a little while, he had almost forgotten.

For a time he lay still and face down on the hard earth. His senses blurred and coalesced into a simple dim awareness that encompassed the dying screams of the mare, the numbing, insistent pain that racked his own body, and the tiny cracks that crisscrossed the ground in all directions. A realization of what had happened dawned gradually upon him, and he cursed the overconfidence that had left him so unprepared. To strike an opponent's horse was an acknowledged foul, regardless of whether the combat was friendly or serious. It was a base and unworthy move, but that was no excuse. Mordred had on many occasions shown himself to be above scruples where fair play was concerned. He should have been ready. Also, it was a move that demanded the utmost skill and dexterity. To roll in the saddle whilst wearing full armor and carrying lance and shield was no mean feat, and Percevale could not help but spare a grudging and bitter admiration for the man's style. It had turned the tables entirely. Now Mordred had won, and he was helpless even to rise and defend himself on foot.

He waited for the expected blow, hoping it would be merciful and swift. Grimalkin's whimpers had by now grown faint; she was conserving her rapidly diminishing energy. He hoped that Mordred would spare a quick stroke for her, for she deserved better than this.

Then he realized that he had already lain prostrate for several minutes and nothing had happened.

Slowly, he lifted his head and looked up, expecting to see his adversary standing there with sword upraised, waiting for his fallen enemy to turn and witness his smile of triumph, the last thing he would ever see.

There was no Mordred. Turning to one side, he could see Grimalkin, lying in a broken fashion, the shattered end of Mordred's lance still deeply embedded in her neck. Her body glistened darkly with sweat and blood, and she was wheezing hoarsely. Puzzled now, Percevale turned his head in the opposite direction, his eyes following the road to Cadras. The small figure of Mordred could still be seen trotting steadily into the distance. He had turned and resumed his journey without a word. He had not even stopped to dispatch the valiant mare.

Wretched and humiliated, Percevale forced himself to his feet. He staggered over to where the horse lay, and with his dagger proceeded to end her slow agony. It was with a keen sense of loss as well as of necessity that he administered the death blow. Grimalkin had held a high place in his affections. Apart from Gawaine, the gray mare had been his only friend. They had been a great team and there were tears in his eyes when he stood up again and removed his helm. He limped painfully over to where Arthur still reclined. The look of sorrow and angry frustration that distorted the great king's once-noble features was a silent reproach to the young knight. He had failed himself. Worse still, he had failed his king. Arthur had been denied his just revenge. Carefully, he helped the king to his feet. Arthur could stand but not without aid. Supporting the king under one arm and with the other leading the king's horse, he stumbled in the direction of the temple entrance. He felt a light breeze stir his face, a cool and welcoming one this time. It blew in the direction of the battlefield. He did not know it, but it would save their lives. He looked up as something cold struck his cheek and slowly ran down the side of his face. A light rain had begun to fall.

5

"And was it all clear?"

He stopped and looked at her with a puzzled expression.

"What?"

"The cellar of the temple. Was it all clear?"

"Oh, yes," he said. "Yes, it was." Hunched upon the chair, her knees pulled under her chin, her face distorted by the shadows in the room, she looked to him rather like a benign and squat dwarf. "Yes," he repeated, "there was a lot of rubble but the entrance was clear. The Druids built things to last."

"What did you do?" She still seemed interested and, unlike him, not a bit tired.

"What I could. It was not much."

What light there was in the chamber filtered through the cracks in the roof. It was enough for him to see that the place was quite empty. A large stone slab which he guessed to be a sacrificial altar stood against one of the walls. There was nothing else. Percevale sat the king at the bottom of the stairs and went on to explore the other chambers. There were four altogether, of various sizes and each connected to its neighbor by means of a tall narrow archway. They were all empty save for the dormitory. Here the monks had left a dozen or so wooden beds, for they had been constructed in the room and could not be carried through the doorway, let alone up the stairs. They had taken the blankets, however. He helped the king into the dormitory and laid him on the nearest bed. Then he began to consider the various alternatives before him.

The first was simply to do nothing; just wait and watch until help arrived. This he quickly discounted; he was quite certain that there was no help to be expected from anywhere.

Secondly, he could take the king's horse and hope it was in a fit condition to ride the rest of the way to Cadras alone. The drawback to this plan was that it involved leaving Arthur behind, and he did not seem to Percevale in a fit state to be left.

Finally, he could mount the king on his horse and walk the remaining distance to the castle. This he dismissed almost as quickly as the first alternative. It would take well over an hour to reach the castle on foot. On horseback and alone he could do the entire journey in less than a third of the time. He still did not like the idea of leaving Arthur alone, but he was underground and out of sight—and there was really nothing else for it.

The king's destrier was in poor condition, but he gamely cantered on and it did not take them long to reach the castle. As he got farther away from the temple, so the scale of the destruction seemed to lessen. Whatever had happened then had not happened to the whole world. He still passed smoldering trees and blackened fields but fewer of them. Farther on the grass was dry and straw-colored, but this was because of the hot summer. Soon the only sign that anything was amiss was the huge cloud, black and swirling, stretching unbroken from one horizon's end to the next. That and the utter silence.

He met no one on the road to Cadras. The single village that he passed was deserted, though there was no telling if the villagers had left before or after the calamity. The refugee encampment that had sprung up beneath the walls of the castle itself was also deserted. A number of still-moist discolored patches on the grass signified where the many crude tents had been pitched. The gates of the castle stood open and unmanned, and he rode slowly into the silent empty courtyard with the feeling that he was entering a place of desolation. There was nobody to be seen, alive or dead. His mount twitched nervously as if it, too, sensed the same atmosphere of dread and hurried flight. Percevale wondered where they had all gone. Six hundred had been left behind at Cadras, not to mention the refugees and the inhabitants of the outlying villages. He could not understand the suddenness of it all. When so many people leave in a hurry, someone is bound to be left behind: the old, the crippled, the very young.

"Were there any other signs of a rapid departure?" Elaine asked. She had shifted in her seat and was now leaning forward slightly, legs crossed, a hand under her chin.

"Oh, yes, several. The courtyard was full of various articles, broken or simply dropped in the rush. They had left the animals in their pens."

"Did you let them go?"

"Yes." He had thought she might ask something like that.

He also chose two good horses, filled a skin with water and a sack with food. Now, he thought, for the infirmary.

He walked along empty stone corridors, the echoes of his footsteps loudly preceding him all the way. On either side the cold, vaulting walls were lined with weapons and pennants, booty from Arthur's victories. One of the heavy oaken doors he passed led into the

great hall itself, the Hall of the Round Table or, to be
more precise, tables, for there were eight of them
altogether, placed end to end in order to make a huge
hollow circle. It was tempting, in spite of his recent
humiliation, to enter the chamber and sit on one of
the unmarked chairs, the ones reserved for newcom-
ers to the order. It was his right, after all. He was a
knight of the Table, albeit of only a few hours. He
fought off the temptation, reminding himself of the
urgency of his errand. Also, he was far from sure that
he was worthy to take a seat in so august an assembly.

He passed on then and continued until he came to
the infirmary. As he expected, it was empty. Even
the absence of the sick, some of whom must have
been virtually immovable, occasioned him no great
surprise now. What did surprise him was that the
Druid physicians had left so much behind. The shelves
were stacked with bottles and jars. The bookshelves,
too, were full. It did not seem to Percevale as if
anything had been taken. Perhaps after witnessing
such a blast from heaven, he thought, they lost all
confidence in the efficacy of their own meager powers. The minds of the Druids worked in funny ways
sometimes.

Taking down a book from one of the shelves, he
began to scan through it quickly. Somewhere in his
mind was the vague hope that just by chance he
might come across a recipe that would heal the king's
wound. Of course, it was no use. The whole thing was
written in the close, arcane scrawl that only the initi-
ated could decipher. He looked through the other
volumes, but he knew his search would be hopeless.
If the Druids wrote in plain language, then anybody
would be able to learn medicine and the monks would
lose their monopoly—and their power. He could not
complain too much about that. Similar motives had
prompted the rules governing knighthood—they had
already been stretched to the limit just to let in peo-

ple like himself. No, he could not object that the Druids had wished to preserve their monopoly of the scientific and necromantic arts just as the knights had tried to preserve their monopoly of the martial ones—but it did leave him angry and frustrated nonetheless and he swept the books to the floor before walking quickly back the way he had come. This time he did not even spare a sideways glance as he passed the great hall again. Putting together with the food and water the blankets, salves, and bandages he had taken from the infirmary, he secured them to the back of one of the horses and mounting the other, a reliable-looking palfrey, he headed back to the temple.

When he returned, the king was still alive; thus one of his anxieties was removed. His condition, however, had deteriorated during that short absence. The skin was drawn tight about his pale face, upon which the scars stood out like livid weals. A distinct yellowness had entered his complexion. He dressed the king's injuries as best he could, applying bandages and ointments where they seemed most needed. Arthur drank some of the water but would take no food. Percevale covered him with blankets and built a fire, cutting up some of the beds for fuel. He quite enjoyed the exercise and ignored the pain it caused his still-bruised body. He imagined that each bed was Mordred.

With the disappearance of the sun it grew quite cold. It was a chill that seemed to signify more than the mere absence of sunshine. The fire helped a lot, though. That and the exercise.

For the rest of the day he sat and watched over Arthur, but his appearance did not improve, even in the glow of the fire. He said nothing, giving no answer to Percevale's occasional inquiries. It seemed that the capacity for expression as well as the color had left his face. He lay back, looking blank and uncomprehending. At first he thought it was because the king was unable to speak. Later he felt that it was simply because he did not wish to.

He had fully intended to stay awake through the night and had deliberately made himself as uncomfortable as he could in order to ensure that he should stay awake.

When he awoke, it was to see the shafts of daylight through the cracks in the chamber roof. It was morning and he had fallen asleep at his post. Even his fall from the stool to the hard floor on which he was lying had failed to waken him.

Slowly, for his body felt stiff, and cursing himself, he got up and looked at the king. He was still awake and Percevale felt sure that he had been awake all through the night. He had slept peacefully while Arthur had lain alone, contemplating his approaching death without solace, even without the silent companionship of an unworthy knight.

Here Percevale stopped again and shook his head in sadness and self-reproach. Many times during the past twenty years he had relived these events but he could not shake off the guilt that still clung to them. Nor, when he thought about it, had he any real desire to. Elaine spoke again.

"You had been through a lot," she said reasonably. "You were tired. I am sure he understood."

"I never knew what he felt or thought about me," continued Percevale. "I tried to persuade him to take food but he could or would not. At intervals during the day I went outside in the hope that someone might come by, someone who could provide more substantial help than I. No one ever did. We were alone, Arthur and I, in a dark abandoned cellar and no help for miles around. I'm not sure who felt the loneliness more, he or I."

*   *   *

He tried to bury Lucan and Bedivere, but something had happened to the earth. He had had enough of wonders by now and so did not marvel greatly at this one. The ground had a hard-baked, almost glazed quality to it. He tried with his sword to hack out a shallow grave, but after a few ineffectual attempts he gave up and returned to the king.

Most of the time he just sat there, absently gazing at Arthur or at the steadily circling dust motes that floated randomly in the splintered light. Sometimes he would leave his post and wander aimlessly through the gloomy chambers. He did not expect to chance upon any new discoveries and so was not disappointed. It relieved the tedium.

Then, toward late afternoon, Arthur spoke. In a broken, indistinct voice he said, "To Avalon." The words were slurred; the poison was attacking his brain now, eating away his lucidity. Percevale rushed to his side. "I must go to Avalon," the king repeated. His lips were badly cracked; they had barely opened, but to Percevale the message was sufficient. At last he had something to do. He had adequate mounts and he had a destination. For a moment he forgot that the king was dying and very probably delirious. For a moment he was overjoyed. Only one problem remained.

"Which way, Sire?" he whispered anxiously. "Which way to Avalon?"

"Go to Avalon," said Arthur. "I must go to Avalon. They are waiting there." Again Percevale asked for directions, more urgently this time, for he could sense the king's desire to reach this place before he died. He sensed also that Arthur had heard nothing. Again and again he repeated his request for directions. Soon he was shouting, crying, his entreaties resounding emptily around the darkening chamber. He had no idea where Avalon was nor indeed what it was. He knew only that here was a dying old man who wanted desperately to go there and he could not take him because he did not know the way.

Several times during the rest of that day and through the night Arthur spoke. Always the same cracked voice; always the same broken message. Avalon. Have to go there. They are waiting. Once or twice, overcome perhaps by a fit of unfounded optimism, Percevale tried again to make himself known. Most of the time he watched dejectedly, waiting for the worst.

Only at the end, tragically late, did the king become aware of his presence.

It was shortly before dawn; the only light came from the fire which Percevale had managed to keep going all night. The drawn features of the king had acquired an eerie glow: ghastly and yellow. For several hours now he had lain silent. Percevale, struggling with a growing weariness, had managed to remain awake. He was not fully alert, though, and when the king grapsed his arm, it was enough to startle him, feeble though the grip was. The young knight found himself looking into bloodshot eyes, wide with disappointment and despair.

"Where is Avalon?" Somehow he had found the strength to shout and his voice, strained and hoarse, echoed through the chamber, mocking him. He shouted again. "This is not the place!" And he fixed Percevale with a look that he would never forget. It was the look of a man who has found himself betrayed in his direst extremity. Percevale rushed to explain, thinking perhaps the king might at last respond, thinking perhaps there was still time. He had scarcely begun to speak when the arm fell away, the head dropped limply back. Arthur, Lord of Albion, died and, incoherent, in mid-sentence, his attendant paused and stared at the now-lifeless shape, dim comprehension appearing on his pained features.

*   *   *

He had finished his story now. He looked down at the bare floor on which his feet were resting and became aware that the daylight was growing stronger. It occurred to him what a strange thing reminiscence was. The events he had recited in such close detail never failed to give him pain whenever he thought of them, which he did involuntarily and often. Yet the experience of recall was often followed by a vague warmth that seemed to suffuse his whole being. It was not a process of catharsis, of recalling unpleasant events and by so doing purging them. It was not that, for the memory never faded and the self-reproach never diminished. Whatever it was, it somehow made the past easier to live with.

Something warm, physically warm this time, enclosed both his hands. He looked up and saw that the girl had come over to him and had placed his hands inside her own.

His first reaction was one of pleasure at this rare contact with another human being. Then he remembered where he was and felt a sudden sense of alarm. But before this feeling, less pleasant than the first, took hold of him, she had released her grip and returned to the chair beside which she now stood. For a while neither of them spoke. Then she looked up, brushing away the hair that partially obscured her face.

"And so you have been looking for him all this time—for Mordred?"

Percevale nodded.

"And have found no clues to his whereabouts?"

"Oh, many clues. Far too many if anything. Most are cold by the time I have discovered their source."

She shook her head in slow disbelief. "So it really was Mordred then who made the wasteland?"

"You do not believe that?"

"Oh, we are taught to believe it, yes. But it does

stretch one's credulity—that one person could cause so much harm."

"I suppose so." He called his attention back from those quietly piercing, familiar eyes. "You are right to doubt in this respect; I do not believe it is the work of men. The Druids on both sides were very powerful. They forged some terrible weapons, unknightly weapons. But this was a magic beyond even their arts, not of this world."

"But it was men who put it to use."

He nodded. "We should not talk of such things."

"Because it is not seemly?" She smiled, not unkindly. "I was nearly eaten alive, remember. I am no squeamish virgin." Then she bent forward and touched his arm gently, for he had frowned. "I'm sorry, I keep shocking you, don't I? I had best return to my own room now."

Percevale nodded. "Yes." There was a dryness in his throat. He had, after all, done a lot of talking.

"Thank you for your story," she added, and without another word she opened the bedroom door and was gone. Straining his neck out of the window, Percevale looked for the sun. About eight o'clock, he judged.

The girl had left the door slightly ajar and he could hear sounds of movement from downstairs. The sort of sounds associated with people getting up and preparing for the day—or so he assumed, for it had been a long time since he had heard them. He wondered at what time his host planned to break his fast. Nothing had been arranged the night before. He had simply been asked to stay for breakfast and had accepted gratefully. He did not wish to make an early appearance when everything was not ready. Nor did he wish to create a bad impression by appearing when everyone else had finished.

In any event, he decided that now was probably a good time. He looked longingly at the bed, for he felt dreadfully tired, then he pulled himself reluctantly upright. Against the wall opposite stood a small table on which someone, at some time during the previous evening, had set a bowl and a jug filled with water. Above it there hung a mirror. Partly curious, partly apprehensive, he went forward and looked in.

He thought he was prepared for a shock, but when he saw his reflection peering back at him, he realized that he was not. Usually when he had need of a reflection—such as for cutting hair and beard, a tedious and uncomfortable task—he would simply polish up his helm and crouch before its distorted image, struggling with scissor and knife. The result was usually less than stylish but it helped him to retain a modicum of self-respect. Then the grotesque face that winced and grimaced back at him did not greatly disturb him, for he knew that the contours of the helm made it so. But now he saw a face angular and worn and realized what a kind deceiver his own makeshift mirror had been. Here was the scar left by a sword blow deflected too late in some long-forgotten duel. He had not noticed that before. Now it stood out, quite livid against the dark shadows below his eyes and the paler shadows of his cheeks.

For several moments he stood there, studying intently the unfamiliar landscape, tracing its contours with his fingers, the lines, the creases, the deep and ravaged grooves from cheek to chin—so many of them! The dull black hair, coarse and uneven; the beard much the same. The eyebrows were dark and heavy and seemed to draw the lines of his forehead in a downward direction, lending his features a hint of distant melancholy. It began to dawn upon him that somehow, and against all reason, he had preserved an almost static picture of himself as a youth of twenty-one. It was a foolish and insupportable illusion and his realization that it was so made this newer, harsher image more bearable. Still far from welcome, but at least tolerable.

After all, he reflected wryly, I was never a handsome man. No, never that. The thought made him smile, rather warily at first, so drastic was the alteration it seemed to effect in the glass. But in time he was able to endure this image too. It is not so bad, he thought. There is some warmth there and some humanity.

He would have to get a proper haircut, though.

After washing and dressing quickly he went downstairs. Faces turned toward him as he approached, but there was not quite the same stiffness, the same air of expectancy in them as there had been on the previous day. They are beginning to get used to me, he thought. Not much, but a little.

The physician greeted him at the bottom of the stairs and after he had finished giving his instructions to the servants, he ushered Percevale into the dining room. There were two others seated at the table, Elaine and her mother. Elaine was not usually so punctual, but she felt that she had to work hard to regain the favor of her parents. Turning up for breakfast with them would be, she calculated, a way of recovering some lost ground.

After an initial polite exchange everyone ate in silence. Percevale wondered where the rest of the family were—the son and the younger daughter.

Answering his unspoken question, Robert said, "You find us a smaller family this morning, Sir Knight."

Percevale smiled noncommittally through the strange but tasty mixture that had been set before him.

"Simon is in the surgery, preparing for the morning's work."

"He is a physician like yourself?" Percevale asked with polite interest.

"Goodness, no," said Robert. "It will be many years yet before he can assume that title. He works hard, though." There was a note of regret in this last sentence and Percevale wondered if the father was thinking of his son or of the rest of his brood.

"Then he will be a credit to his family," he said.

Robert sighed gently and said nothing.

The meal over, the servants entered and cleared the table. From their manner and their bearing Percevale concluded that they were of the better type of retainer, the sort that worked efficiently and unobtrusively and could be trusted not to run away with their employer's valuables. Ralph must have been a disappointment. He caught this piece of malice and crushed it before it could go any further. Yes, they were good servants—the kind who worked at Arthur's court. They complemented well their surroundings.

His reverie was broken by the scraping of chairs as his hosts rose from the table. Percevale hurriedly stood up and bowed as the ladies left the room. Normally, he supposed, I should now thank my host for his hospitality and take my leave. In the circumstances there seemed little point in doing that. Should he let on that he knew? He could tell that the physician was embarrassed and not quite sure what to say next. Percevale decided not to say anything that would make him feel worse.

The silence between them was becoming strained when, with timely precision, a series of knocks sounded on the door outside. As it was opened, Robert seemed to find the words he wanted. He pulled the curtain across the doorway, leaving a small gap for his expected guests.

"Shall we sit?" he suggested nervously. "There is an important request I have to make of you—and some people I should like you to meet."

6

Another good burning.

King Clarivaus breathed deeply several times and savored the sharpness of the wood smoke as its faint scent drifted past his nostrils. They had left the village far behind, but still the smoke rose, billowing vigorously against the clear sky.

He was standing on the crest of a hill. From this vantage point he could see, all around him, a landscape of almost unbelievable greenness that rolled gently and peacefully. Here, on the westerly edge of the South Downs, the violent forces that millions of years ago had thrown up vast mountain ranges and torn open giant rift valleys had been on their best behavior. A tiny ripple in the earth's crust had created this rich natural garden, carefully proportioned, where the colors of the seasons appeared clearer and more distinct than in many other places.

Clarivaus did not like it. It lacked the harsh masculine quality of the moorland and granite hillsides of his home. And so it gave him some pleasure to contemplate the thick black pillar of smoke rising from a distant fold in the hills. That will teach them to forget about the men from the north! Not that there

was anyone left alive in that particular village to pass
on a reminder.

He turned in the opposite direction to see how far
the army had gone. Some parts were making faster
progress than others; in the glaring sunlight it seemed
to him like a thin, black, segmented worm. Shielding
his eyes, he saw a tiny dot detach itself from the rest
of the column and head toward the spot where he
stood.

Of course, there were those who doubted his policy. At the last meeting of the council they had formed
a sizable minority. Next time they might be a majority. That did not bother him; he had little time for
democracy.

As usual, it had been Sir Marhaus who had been
their spokesman.

"Why do we not simply kill the men and settle the
villages with our own poor?" he had said. Marhaus is
getting too clever by half, he thought. Perhaps he should
revoke his title. He could do that.

The black dot was getting larger. Soon it became a
rider on horseback. It's good to be wanted, he thought.

"It seems to me senseless to waste good lands and
good buildings in this way," Marhaus had continued.
"What did we come here for if not to settle?"

"You're a fool, Marhaus," he had replied, not being
one to mince his words. The knight had reddened and
lowered his face. "You're all fools." Then he quickly
changed his tone, pleading with them, appealing to
their reason. "Do you not see, my friends, the sword
must be appeased before we can use the plow." At
this a few frowns had appeared—some of the chieftains were none too bright. "Our people will not settle easily to farming and husbandry; it is not their
way." There were fewer frowns this time, and a few
nods of agreement. "Let our people burn and kill
until they have had enough of blood and fire. Then, if
they wish, they may settle the villages. The damage

we do this way is not so great. The land is unharmed and the buildings are not to our taste anyway. If our people can vent their bloodlust on these foolish southerners, then they may feel less inclined to turn their energies upon us, their rulers."

He had resumed his throne then, well pleased with his largely impromptu speech. The federation of the northern tribes had not been easy, and there were many who still refused to accept it. Before the long and bloody march south, there had been mutinies and discords among some of the warrior groupings. Recently, the number of such incidents had declined. Yes, some of the chieftains had thought, it is a good theory. Others were pleased simply because their career of murder and rapine looked like it was being extended. In the end he had won by a narrow but respectable majority. He was not worried about the next meeting. If things looked bad, he would simply postpone it.

Of course, there had been times when he himself had entertained doubts. Were there not better things in life perhaps than mere destruction? He knew of men who claimed that there were or who acted as if there were. There were those who took pleasure in their women and their children, in their skills as craftsmen or as artists—counting themselves far happier than the proudest, most accomplished warrior. Well, he had tried all these things at one time or another. He had tried them and had found them wanting and had returned all the more readily to the life he knew best. There was nothing to beat it really.

Hoofbeats sounded behind him. He did not turn. Their thundering stopped. He could hear the harsh breathing of the horse and the creaking of leather as the rider shifted in the saddle.

"My lord?"

He gazed at the smoke for a while longer before turning. A young man was looking respectfully down at him. His long, matted hair and thick beard made him difficult to recognize. Being on horseback, he was clearly a knight, but he had so many knights these days. He would have to do something before there were more knights than footsoldiers.

"Sir—" he began, taping his forehead.

"—Tristram, my lord."

Now, where had he heard that name before? Never mind, he seemed a worthy enough young man—eager, bloodthirsty, the sort who would probably go a long way with a little help.

"Sir Tristram," he repeated, and looked at him inquiringly.

"My lord, the column is over a mile distant now. You are alone here. There are fears for your safety."

"Are there indeed? Who sent you to fetch me?"

"No one, sire." The young man blushed slightly and lowered his eyes. "I came of my own bidding."

Definitely a go-getter, thought Clarivaus. Yes, he would go far. "Very well, bring me my horse."

The knight dismounted quickly and ran to untether the horse that stood munching peacefully at the rich hillside grass. When he returned, he stood by the horse and cupped his hands, for there was no stirrup.

"No, no, I don't need that. In another ten years perhaps but not"—with a practiced dexterity he lifted himself into the saddle—"yet." He could sense the young man's surprise at such unexpected agility and was pleased by it.

"Ride beside me, Sir Tristram," he said, and the young man blushed again, this time with pride.

"Did you enjoy our little fracas today?"

Tristram smiled, not at the king's wit but because he had found favor.

"Aye, my lord. Yet I wish they had put up more of a fight."

"My feelings exactly." Clarivaus brightened visibly. He was a perceptive fellow, this. "I couldn't agree with you more. They're nothing but a bunch of milksops. Sending out their old men to remonstrate with us"—he shook his head angrily—"they deserved what they got. And yet it's not much fun for you young folk when they don't even have the decency to stand and fight. Sharp of you to see that, my lad." He smiled approvingly at Tristram. The young knight's smile broadened and his blush deepened that such praise should be bestowed upon his unworthy self and he thought to himself, It's not sharp at all, you old fool. You complain about it every time you're in your cups.

"Still, I tell myself that it's necessary, even if it is a bit of a bore sometimes." He fixed his companion with an earnest gaze. "You do see that it's necessary, don't you?"

The horses were nearing the bottom of the steep slope and Tristram had a difficult task controlling his mount while returning that searching look.

"Sire?" He did not wish to seem too wise, though he had a pretty shrewd idea of what was coming next.

"These people." The king made a wide dismissive gesture. "They have lost their right to the land. If they will not fight for it, then they should not keep it."

Tristram nodded. Yes, he knew what was coming next.

"They are soft. Degenerate."

He nodded again, not too eagerly.

"You know why they didn't try to fight?"

Tristram raised his eyebrows in interested inquiry.

"Because they don't know how to. Long ago, in the days of King Arthur, they were a formidable race. Even my father acknowledged Arthur as his lord. Then they fell out among themselves and the gods destroyed them all. None of that kind are left anymore—just these placid, docile creatures. They have forgotten about the old days. And they have forgotten about the north. Well, they have had their peace and if they have chosen to spend it wallowing in luxury and idle self-deception instead of learning to defend their lands, then they can hardly complain when we come to take it away from them."

Tristram nodded his agreement. I was right, he thought. It's the one about our manifest destiny. It is not only our right to take the lands of the southerners, who have lost them by default; it is our solemn duty. He had heard it many times.

"So we have a right to their lands, sire," he said, subtly prompting. "The right of conquest?"

"More than that—an obligation. A duty to show ourselves worthy of the soil. A duty which this corrupt race"—he nodded his head in the direction of the village—"have clearly neglected."

This last declaration was followed by a conclusive snort, indicating that the truth of the matter was perfectly obvious and further comment was unnecessary. Sir Tristram responded by inclining his head thoughtfully and hoped that this would suffice—it did—and they continued for a while in silence.

Soon they drew level with the rear of the column. At the very end were the cattle and other livestock, their numbers swollen by this latest raid. The herdsmen turned and bowed when they saw the riders. Next they passed the wagons, twenty of them, drawn by oxen. Mostly they carried plunder—milled corn, clothing, a few weapons, and some choice farming implements. A few were set aside for the very young—of whom there were many—and the very old—who were fewer in number. Then there was a gap, gradually lengthening all the time, between the baggage train and the main body of the army—the unarmored fighting men, their women and children. By nightfall the wagons and livestock would be far behind, but this did not worry him. In this country there was no danger. Heads turned as the riders drew closer, then

a hoarse and subdued cheer passed along the straggling line of footsoldiers. These numbered nearly a
thousand altogether. They wore neither helmets nor
armor unless they could acquire it by right of plunder
and there had been precious little in the way of armor
to plunder in the campaign so far. Each man carried a
sword, a wooden oval shield, and a thrusting spear. A
few, those who were skilled enough, also carried throwing spears.

Clarivaus slowed his pace as he rode past. "You
have fought well, my brothers!" he called.

There was little in the way of reply. The men who
composed his infantry, the largest part of the army,
were poor and, in their own eyes as well as his, insignificant. The youngest of them aspired only to a pro-
fitable season of bloodletting with perhaps a pliant slave
and a few choice trinkets to show for it at the end;
the older men, most of whom had already more than
satisfied these ambitions, hoped for modest plots of
land and fine sons to help cultivate them. Whatever
their hopes, they all knew their place. Some raised
their shields in salute, some cheered again with vary-
ing degrees of enthusiasm. But none ventured to speak.

Clarivaus quickened his horse's pace until he reached
the head of the column. Here the cheering was loud
and heartfelt, for these were the knights, his armored
cavalry. He had originally intended to keep their number at a round hundred, but there had been so many
deserving cases lately in addition to the many petty
chieftains. Two hundred and thirty-five men on horseback rode at the head of the army now. As befitted
their status, they all wore mail shirts and iron helmets. In addition to his sword and shield, each knight
carried a war ax or a wooden lance and sometimes
both. This elite group had been of little value in the
campaign so far. There is little point in deploying
armored cavalry against an enemy who cannot surrender quickly enough. Many, he knew, had not stained

their weapons once this season. Still, he thought, give it time.

He halted and watched. The knights rode past, stiffly erect in their saddles, conscious of his critical appraisal.

"You have fought well, my brothers!" he shouted. "Which is more than can be said for the enemy, ha!" Several of them laughed at this. A few shouted back.

"Find us some men to fight, sire. I am tired of fighting women!"

"What's tiring about fighting women?"

"Why don't some of us join the enemy? It might even things up a bit."

Clarivaus laughed and returned their banter. Though they had had little opportunity to show their mettle, they were well pleased with themselves. They have a right to be, he thought. Since they had crossed the Thames, his column alone had destroyed four settlements without a single loss to themselves. No doubt the other warlords were enjoying similar successes. At this rate, they would have the whole region sewn up before the fall, just in time to gather the harvest and prepare for winter. He turned to Tristram and said, "Ride with me at the head of my kinsmen." It will be good policy, he thought, to discomfit some of those who take my favor for granted. There were some among the council, he believed, who were becoming too powerful. Cliques were beginning to form. He would have to put a stop to that. Marhaus he would reduce to the ranks—that would take care of him and the other humanitarians. Then there were Colegrevaunce and Kay; they were inclined to throw their weight around a bit. Elevating this obscure young man would help take them all down a peg or two. Yes, he thought, after all, I can always send him packing in a day or two.

"Your Majesty does me too great an honor," Tristram replied. I just hope it's all worth it, he thought, listening to his interminable lectures, laughing at his inane jokes, earning the jealousy and hatred of my friends. For a while he watched in ruminative silence as the king spurred his horse and galloped away to take his place at the head of the column. He did not look behind him to ensure that he was being followed. Tristram paused only for a moment. Then he urged his horse forward to join his lord.

7

Later, expressing a desire for solitary reflection,
Percevale was escorted outside. He expected
perhaps a seat against a sunlit wall or beneath
a tree. What he found left him almost speechless.

"It is my wife's work," Robert proudly remarked.
"It is quite unique in our little community."

It was so long since he had stood in a garden, and
this by any standards was a fine one. For a little
while he gazed about in silent admiration, then, taking
his time, he followed a pathway that ran beneath a
high stone wall covered in greenery, admiring the
well-turned beds of flowers and the tall shrubs that
he passed.

The profusion of color dazzled and confused him.
He had never been able to master the sometimes absurd names the gardeners of Albion had given their
creations. Some bore a faint resemblance to plants he
knew in the wild. That might be mallow, those tall
flowers toadflax, yet they were varieties he had never
seen before. But if he could not fully comprehend the
gardener's art, he could admire it. To take the color
and tranquility of a woodland glade and shape it in
plant and stone outside its owner's very doorway; it

took a special sort of genius to so combine art and nature.

So what was it doing here?

He wandered on.

There was much to see. Even though the garden could not be so very large—common sense told him that—its designer had created a clever illusion of scale. A number of smaller paths branched sideways to disappear behind bushes or rocky archways. Peering through one such archway, he saw a path that led directly to the center of the garden. Here, surrounded by a square of closely cropped grass, stood a sundial on a stony plinth. Percevale decided to keep to the main path. A man could almost get lost here, he thought. Presently he came upon a stone bench that had been set into the wall and partially enclosed by a screen of flowering shrubs. It had been so placed as to catch the full force of the early morning sun. Gratefully, for he wanted to think rather than to feast his eyes, he sat down, spreading his knees and resting his head against the warm orange stone that rose behind him. For a moment he would try to forget about the momentous issues that were so exercising the minds of the four men in the house. He closed his eyes and felt the sun's rays warming his face. The words of an ancient rhyme sprang to mind.

> Maytime, fair season,
> Perfect is its aspect then,
> Blackbirds sing a full song,
> If there be a scanty beam of day.

There was more, but he had forgotten it. Another knight would have been able to recite it with ease, together with many more of the old songs now lost. But in Gawaine's school there had been no time for mastering any of the cultural activities so prized by the generality of knights. Gawaine could teach his squire how to kill a man with one hand or disarm an opponent when one's own sword was lost. He could not teach dancing or singing or how to pay court to a lady, and so he had convinced them both that such activities were but idle conceits and had no part in the making of a knight. Well, perhaps Gawaine had been right. All the same, he felt that something was missing from his education, when he could bask lazily in the warm sun, savoring the honeyed scents of unknown plants and listening to the pleasing harmony of birdsong, calling to mind some apposite words— only to get stuck after the fourth line. It left him feeling rather unsatisfied.

Well, it had been nearly twenty years since he had last read a book. There was no mending it now.

There was something else rather more unsettling than these supposed flaws in his professional training.

A disquieting thought was beginning to form in his mind. At first he had merely been pleasantly surprised at the extent to which this sheltered community had preserved so much of the old civilization. On his many travels he had come across settlements where the inhabitants still possessed and half-understood such crafts as casting in iron or building in stone. In some places even, some of the more esoteric arts survived, such as literacy or medicine. Such knowledge had become dangerous for its practitioners in the years immediately after the war—they were now few in number and widely dispersed. Never had he chanced upon a place where more than one, perhaps two half-remembered fragments of that vanished society remained. Until now. There was something even more improbable that had to be considered. These people had not merely preserved much of the technology of the Arthurian period, they had progressed beyond it. There had been much fine architecture in Arthur's

day. There had been the castles, as impregnable as
they were elegant. There were the great universities
of York and Durham. But Albion's had been a rural
civilization. There had been a few towns and these
had been simple affairs: a few huts clustered about a
temple and a space for a weekly market. Even the
capitals of the two kingdoms, Glastonbury and Colchester, for all their status and strategic value, had
been little more than fortified villages.

Then there was the glass—and this garden, of
course. What was such a beautifully wrought space
of ground doing behind the house of a bone setter?
Earlier, indoors, one of the councillors had spoken
of a manuscript machine. Percevale had no idea what
it was or how it functioned, but he had no doubt
it betokened yet another marvel.

It puzzled and disturbed him, this haven of industry
amid a world that was quietly settling into decay
and ruin. But it intrigued him more.

Footsteps padded softly along the narrow pathway.
He felt a shade cooler as a figure stopped directly in
front of him, momentarily blocking the path of light.
He opened his eyes and looked up.

"I hope I have not disturbed your reverie, Sir
Knight."

Somehow he had not expected to see the mother
standing there. (Why did he feel that slight pinch of
disappointment?) He had begun to think that she
was avoiding him for some obscure reason of her own.
She moved a little to one side so that part of her
seemed for a moment to be surrounded by an aura of
sunlight, lending an insubstantiality to her outline,
like dazzling gauze.

"I have disturbed you." There was the faintest trace
of genuine concern in her voice. "I am sorry."

"No, no," he assured her. "It is nothing. I was
admiring your beautiful garden." Remembering his

manners, he rose quickly to his feet. "I suppose I must have been dozing."

"Did you not sleep well last night?" She fancied she had heard voices early in the morning. She could not be sure.

"Tolerably well, I thank you. I am unaccustomed to these comforts."

"Ah." Was it just his imagination or was she really incapable of making even a noncommittal grunt without seeming to invest it with significance?

He stood before her, feeling gauche and awkward, just as he had felt the previous evening. She had not moved back when he had stood up, and he was close enough to feel her breath on his chin. It was warm and fresh and not unwelcome. Presently he found words.

"Lady, will you sit?"

Smiling graciously, she did so. Reaching up, she tugged at the mass of greenery covering the wall behind. A token handful of leaves and twigs came away. She crushed these slowly between thumb and fingers, releasing their pungent, slightly spiced odor before absently letting the mangled bundle fall to the ground.

"I must get this seen to," she said as she gazed in brief puzzlement at her now-stained hands. "These creepers can pull a wall down, you know. Do you like our garden?"

Percevale nodded with partly feigned enthusiasm. "It charms the eye and calms the mind. It is a fine place in which to seek repose."

"My husband and I sometimes come out here during the light evenings and play backgammon. Do you play backgammon?"

Percevale shook his head. "Sadly no, lady."

Sometimes, during his more introspective moods, he had puzzled over the convoluted logic that had shaped his strange destiny. Why had he survived the great calamity rather than some other knight more accomplished and better educated?

However, if she was disappointed, she did not show it. "No doubt you have seen gardens more richly attired than this," she said.

"I can remember a few such as these, lady," he replied honestly. "None more so." Not even Cadras.

She was clearly pleased with his reply. "Yes, well, I have had plenty of time to make improvements." He looked up sharply, which seemed to gratify her further. "Did my husband not tell you? I once lived in a castle."

Of course. That would explain much. No doubt she had seen better days. This must be a galling existence for her.

He wondered if he had known her husband. Those had been crowded days and he did not feel it wise to ask, but it was possible.

But she was interested only in stimulating his curiosity, not satisfying it. "My husband tells me that you think we should all leave."

"Your husband and his colleagues have decided to ignore my advice."

"Perhaps now you understand something of the reasons for our reluctance. It has taken many years of toil to create all this."

Percevale did not but he remained silent.

"Will you stay and help us?"

"It seems I have little choice in the matter. My horses and accoutrements were taken during the night and hidden—a poor kind of hospitality if I may say so, lady."

"You are right, of course. It was not well done," she conceded hastily. Returning to her more immediate preoccupations, she added, "So you will help our men to fight and defend our town?"

"If they have it in them to fight, yes, lady." This was not said in malice. He simply had his doubts whether people so accustomed to a secure and prosperous existence could, at such short notice, find the will to defend it. His discussion with Robert and his fellow councillors a few moments ago had given him little reason to feel optimistic.

"How many menfolk have you in the town?" he had asked.

The four burghers standing around the long table in Robert's dining room had looked thoughtfully at one another.

"Among the workers?" said the town clerk. "A good thousand or so who are of the right age. I have the exact figure somewhere."

"It is no matter. Have they weapons?"

"Oh, no," said Oliver, the mayor. "We don't allow that." He was a tall, impressive-looking man who might have appeared more imposing still a few years ago before he was seduced by the comforts of his present existence. "Ours has always been a peaceable community," he added.

"Then they must be furnished quickly," said Percevale. "Can this be done?"

"There are two forges in the town," said Robert. "It can be done."

"And gentlefolk," Percevale asked, "how many of those are capable of bearing arms and riding a horse?"

The councillors looked at one another in bewilderment and surprise. "Do you mean people like us?" their expressions seemed to say. It hasn't really sunk in yet, thought Percevale with a mixture of impatience and wry amusement. To spare them further embarrassment he said, "What of the peasantry of the district? What is their number?"

More surprised glances were exchanged. Somebody

coughed uncomfortably. Then the mayor spoke again. He shook his head disapprovingly and drew a sharp breath between small gleaming teeth. "Oh, we don't use that word these days, you know. Not these days."

"Peasants?"

The mayor winced slightly. "No, not these days," he repeated.

"They are slaves then?" Percevale asked ingenuously.

For a moment they looked at him as if undecided as to whether he was serious or not. Then Oliver laughed a short nervous laugh.

"Slaves? Good gods, no! Anyone would think we were living in the Dark Ages."

He turned to his companions as if seeking confirmation, and they, too, smiled and threw up their heads as if it were all rather a good joke. But Percevale knew he had touched upon a sensitive subject.

"They are agricultural laborers," explained Robert eventually.

The others nodded. "Salt of the earth," echoed one.

"Peasants then," said Percevale, who had always understood the terms to be interchangeable.

"Certainly not," protested the mayor.

"The term carries with it certain connotations," Robert explained. "Feudalism is dead. We feel that the language of feudalism, too, should be buried."

"I see," said Percevale, who was beginning to find their senseless quibbling irritating. But he suppressed the impulse to throw up his arms in angry frustration—they still had his equipment even though he had managed to extract a promise of its eventual return—and begged leave instead to pause and reflect. They had looked worried at this, but had complied readily enough. The physician, the only one among them with a sound head on his shoulders, Percevale had already concluded, had bade him make use of the garden and there deliberate at his leisure.

"But they will fight, they must," protested the lady Anne with a sudden vehemence that took him aback. It was the first sign of any spirit he had so far encountered. That and, of course, the daughter's still only partly explained foray into the wasteland. Perhaps it is the women I should train for battle, he thought.

"If they don't, then all is lost," she said. Her arm, in the wide sleeve of her robe, made a graceful sweeping gesture that struck him as almost theatrical in its intensity. But there was nothing contrived or artificial about her concern for what was obviously closest to her heart. Percevale had never considered himself blessed with a sharp perception, but he was sure that she had no fear for her own life, still less for her husband and children.

"These barbarians, they would keep pigs here," she muttered bitterly.

If they did so much, thought Percevale, it would be constructive for them.

"They are scum," she hissed. "I despise them."

The erect and impassive demeanor that had earlier impressed and slightly overawed him, reminding him of those vanished days, had now vanished. In its stead was a primitive racial hatred, a fierce and violent emotion, for years submerged beneath an elaborate cultural overlay, now brought to the surface in defense of something prized, something threatened, something, in Percevale's eyes at any rate, ultimately trivial.

Still, it gave him renewed hope. If such a fine lady could be moved to such a passionate outburst over her flower beds, could not the menfolk be similarly aroused in defense of their livelihoods and their lives? Civilization and the easy living it engendered was, as his companion had so vividly demonstrated, a veneer and a pitifully thin one at that. It might not take so much to strip it away. What lurked beneath was ugly and ignoble, but in a situation like this it could be useful.

"They are like animals," she said. There was a note of fatigue in her voice now; her venom was weakening.

Yes, he thought, and the sooner we start behaving like animals ourselves, the better our chances will be.

Twenty years ago he would have been profoundly shocked to find himself thinking in such dark and pessimistic tones about his fellow men, but then a lot had happened in twenty years.

Looking up, he noticed that she had made some effort to pull herself together. She looked flushed and somewhat chastened, as if aware that she had lost, temporarily, some of her dignity in his eyes. Well, that suited him well enough. He could, with some confidence, confront her more or less as an equal.

"We may find a way of thwarting them yet, lady," he said, trying to soothe without raising false hopes.

If she had hoped for more, she seemed ready enough to settle for this. Now she turned her attention to the other matter that had brought her here.

"What do you think of my daughter, she whom you rescued?" she asked.

To this unexpected question Percevale gave the usual reply a gentleman gave when wishing to be polite and noncommittal. "I find her modest in her bearing and fair in her speech." It was a reply which he felt satisfied neither of them.

"She is an impulsive girl, you know." Percevale nodded, hoping that she would offer some explanation for Elaine's behavior. "She is easily led." She looked at him through lowered eyes. "I daresay she is very taken by you."

Despite the form of words, Percevale did not think this was meant entirely as a compliment. Clearly, she was hinting at something. He wondered how he could politely forestall further discussion of what might become an embarrassing and delicate topic, when she rose from her seat.

"The council is no doubt waiting upon your delib-

erations," she said. "Shall we go indoors?" Her tone
had changed quite suddenly. She was now once again
the rather cold, quietly impressive woman he remembered from the previous day, except that there was an
added note of displeasure, barely discernible, in her
voice. Hastily, he stood up. Even now, after she had
revealed some of the less attractive aspects of her
nature, he found the mask imposing. In silence he
followed her back, for the pathway was too narrow
for two to walk astride without brushing shoulders.
Once again he found himself admiring the illusion of
scale that the garden's designer had so cleverly contrived. Again, too, he had the unsettling feeling, foolish and unfounded though he knew it to be, that if he
strayed out of sight of the main path, he would not
find his way back.

In the old days it had been customary for gentlemen to escort their ladies around the castle perimeter, usually before the evening meal. He had seen
them many times at dusk, pacing their steps to a
measured, thoughtful rhythm, their heads bowed in
deep conversation, or turned upward admiring the
view. Taking the air (but staying well clear of the
moat and its noxious fumes). Often on such occasions
he had waited on Gawaine, a reluctant follower of the
custom and an even clumsier courtier than himself.

No one seemed to know how this practice, observed
punctiliously by all, had originated, nor what purpose
it served. Looking back, it seemed rather a silly idea.

But at least you couldn't get lost then.

8

Summer or not, the mornings were still cold. Mordred lay in bed and watched the sunlight stream through yet another hole in the roof. It neither warmed him nor improved his temper. I'll not patch that one up again, he said to himself. I've done it once this year, I'm not doing it again. He observed that it was directly in line with his feet. In the winter then, he grudgingly conceded.

Soon he would get up and begin the business of the day. Tedious though much of it was, he was not greatly tempted to postpone it. Amid the quantity of mundane tasks there were important things to be done and this might be a day for doing them well.

But first things first. Abiding by the ritual he followed every morning, he let his eyes slowly scan their immediate horizons.

Starting on our left, we have a seat. It is a plain instrument but serviceable. I made it myself, from applewood. The tree was barren, but the wood was sound. It bends, you see, but does not break. It is used for visitors, so there is little call for it. Behind the chair is the wall, circular because a circle is the most efficient shape. It is not in as good a state of repair as

it should be, but then I am not as young as I was. It is
constructed from mud and wattle and has withstood
three consecutive winters. This is the fifth hut I have
built, though the first on this particular site. The floor
is pressed earth and stones strewn with dry grass.
You would be surprised how well it has lasted.

Next we come to my table. Like the stool which
stands before it, it is made from elm. I did not make
the table or the stool—I was not brought up to be a
craftsman after all—but I paid a good price for them
both. On the table are my writing implements—two
goose quills, a knife for sharpening them, and a
jar of ink. Oh—sorry about that—remains of last
night's supper. Beneath the table are two piles of
parchment, one containing blank sheets, the other
containing full sheets. This latter pile, the one on the
left and, sadly, smaller than the right-hand pile, is
my magnum opus, part of it anyway, of which more
later. The parchment comes from the skins of sheep. I
have four at the moment in a small pen outside and
soon they will commence their incessant bleating as
they do every morning at this hour. It is a primitive
medium, parchment, and when I first started, I found
the task of preparation barely endurable. Killing the
animal, removing the wool, stripping the skin, drying
it. All that before I could write a single word! In the
old days we had paper made from wood pulp, but the
old days are gone now and one must make do with
what is to hand.

Speaking of paper, these are my bookshelves next to
the table. Yes, I know they are stocked mainly with
food and bric-a-brac, but there are also some books.
They are from the old days. Of course then I had a
whole library to my name—one of the largest in the
land and unlike Arthur's I had actually read everything in mine. You name the volume, I had it. Homer,
Hesiod, Plato, Aristotle—now Plato, there was a writer
with a true grasp of the political realities. A brilliant

book, *The Republic*. Some of his proposals were a bit
eccentric, I grant you, but the underlying theme was
broadly correct. By comparison, Aristotle seems in-
sipid. I never had much time for Aristotle. Oh, yes, I
had most of the Romans too. Some of the others at the
court used to think I was unpatriotic, reading the
works of the enemy and all that. A parochial lot they
were in those days.

We pass on to the doorway, at present covered with
a curtain. No, it's not too bad in winter, not after the
first one anyway. Beyond the doorway are the pens
where I keep my livestock—four sheep, I have already mentioned those, a goat (for milk and cheese),
and the pigs (for companionship and, alas, one day,
for breakfast). Then there is the oven in which I bake
my bread. Then there is the small stretch of ground
on which I grow the corn which, considering its position, thrives pretty well. Also there is a spring nearby.

Returning indoors, we move to the other side of the
doorway, where there stands a small screen on the
other side of which there lies a pallet of straw. In
front of this pallet, in the exact center of the circle, is
my fireplace. The smoke, you see, goes through the
aperture in the roof. It does, but in the process it fills
the whole hut. Again that is something to which I
have become accustomed. On the pallet, my bed, lies
Mordred, pondering on his surroundings and reflect-
ing with ironic amusement on the sheer amount and
variety of materials needed to sustain his simple life.

There were good reasons for this daily itinerary
together with its accompanying silent monologue. For
one thing, although the general pattern was identical
each morning, the details were always new. There
were fresh insights to be gained every day. Also, this
conducted tour acted as a warming-up process, preparing his brain for the more arduous monologue that
he would shortly resume at his elmwood table on his
elmwood stool.

But first there were the tasks of the morning. A loud solitary bleat from outside, closely followed by a chorus of similar calls, told him that it was time to get up. He threw aside the thick sheepskin blanket and slowly pulled himself upright. Straightening his back, he breathed deeply six times. Such regular observances, he believed, helped to keep him a relatively fit sixty years old—or was it fifty-nine? Passing through the curtain, he went outside where, behind the hut, a little way off, stood the latrine. Above the hole was a raised wooden board with a circular hole in the center. He positioned himself carefully, sat back, and waited, exerting only the minimum of effort. Until quite recently he had been able to manage simply by crouching over the pit; age did bring some advantages.

He looked up. After the steady and unseasonable rain of the previous few days, the sky had at last cleared. Apart from that, it had been a fine summer so far. There was still a chill in the air, but it did not greatly bother him now that he was up and about. He looked around him, surveying a wider landscape now. To his left was a wide plain of gorse and heather which rose slowly in the distance, eventually becoming the far-off Mendip Hills. To his right the vegetation was much sparser and drier; even in the wettest weather it was like this. Eventually it died out altogether, for no plants grew in the wastelands and those that managed to survive on the outermost boundaries were sickly and barren things.

And yet, for Mordred this was a good place in which to settle. Few people were foolhardy enough to venture near, so he was sure of being left well enough alone, and twenty years was ample time in which to learn where, even in such unpromising soil as this, were the places where crops could grow and animals feed.

Nor were the other permanent inhabitants of the

district a great drawback—certainly they were not to
be feared. During his long self-imposed exile he had
come to know the backgrounds of many of these sad
and lonely creatures. Many times, especially in the
years immediately after the war, he had chanced across
the cold, stiff body of a hideously deformed child,
brought to the edge of the wasteland, probably in
secret, by its horrified parents and there left to die.
Others, perhaps luckier, perhaps not, had been kept
alive for some while until mounting aversion or chance
discovery by neighbors had forced the creature to
seek refuge in the only place where it would be safe.
How many of these mutants there were he could not
tell, for though their death rate was high, there were
still plenty of new births to swell their number. And
the ones he had encountered had been on the edge of
the wasteland. Farther than this, few humans, certainly not he, would go, and who was to tell what
horrors there resided? For it was widely held that
mutants, too, could conceive.

"Ah, well," he announced to the sky in an effort to
banish these unsettling speculations, "I look after them
and they leave me alone." His ablutions completed, he
rose and washed himself from the bucket that stood
beside the latrine. Then he shoveled in some soil.
Peering through the hole, he noted with satisfaction
that it was not yet half full. That left him another
week or two until he would have to dig a new one. He
went back to the hut, his speculations on the subject
of mutants in general having reminded him of one in
particular, a shambling one-eyed creature whose huge
head and arms were out of all proportion to his small
yet muscular torso and legs. I wonder what has happened to him (or her), he thought. Mordred counted
this particular specimen as one of his more notable
successes. During their first encounter, when the creature had burst into the hut with the blood of a sheep
on its lips and the unstated but fairly clear intention

of eating the sheep's owner as well, Mordred had quickly persuaded it—with the help of his sword—that home-baked bread and goat's cheese was not only less likely to put up the sort of resistance an animal or man might put up but was also rather tasty. Since then the creature had become a regular visitor. On the next visit, Mordred resolved, he would give it a name and endeavor to teach it some words—one needed some diversions in a place like this.

But there had been no visit for several days and Mordred began to suspect that perhaps it had come across a weaker member of its own kind (kinship among the mutants was tenuous and fleeting) or a lost traveler and reverted to its former habits. If so, he would need his sword again.

Mordred was a little saddened by this thought. He took a keen interest in the welfare of his unfortunate neighbors. After all, he reflected with an irony that was neither bitter nor grim, I'm like a father to them.

Inside the hut he exchanged the jerkin in which he had slept for another, identical one. Sometimes he wondered why he bothered. After all, neither had been cleaned now for several months. And yet he did bother. In preserving a distinction between the clothes he wore in the daytime and those he wore at night he felt he was preserving one of the qualities that marked a civilized being, albeit one that is a little down on his luck and has been for the past twenty years or so.

Another wooden bucket of water stood on the floor beside the bed. Kneeling down, he splashed water on his face, drying himself afterward with the discarded jerkin. Several times he ran his fingers through his long gray hair and rubbed his eyes to remove any deposit that might remain. Now for the animals. Again he went outside and moved aside the gate of the wicker sheep pen. The animals needed no coaxing to leave. They were hungry and the ground of the pen was nothing but dry earth. Outside, there was plenty of pasture and they ran out, searching eagerly. In the evening he would return them to the pen. They never strayed far from the comforting sight of their home and he had never lost any yet—save to his nocturnal visitor with the one eye.

That done, he fed the pigs; Guinevere, the fat sow, and her offspring, Lancelot, Isolde, and Kay. Kay was a runt and Mordred had been promising himself for several weeks now to kill it, for there was little point in letting such a weakly creature survive. Yet something had stayed his hand and indeed the little thing was doing quite well. Mordred had little regard for his sheep; they were useful enough but noisy and stupid. For the pigs he felt an affection he had never felt for their namesakes. Leaning over the pen where the little ones were now kept, away from their mother, he threw an extra handful of turnip slices in the direction of the runt. The little animal wolfed them greedily before any of his fellows were aware of what was happening. Then it looked at Mordred in the same unselfconsciously appealing way it had looked when he had been about to cut its throat. Mordred smiled back and returned indoors.

On the shelf below the remains of his library there stood the bread crock. Removing the remnants of the previous day's loaf, he noted before returning the lid that there was enough bread to last another three days. That was a pleasant thought upon which to dwell for a moment. Three days of comparative leisure before he would have to grind and mix and knead and bake enough bread to last a further week. Breadmaking took a whole day and Mordred considered it a tedious and laborious task. He ate some of the bread, returned the rest to the crock, then washed it down with a beaker of goat's milk. Gods! I haven't seen to Annie! He brushed the food from his beard and hurried outside. Murmuring his apologies, he untethered the goat and moved the unprotesting animal to a fresher area of pasture, where he tied it to the base of a strong bush.

This time when he returned to the hut he went straight to the table and sat down. To one side of the table, precariously fastened to the wall, was a narrow shelf. From this he took his penknife and sharpened the goose quill which he had selected for the day's work. Reaching beneath the table, he pulled up the pile of completed parchments. It did not matter how many times he read them, they always seemed so fresh—and he was always revising.

He turned the parchments over, for the first sheet was at the bottom of the pile. This he did not bother to scrutinize; it was simply the title page: "The Boke of Mordred." Not inspired, perhaps, but adequate. It would do until something better came to mind. He turned to the next sheet.

CHAPTER THE FIRST

Mine was not a happy childhood.

Mordred sat back and smiled, thinking, as he always thought when he read it, what an opening! No rambling introduction, but a bold statement of one of my central theses encapsulated in six words. That should make even the most jaded reader sit up and take notice.

There were occasions when he had been tempted to change his opening sentence and adopt a somewhat more conventional prose. But the novelty of it had struck him from the beginning and had never left him since, even though he had read it over several hundred times.

He read on. Occasionally he would stop and make alterations. Nothing major; a changed adjective here, a rearrangement of syntax there. As for the basic structure, he trusted to first instincts. Of this he had changed nothing. He was perfectly satisfied with it.

The later chapters presented more problems. Now he began to look pensive. His face creased and the occasional frown appeared. Sometimes whole paragraphs had to be struck out. These chapters dealt with the period after he was taken from his mother and was brought to Arthur's court as heir to the throne. In this part of the narrative he chronicled some of the important events in and around the royal court, dwelling at length on the character of Arthur himself. Extensive revision is required here, he reflected with some annoyance.

At last he came to his work of the previous day. Now the frown deepened and settled. He had worked hard yesterday, harder than he had done for a long time. When night finally came, he had crawled into bed exhausted but happy, feeling a sense of achievement and tired euphoria which he could not remember having experienced since his first (and last) drunken orgy the day after he was made knight by Arthur at Cadras. There had been times during yesterday's sustained bout of creative endeavor when his quill had seemed to acquire a life of its own; almost as if it had established a direct link with his subconscious memory, a link that circumvented the mechanisms of hand and brain. Now he threw aside each sheet in growing dismay. He laid the quill aside. No revision was possible here; this would have to be rewritten entirely. Anxiously, he counted back through the sheets of parchment. Twenty-one sheets, about two hundred words to a sheet—four thousand words! The most he had ever written in a single sitting and it was all so much ordure. Even the style was different, reminiscent of the florid, heroic language of the minstrels and storytellers. There was little of the hard, searching analysis he had perfected elsewhere, just a recital of heroic deeds and improbable characters. Clearly, the atmosphere of the court had made a deeper impression on his inner mind than he had hitherto guessed. It would have to be brought under firm control. Sadly, he laid aside the final sheet. There were some passages which might yet provide useful material for a second draft, but on the whole it was quite devoid of merit. He rolled the twenty-one offending sheets and tied them in a tight cylinder, placing it to one side. They would have to go, of course, all those tales of dragon-slaying and unlikely mystical guests. In their place he would write the truth—the scandals and the institutionalized corruption, the shady diplomatic deals with the Italians, the exploitation of the peasantry under the guise of benevolent feudalism, all these he would expose to the world. Not that he was under any illusions concerning the reception his thesis would receive from the contemporary reading public. Faced with the choice, they would prefer the comforting warmth of the legends to the cold reality that he offered. But this work was not intended for the present. Mordred had decided that long ago. History was to be his judge, and he had already earmarked the spot where he would bury the completed manuscript. There would come a time, he believed, when men like him—rational, clear-headed, with a strong desire for order—would be the rule rather than the exception. Such men would find his book and read his words with sympathy and understanding.

But not that, he suddenly thought, casting a worried eye upon the discarded roll on the table. Next breadmaking day I shall light the oven with it.

With a sigh he pulled out a clean sheet and dipped the quill in the viscous substance that served as ink. Now he would have to start all over again. He could

not hope to write four thousand words, especially
when he was in such low spirits. Less than a quarter
of that was more usual for a daily output. Ah, well.
With more sighs and mutterings he began to write.

9

In the center of the town square a wooden platform had been hastily erected. The walls around the square were covered with posters, their loose corners rippling gently in the cool evening air, all announcing that evening's meeting.

Percevale had not yet seen the mayor's manuscript machine, but he wondered greatly at its ability to achieve in a few hours what it would have taken Druid scribes many days to do in the old days.

"We have also sent a leaflet to every household," Oliver had announced proudly. "There should be a good attendance."

And indeed there was. Percevale stood beside the platform and watched as a steady stream of people converged on the square, filling it with the din of their collective murmurings.

From their crowded dwellings in the sunless back streets they had been summoned, but they came without eagerness. Percevale could sense among the growing audience a spirit of reluctance and weary resignation. Their appearance struck him as less than inspiring. They lacked the bucolic good health of the rural peasant. Not that they appeared undernourished—indeed some were positively fat.

Naturally there was a marked (and in his view very proper) contrast between these folk and their more affluent neighbors, yet the mass of them appeared far from indigent. Many wore the brightly colored clothes of checked and plaid wool that in former times were worn only by the Celtic nobility. Percevale was not offended by this, believing that a certain modest prosperity among the lower classes was quite allowable and probably beneficial. But he was puzzled. He had seen examples of most of the forms of social organization that had struggled into existence after the war. For the most part, they were either oligarchies of one sort or another or cruel distortions of feudalism, and sometimes simple slavery. All had one thing in common: the majority lived lives of privation and desperate misery.

It had not been so in Arthur's time. But even then the wealthiest peasant could not have clothed himself as richly as some of these simple townsfolk.

What disturbed him rather more than the crowd's sartorial elegance was its latent hostility; it seemed to charge the air around him. He turned to the councillors, wondering if they, too, could sense the dangerous atmosphere. They appeared pleased and were smiling and congratulating one another on the excellent turnout. Oliver was wearing his chain of office. Presently, he broke in on the subdued conversations of his companions with a polite cough.

"I think we can probably start now," he suggested softly.

Several hundred people now stood in the square. The murmuring had stopped. In its place was a resentful and expectant silence. Percevale began to feel uneasy. It was a feeling not lessened by the presence, around the edge of the crowd, of six or seven armed militia, the nearest thing the town possessed to a

standing army. If these people get out of control, he
thought, they will prove nothing but a handy source
of weapons.

He had encountered feudal levies before and they
had been no more willing to risk their lives for their
lord or king than this crowd seemed to be for their
town. But there was something here that could prove
more powerful and dangerous than the helpless cowed
resentment of reluctant peasant conscripts. Percevale
had the distinct impression that these people had
both the will and the capacity to resist. All it wanted
was the mainspring.

Oliver climbed onto the platform. Percevale wished
they had not taken his sword. Better still, he wished
he were twenty miles away. Of course, then he would
never have met the damosel.

The mayor had left his entry a little late; the crowd
had become restive again. For a moment he looked nonplussed, as if he had expected his presence alone to
silence them. The noise continued. He raised his voice.

"Ladies and gentlemen!"

The crowd fell silent. Many looked up in surprise
at being so addressed. There were a few laughs.

As speeches went it was, Percevale conceded, quite
good. Oliver spoke to them in language that was plain
and unadorned, telling them of the danger that was
fast approaching. They listened attentively as he told
them of the choice that faced them—to leave immediately or to remain and fight. There was no possibility
of a peaceful settlement with the invaders, for they
were barbarians and knew nothing of peace treaties
or terms of surrender. Then he introduced the knight,
who, standing at ground level, was invisible to most
of them. He said that the town council had decided to
defend the town against the invaders and that Percevale
would train them and lead them into battle. Training
would commence the following morning and all able-
bodied men were expected to attend. He concluded

by expressing the hope that all the men of the town would respond wholeheartedly to the call to arms and do their duty for the sake of their families and the community in general. Then he turned and smiled down at his colleagues, rather pleased with his eloquence and his brevity.

At first it seemed his words had the desired effect. The faces before him registered alarm when told of the menace from the north, doubt when told of the council's decision to defend the town, reluctant approval when they learned that they would have expert leadership and training. They were far from enthusiastic, but it seemed as if they could be won over. Then: "And what, pray, will the councillors do while the rest of us are fighting for our lives?"

It was impossible to pinpoint the source of the question amid so dense a crowd. Robert quickly mounted the steps and began busily scanning the square.

As for Oliver, he should have parried the question easily but he hesitated. He had spent a long time preparing his speech but he had not bargained for hecklers and he had little aptitude for improvisation. For a few seconds too long he stood puzzled and angry, wondering at the impudence of the remark and what to reply.

"Oh, they'll be busy drawing up battle plans and such, I expect." A woman's voice this time, again impossible to detect. Some laughter followed.

To the mayor it was a straw and he grasped it thankfully.

"As a matter of fact, yes," he replied hastily. "There are many details of organization to be worked out—" Then he stopped. It was a very obvious trap and he had blundered right into it.

Outrage and amusement mingled to create the uproar that followed.

"I'm not risking my life to keep such as you in clover."

"The town is not ours. Let the rich fight for it if they want it. I shan't."

There was more but it quickly became lost in an undifferentiated roar.

Angrily, Percevale climbed the by now crowded platform. "Fool!" he muttered. It was not his intention that the hapless Oliver should hear this, but he little cared if he did. Looking about him, he could see that things were rapidly changing for the worse; the purpose of the gathering now quite forgotten as hundreds of people seized this opportunity to let off steam or vent some of their inchoate resentment. One large group at the edge of the square was singing raucously and Percevale noticed several of the militiamen moving gingerly toward them, their truncheons held nervously at the ready. He turned to Robert.

"Unless you disperse your soldiers quickly, you will have a riot on your hands." And he pointed to where the militiamen were slowly converging on the singers. Robert nodded and gestured fiercely toward the edge of the crowd. Several people there waved back good-naturedly and some returned messages of endearment.

Fortunately, the sergeant-at-arms saw and correctly interpreted the physician's signals. Discreetly, he ordered his men to a safe distance. Robert turned and sighed with relief.

"They'll get fed up soon and start drifting away. Thank gods it wasn't any worse."

Some of the crowd were already turning away and wandering back the way they had come.

To the mayor, who was muttering indignantly to himself, Robert said quietly, "Not a very encouraging response, I fear, Oliver."

"I'll find out the names of those troublemakers and have them sent packing," came the angry and injured reply. "How dare they? After all we've done for them, how dare they?" For no good reason he rounded upon his colleague. "I'll warrant your son had some part in this."

For a moment Robert could only look at him in disbelief, then he shook his head lightly and forbearingly. "Shall we go down, gentlemen?" he suggested. "There seems little we can do here."

As he led the way down the narrow flight of steps, he turned to the knight. "I fear that you may not have many volunteers tomorrow," he said.

10

In the dim light of a cold afternoon Mordred wrote:

I have never been what you might call a romantic person. Perhaps this was partly a reaction to my father's excesses; at any rate, the pursuit of love has never interested me so much as has the pursuit of knowledge, and the absurd conventions governing the former have always seemed to me petty and demeaning to both sexes.

And yet I fancy I understand women better than most men do. The greater part of my youth was spent among women. I had no brothers, only sisters—seven of them. And there was Mother. Then, after her death, I was sent to the court. The boys and, later, young men who were compelled to associate with me often did so grudgingly and with few exceptions I resented their company as they did mine. But the womenfolk made much of me. I think they liked to spoil me and at the time that was just the sort of attention I needed.

99

I have learned to respect women. I have had few as lovers (and this is a matter for passing regret), but there are many who have been my friends.

There are some upon whom I look with a less than favorable eye. One is Lile, who was my nurse for several years after my arrival at Cadras. She was a large, comfortable woman whose benevolent and vacant smile I recall vividly even now. It was she who told me that Mother had been a queen of Gaul and had taken fever and died when I was very young. In doing so she nurtured an illusion which made the truth—when it was finally and belatedly revealed to me—so much harder to bear. She meant well, I know, but she was a foolish woman and did me a great disservice.

And there was Guinevere. So beautiful and so sickeningly conscious of the fact.

Yes, Reader, like so many others, I did conceive a youthful passion for Guinevere and she, because she was flirtatious and promiscuous, responded favorably to my clumsy overtures.

Not that I was completely naive. I knew as I ascended the narrow winding staircase that led to the private entrance to her chambers that I was not the first to keep this furtive rendezvous, nor would I be the last. No matter. For one night I should be Lord of Albion and the legendary Guinevere would be my queen—or so I thought.

At the top of the staircase a tiny door, concealed on the inside by a tapestry, led straight to her bedroom—Guinevere did not like to waste time. I did not stop to knock, but burst in, dizzy with anticipation, my heart pounding fiercely (for it had been a long climb and I had run all the way).

Guinevere looked up from the book she was pretending to read. Her eyebrows rose in a tiny gesture of mock surprise; upon her pale lips appeared the merest smile.

Oh, it gave me such pleasure to contemplate her thus. She was reclining on her bed, her magnificent red hair spread about her like a carpet of autumn leaves (I apologize for the drunken imagery but she had that effect on me). Gods, she was beautiful!

She put down her book and with a slight languid gesture beckoned me forward. "Enter, good Sir Mordred," she whispered. Then, putting her hand to her mouth, she gave a soft, girlish laugh.

I must confess, at that point I hesitated. Such wanton coyness, charming enough perhaps in a girl of fifteen, seemed merely hollow and affected in a woman of thirty.

But it was only a moment's caution. I had no illusions about Guinevere's intellect and though I was far from certain what it was I sought, it was not her conversation.

I threw myself down beside the bed and took hold of her arm—a little roughly, I fear, for she cried out, "Take care, Sir Mordred, or you will crease the cloth!"

She was still smiling, however, so, my confidence only partly shaken, I released her arm and directed my attentions instead to her heart, assailing it with the generous outpourings of my own—no, I shall not repeat them; I am too ashamed.

Guinevere must have heard such banal utterances many times before, yet, to her credit, she listened attentively enough to mine; at

its conclusion she even appeared quite flattered.

"Why, Mordred." This time her smile was
not at all affected but warm and genuine. "I
had no idea. I always took you for such a
bookish fellow." Her brow fluttered as she
added lightly, "I was reading a book when
you entered."

Not wishing to be sidetracked when I
seemed so close to my goal, I hastily stammered, "Lady, may not the heart of a scholar
beat as true and as full as that of any uncouth warrior?"

This evidently pleased her; perhaps, after
all, she was not accustomed to this sort of
treatment. At any rate, her smile broadened
measurably and she patted her bedcover in a
fashion that was anything but coy.

I was there at last!

I could stand upon burdensome ceremony
no longer. Leaping upon the bed, I clasped
her in my arms, my whole being afire with
ungovernable passion. "Ah, lady!" I breathed
hotly. "Long have I awaited this moment!"

But even as I held her thus, my senses
clouded with lust, I sensed that something
was terribly wrong. Guinevere still smiled,
but a fixed and strained quality had entered
her face and in her eyes was a look of determination, even panic. I had not expected this.
As she wriggled uncomfortably in my grasp,
I felt my passion wither rapidly and became
suddenly and vividly aware of how foolish
and indiscreet my behavior was.

"No, no!" she squealed. "It is the wrong
time."

"Of the month?" I stammered abjectly.

"No, silly." With great ease she pushed me

away. "I wanted to talk to you, Mordred." She pouted her lips and frowned girlishly but on her brow I could see many creases and her face was blotched, in places almost purple. I began to feel annoyed with myself. "You're such a close one, you know. We ought to get to know each other better. For your father's sake."

Her manner now was firmly maternal—did I not say that women liked to mother me? And she, after all, was my stepmother, though she had chosen an ill time to remind us both of the fact. Still, the damage was done. My appetite was quite gone and hers, I fancy, had been slight and tinged with guilt—for all her playful manner.

So we sat and talked for an hour or so. It was a rather one-sided conversation; she with folded arms fixed me with an earnest and matronly gaze while I tried my best to hide my disappointment and appear dutiful and attentive—not very successfully, I fear, for at length and heaving a great sigh, she rose and went to the main door of her chamber. She opened it and in came a trio of ladies carrying what seemed to be various punitive-looking instruments. They looked at me uncertainly, but Guinevere, who clearly had faith in their discretion, was impatient for their ministrations. "Come on, girls," she commanded. She was sitting on the edge of the bed, her spread over the coverlet, her arms languidly stretched above her head.

With scarcely a glance at me they began to undress her. I had become as inconsequential to them as I was to their mistress. I did not wait to learn the secret of Guinevere's enduring beauty—though my curiosity was aroused. Mumbling a hasty farewell, I left almost unnoticed.

"Come again," she murmured as I turned in the doorway. "Soon?"

But Guinevere, I had decided, was not worth making a scandal over. In later years I came to feel sorry for her. It is true that as she grew older her indiscretions became increasingly embarrassing, but in Arthur she had a lot to put up with. We even became friends of a sort; that is, she would complain to me of Father's unreasonableness and I would provide a sympathetic ear. Yes, upon reflection, I find I can harbor little bitterness toward Guinevere. It may be that as a result of that unfortunate encounter I was afterward chary of romantic involvements. But had it been otherwise, I might never have met—too late, alas—the one great love of my life.

At which point Mordred stopped. Slowly, as if with great effort, he laid down his quill. It did not surprise him to find his hands trembling violently all of a sudden or to feel his breathing dreadfully short—this had happened before many times. But it saddened him. "Oh, my dear darling," he whispered hoarsely into the damp emptiness that surrounded him. "Shall I never be able to write about us?"

Taking his sleeve, he hurriedly wiped his eyes. Not because he was ashamed of his tears but because there was somebody outside the hut.

He rose from his stool but did not reach for his sword. His visitor was making no effort to conceal his approach and anyway he recognized those wary shuffling footsteps well enough. For this reason he did not pull aside the curtain or step outside. He stood back and waited.

The footsteps circled the hut once, then stopped outside the doorway. For a moment all Mordred could hear was the sound of his own breathing, more relaxed now, and that of his visitor. Eventually he said coaxingly, "Is it you, my little friend? Come on then, come on. There is no one here save myself."

The curtain parted slowly and the creature, wearily and cautiously, dragged itself in. Its distended head, partially bald and covered in unsightly sores, drooped sideways in a gesture of permanent mocking inquiry.

Mordred pointed to his bed. "Go and sit down. You must have come a long way. Go on."

The creature did not understand the words, but it comprehended well enough the soothing tone in which they were uttered. Carefully, for nearly every movement caused it some degree of pain, it arranged its misshapen form on the straw pallet, finally letting out a sob of gratitude and relief.

Mordred broke some bread and threw it across the hut. "You are a welcome distraction. I was beginning to feel very sorry for myself." Reaching for another crust, he chewed on it thoughtfully. "Now you have reminded me what real despair is."

The creature eyed attentively the tall kindly human whose shoulders were so much farther from the ground than its own. It struggled to attach some meaning to the words that were directed at it, but they were simply sounds, no more. It shrugged, and with its hardened gums began to gnaw ravenously at the stale, delicious bread.

Mordred watched with interest. "I really should give you a name," he said. "You look at me with such a distrustful gaze as you eat my food, yet more than once you have dragged your broken-backed form who knows how many miles to visit me. Therefore you are to be considered a friend and friends must have names. I will call you"—here he paused—"Agravaine. He was

a friend too." He shook his head sadly while the creature, discarding the loaf's outer crust, turned on its
side and, after laboriously tucking its stunted arms
beneath its asymmetrical head, looked at Mordred no
longer warily but with something akin to polite interest.

"A trifle pettish at times. Uncommonly vain too." He
smiled gently. "Something of which you cannot be ac-
cused." Extending an arm, he approached the bed.
"Take my hand, Agravaine."

But the creature would not, and, whimpering, re-
coiled. Nor, in spite of repeated coaxing, would it
attempt to speak its name.

"Not even a grunt," Mordred muttered. "I suppose
it is a bit of a mouthful and you are tired, no doubt."
With a disappointed sigh he went over to his desk
and began busying himself among the piles of parchment. "Well, just as long as you do not intend staying
the night you are welcome to rest here."

He knew there was little fear of that. At dusk or
shortly thereafter his guest would slink off, perhaps
uttering a farewell grunt, perhaps not, as it vanished
into the night. Mordred, like most humans in an age
when artificial light was rare and precious, feared the
dark. But the mutants seemed to thrive upon it.

"One day I shall make a study of your folk," he said
to himself as he searched among the papers. "But first I
must complete my present task. And more urgent
still—ah, here it is!—I must dispose of this."

But first, he read it through again. "Listen," he cried
at one point. "Just listen to this:

> Thus Arthur and Lucius, eager as lions,
> drew their swords and put their shields afore
> them and gave many great strokes. Then
> Lucius gave Arthur such a buffet that he fell
> to the ground. But when Arthur felt himself
> hurt he was full wroth and he smote Lucius
> with Excalibur that it cleft his head. Then

when it was known their leader was dead,
the Romans with their allies put to flight
and Arthur and his knights followed and slew
full ten thousand of them, for though they
were full courageous, yet they were no more
to King Arthur and his knights than are straws
to the wind.

"What nonsense it is." Fiercely he rolled and retied
the twenty or so sheets. "That is not how I want it to
sound. It was not like that—we never killed above
four thousand Romans, for one thing—they ran away
too fast." He waved the bundle before his uncomprehending guest. "I have nightmares about this, you
know. I wrote it when my brain was afire and have
regretted it ever since." Gripping the offending chapters tightly as if they might otherwise fly away (which
he sometimes feared they would), he began to pace the
narrow confines of the hut thoughtfully.

"I have this foreboding. Groundless, I am sure, but
no less terrible for that. I imagine that all this"—he
gestured briefly in the direction of the desk—"is somehow lost forever while this bauble is all that remains.
Worse still, I imagine people believing it." His shoulders slumped dejectedly and he shook his head. "Yet I
cannot burn it. I was going to—into the oven with the
lot. But I find I cannot destroy my handiwork so
completely." He looked into the eyes of the creature—
one sightless, the other largely vacant. "Why is that?"

The creature, which was capable of some thought,
could also sympathize. It let out a stifled sob.

Mordred tugged fretfully at his beard for a while.
Then an idea took shape in his mind. He visibly
brightened. His shoulders rose.

"I shall bury it. That's it. I shall put it where I put
the rest of my shit." Laughing, he turned to the creature. "What do you say to that?"

The creature recognized laughter. It could also

imitate it after a fashion. Throwing back its head, it gave vent to a long drawn-out howl which caused the astonished Mordred to clap his hands with delight and shake his head. Reaching for an empty jar, he removed the lid and placed the sheets inside. "I shan't be long," he called as he left the hut. "What an interesting fellow you are!"

As it watched Mordred go, the eerie howl died on the creature's lips. That small bundle which the human seemingly despised yet guarded so jealously had aroused its primitive interest. After waiting a moment, it climbed off the bed and with painful stealth crept to the doorway just in time to see Mordred, a smile of deep satisfaction on his face, drop the container into his privy.

Inside its clouded mind the creature thought it understood; nodding and grunting, it dragged itself back to the bed, and by the time Mordred reentered, it was already beginning to lay its plans.

Mordred went straight to his desk. He felt a sudden urge to resume writing. "That's a weight off my mind. I hope you will excuse me, but this is an important chapter and I must continue while the ideas are still fresh." With short rapid strokes of his penknife he began to sharpen his goosefeather quill. "You see, it is one of the few chapters which treat of personal matters. I do not greatly enjoy writing in this vein, but the reader does expect the occasional"—he grinned to himself—"spice. And this is supposed to be an autobiography, after all." He turned dutifully to his guest. "You will not mind?"

But the creature, too, was preoccupied. Mordred dipped his quill into the thick black ink and began to write:

> I do not wish to seem unduly harsh on Arthur. He had his qualities. Above all, he had *gravitas*. He was tall and kingly in his

bearing. a trifle round-shouldered perhaps, but that served to strengthen the impression that he was beset with many cares. And he always spoke well of Mother—never without affection and often with sadness. It does not lessen his guilt in that deplorable matter; I can never forgive him for what he allowed to happen, but I accept that it was through weakness rather than evil that he erred. For the rest, he loved her well enough and probably treated her better than those other poor women—yes, I include Guinevere among them. For all her faults she deserved better than Arthur.

He stopped then and turned around. Despite his many years of solitude, he was still a gentleman of the court and as such was mindful of his duties as a host—even to a guest so plainly deficient.

"I wonder if you remember your mother? I'm sure she'll never forget you." Pursing his lips, he repeated the word slowly. "MO-THER. Does that mean anything to you?" He shrugged. "Well, never mind. If it comes to that, I can hardly remember my own, not in any physical sense, that is. I was but four years old when she—died. But"—he slapped his chest—"her presence is very much with me. Had she lived, I might have become less attached to her. I find it inconceivable to my mind, but I know that sort of thing happens as one grows older. As it is, I have always felt her loss keenly." Pausing a moment, he contemplated the creature's outlandish contours. "She was a good person. She could have done something for you. Perhaps she could have cured you. Whereas I—" Stretching, he stood up. He had written enough for one day, he decided. "I cannot even teach you your name." Going over to the bed, he crouched so that both their faces were level. "Come on now, once more. AG-RA-VAINE."

But though Mordred persisted for several minutes, his guest was not in a receptive mood. It was thinking of the human's treasure and considering how best it might be retrieved. The dung did not bother it, but the human did. It would be simple to return late one night and kill the human as it slept. But unlike others of its kind, the human had been good to it. The creature would not harm its benefactor if it could be avoided.

But it would have the treasure.

11

Of course Simon would have nothing to do with such an affair," Elaine pronounced emphatically. "Oliver knows it as well as Father. It is an infamous suggestion."

"The mayor seems to think he is some sort of malcontent."

"Nonsense. He is jealous of our family, that is all. My brother is an idealist but he would do nothing that is outside the law. Nor would he do anything to upset Father."

"There is no harm in having ideals, certainly," said Percevale, who thought that on the whole he approved of the physician's son. "As long as they are the right kind."

It was later that same evening, though still light. After supper Percevale had gone into the garden. Elaine had followed soon after and sat down beside him. They were not left entirely alone. From time to time Robert would emerge apologetically from the shrubbery on some pretext, or his wife on another. At one point he espied them muttering together in a corner where they thought themselves unseen. It did not greatly concern him.

"Do you think this business was organized?" Elaine asked him.

"No, I do not. Such things are to be expected. It is rather a lack of fortitude on the part of your council that is to blame."

"What did they do wrong?" she said plaintively. "Oliver told the people of your news and asked for help in repelling the invaders."

"Precisely." There was perhaps more sharpness in his voice than he had intended. "Your peril is extreme, yet your council discusses the issue with your townsfolk as if they had a choice in the matter. This situation calls for leadership, not consultation." Seeing the frown that had appeared on the girl's face, he checked himself. "Forgive my intemperance. There is in this affair something that makes me angry. It was not my wish to stay here, after all."

She smiled faintly. "I can see that our way of doing things must seem at times strange to you. Certainly it is different from the past. But you also must try to understand us. It is how Father and the others have tried to make it. They are striving for something better, something fairer."

"There were many among the crowd tonight who did not seem to think they were having much success in this."

If the remark struck her as unkind, she did not show it. "They have a long way to go and it is true that there are some who do not like our way of doing things. But Father and the others, they try hard. And there is little poverty here. Surely you noticed that?"

"Indeed I did," Percevale admitted. "Your rulers seem benevolent, your people well looked after. Yes, in many respects you have come far." He paused. "But such qualities alone will not save you from the peril that is nigh."

"I suppose you think the old days were better," she said. "Of course I can see why you should."

"Oh, life then was far from perfect, that I freely admit. But then, Arthur had a whole kingdom to manage. And innumerable wars. He, too, tried hard. Like your brother, he was something of an idealist, you know."

Elaine sighed gently. "Ah, well, for my part I really do not understand any of this." Her slender hand dismissed the world of politics with a decisive sweep.

He did not really believe this. He thought she was too astute not to notice the significance of events about her. "And yet you say there is some resentment," he repeated.

"Oh, yes," came the vague reply. "But quite unfounded, I am sure." She looked at him for a moment, then, realizing that he wished for more information, continued.

"Poverty is relative, I suppose," she said. "Those who have sufficient look at those who have more and they are envious."

To Percevale this all seemed rather glib. Had not the poor peasant always envied the good fortune of his richer brethren? "Societies do not collapse because of jealousy," he observed, "however sinful it may be."

"Ours is not an unstable society," she replied quickly. "Why should you think that?"

Percevale did not reply, and she continued. "Of course, some of the townsfolk do not like the restrictions that are placed upon them."

"Such as?"

"In the past, when the town was first built, things were not as they are now. We were all pretty much the same then; all refugees, possessing nothing save what we could carry. I was only a little girl then, but I can remember clearly how cold those first winters were.

"But we were all survivors and that bound us together; made us forget our origins. Everyone worked together and everyone worked hard.

"Yet after a while rank would appear again. A natural process, some would say, though there are others who maintain it was better before in spite of the hardship."

"Your brother for one?" Percevale suggested.

"He believes that social distinctions are artificial," she replied. "There are no distinctions of rank among the gods."

But we are not gods, Percevale thought, and it is surely the gravest blasphemy to suggest that we could become like them. "And you," he probed, "what do you believe?"

"Oh, I don't know." The tone of her reply suggested to Percevale that it was an issue with which she had struggled before—without resolve. "All I remember of the past is the discomfort. I do not think it is right that the townsfolk should be so severely restricted as to where they may erect their dwellings. And I do not think it just that a servant should have no redress against an unreasonable employer. Yet, if I question these things, I am told that it is the best possible arrangement. The townspeople, I am told, are esteemed for their qualities of strength and their capacity for patient hard labor. When they are too ill to work, their families receive succor from the council; when they are too old to work, they are provided with a regular allowance; and when they reach an age when they can no longer fend for themselves, they are taken to a rest home, where they may spend their final years in comfort and security. There is a minimum wage which I am told is fair and realistic. My father and his colleagues, on the other hand, are enterprising and energetic. They are the natural rulers, and it is their job to carry the burden of leadership. If you were to question Father on this, he would probably claim that his class is the worse off of the two." She raised her face then and looked at him. "Well, I hope my little digest has proved informative."

"Oh, yes; yes, indeed."

For a while silence fell between them, the girl's manner becoming pensive and withdrawn. Percevale, contemplating her strong profile with its firm and prominent chin, its trenchant nose inclining to the aquiline, wondered why he had first thought of her as a frail and insubstantial being. Was it the circumstances in which they had met or was it because he had been firmly tutored to believe that all maidens—virtuous ones anyway—were really rather helpless and ineffectual? Then there were the eyes. He could not see them now, only the softly angular concavity marking the boundary between forehead and cheekbone. But when turned they drew him. I have seen them before, he thought with growing conviction.

She turned then, almost catching him in his artless study. Concern was on her face now. "How have you lived all these years?" she asked suddenly.

"There are many ways in which a trained warrior may earn a living," he at length replied. "In the northern kingdoms they still hold tournaments—after a fashion. They are not quite up to the standard to which I am accustomed, but they pay well enough."

"I did not know the northerners still followed the old ways."

"Well, they are not quite the old ways as I remember them. Let us say, rather, that they have adapted the chivalric tradition to suit their regional and emotional needs. Jousting, for example, is a far bloodier affair than it was in Arthur's day. At least one of the combatants usually dies of his wounds."

"And they have knights?"

"Some of them call themselves knights, yes. Some have even adopted the names of the Round Table. I have defeated several Lancelots in my time. I never could have beaten the real one."

"Yet they burn and pillage and rape and murder."

"Their code of knighthood does seem to admit of

broader interpretation than ours did," Percevale agreed.

"Does it not anger you?" she asked. "Isn't your sense of propriety revolted by it?"

"Ah, yes." Quietly he admired the way her lips quivered as she spoke thus. *She feels for me,* he thought with gratitude. Then he sensed her disappointment with his sanguine reply. Immediately he regretted the inadequacy of his response and wished that he could muster an indignation to match her own.

"Sad to relate," he said, "we are partly to blame—the old guard, that is. Some of us set rather a bad example during those last days."

She was curious and wanted to know more and so Percevale went on to reveal something of the venality and scandal that had cast such a shadow over the final period of Arthur's reign, and had, so some of the chroniclers claimed, been a major cause of the downfall of the house of Pendragon.

"Not the majority, you understand," he here interposed hastily and firmly. "There were a disreputable few whose misdeeds gave the rest of the table a bad name.

"There were some who said later that it was Mordred working his poison and his subtle crafts. His mother, Morgause, it was said, had been an evil woman, a witch. Well, there was some truth in that, but she was not as bad as some have painted her, nor was she a very competent witch. She did not deserve her fate."

"What was that?"

Percevale sighed. "They burned her."

"That's awful."

"Arthur tried to stop it—he was awfully fond of her. But"—he shrugged—"there are some rules that even a king must obey."

"It must have affected Mordred terribly."

"He was very young when all that happened. He didn't learn about it until much later."

"All the same."

"Arthur tried his best to make it up to him. He felt

terrible about the whole thing, naturally. No more witches were burned during his reign."

"That cannot have been much comfort to Mordred." She was not being consciously ironic.

"No." Since their conversation had begun, the sun had slowly gone down and he contemplated the dense greenery, now bathed in the cold pale colors of the failing light. Out of sight, but not quite out of hearing, the garden's nocturnal dwellers were beginning to stir.

"How he must have hated you all."

Beyond the narrow path Percevale could hear the busy scufflings of unseen animals. He thought, how pleasant it would be if some small creature were now to emerge from hiding and stand at my feet that I might contemplate and not kill it.

He sensed her eyes upon him. "Oh, yes, he hated us all. But that is no excuse. Besides, Mordred was a catalyst, not the cause."

"What about courtly love?" she asked.

He smiled gently at her eagerness. "So you are not above entertaining illusions after all. Well, I am sorry to disappoint you, but in my time at least, that was something of a vanishing art—guilty affairs in dark corners—that is what I remember." Bending forward, he peered vainly into the undergrowth. "What creatures inhabit this place?"

"Oh, mice, voles, shrews—some hedgepigs. Tell me about Lancelot and Guinevere—wasn't that special?"

"Only in the sense that theirs was the most sordid affair of the lot. No less so for being the most spectacular."

But most of the knights, he insisted, had been of finer mettle and of these none had been finer or more noble than Gawaine. He told her how after Gawaine's death, his murder, his will revealed that he had owned nothing more than his horses and his weapons—his lands had long been sold to help pay for the king's wars and his own adventures. All that he left he had bequeathed to Percevale, "my most industrious pupil," to inherit when he attained knighthood. Thus he,

Percevale, bore the Gryphon emblem of Sir Gawaine of the house of Lot, of Orkney.

"So it was not such a fine tradition after all," she observed. "Mother has often said so."

"There is nothing wrong with tradition," Percevale insisted, "only with the character of some of those who claimed to uphold it." He frowned. "Why does your mother say that?"

"She has always held the ways of Chivalry in low esteem. She used to work in the household of one of the great lords of Albion, you know. If such things went on as you have described, it is not so surprising that she has a rather jaundiced view of the past."

"What position did she hold?"

"Nothing of great importance. A personal maid to the daughter of some great lady. I do not know the details. She doesn't talk about it much."

Percevale was silent for a moment as he tried to conceal his disappointment. Still, the misconception had been his—she had said nothing about her former rank. Twenty years ago hers would have been a humble enough occupation. But in the aftermath of the war, when most of the noble widows and their children fled to Gaul or even to the hated Italians, she must have represented a very good catch indeed. To a humble physician she must have seemed a lady of high merit.

"Anyway," Elaine continued, "she managed to amass a modest fortune, so her position could not have been that humble."

"And your father married her?"

"Or she married father. I can't imagine her letting someone else make that choice." She paused, staring reflectively at her hand which lay on the bench like a white ghost amid the settling darkness. Her next words seemed to be uttered with difficulty.

"Father tries so hard to make her happy." He looked at her and smiled uncomfortably. "It is not his fault she is unhappy. She does not know what she wants. She professes to hate the past yet at the same time she tries so hard to relive it. This garden of hers—"

"It is very beautiful. A fine achievement."

"It's her obsession," she said with quiet conviction. "It's unhealthy."

"Perhaps you should persuade her to talk about it. She might feel better than. I sometimes do."

They both smiled then, remembering the first morning he had woken in her house. Then she shook her head.

"Oh, she never talks to me about those things. Sometimes to the others if they press, but not to me."

He would have questioned her further but she wanted to change the subject. "So, you alone are left to uphold these fine knightly traditions?"

"As far as I know. There is also Mordred, of course."

"Yes, Mordred." She stretched out the final syllable by the barest fraction. It hung in the air like an echo. "Do you really think it's right?"

Percevale raised an eyebrow. "How so?"

She looked away as she spoke, lacing her slender fingers nervously, he thought. "It's just that it seems such a mean and futile little quest—chasing after an old man to avenge a crime committed all those years ago."

"Crimes, not crime," he corrected her gently. "Mordred is guilty of more than one atrocity."

"Anyway, it's still hardly inspiring, is it? I do not consider it worthy of you. Now, if you were looking for the Grail—"

"It's been done."

"Or Arthur's sword. Wasn't there something special about his sword?"

"Caliburnus. Excalibur, the Latins called it. It was rumored to have magic properties."

"There you are then," she declared with a conclusive air. "You could look for that. That would be a worthwhile quest."

"I already know where it is. Arthur was wearing it when he died. He was wearing it when I buried him in the courtyard of Cadras."

They remained there for much of the afternoon.

She asked him many questions and he answered as well as he was able.

"I have heard stories of knights who would erect their pavilions at roadsides or fording places and challenge all passersby to joust with them before continuing their journey."

"There were some who practiced the custom," Percevale said. "I never did."

"It strikes me as rather silly and self-indulgent," she said.

"Self-interested rather," Percevale said. "There was, of course, an element of posturing, but essentially the idea was to discourage would-be trespassers. Even in Arthur's day, seizures of land by force were not uncommon. A willingness to defend one's boundaries in this admittedly unconventional manner might do much to dispel any suspicions of weakness that an intending aggressor might hold. Also, it was good practice. Between tournaments, jousting partners were sometimes hard to come by."

She asked him about the tournaments that were held in the northern kingdoms.

"They are not such colorful affairs as those of old, nor are participants unduly encumbered by regulations governing behavior on the field. In fact, to the best of my knowledge, there are no rules at all."

She winced at this.

"Yes," continued Percevale musingly, "the men of the north have a refreshingly prosaic view of tournament art—they like it to be as convincing as possible. For the winners the rewards are substantial."

"And for the losers?"

"Oh, death usually. And if not, severe injury. As a people, they are remarkably philosophical about such matters." Correctly reading the pinch of anxiety in her face, he added, "I do not kill my opponents if I can help, but it is often difficult not to, for they do not share my compunctions."

"It is not my idea of earning a living," she decided.

"Nor mine. I compete only when necessity calls."

"And when all this is over, you will return to it, I suppose."

"I suppose so."

"And your search for Mordred?" She rose to go indoors. A cold breeze was blowing through the garden, raising goose pimples amid the scatter of soft, downy hairs on her bare arms.

"I suppose so," he repeated, rising also.

For a moment they stood there, Percevale held firmly by her unwavering gaze and feeling a sudden urge to forget all about Mordred. He had only to approach a little closer to see his own double reflection in those beckoning eyes, dark and crystalline and so naggingly familiar. For a magical, absurd moment he was back in the charged atmosphere of the great tournament at Cadras, a young squire pathetically yearning for an opportunity to prove himself. In similar circumstances a modern hero would perhaps succumb to more fundamental urges. Percevale had been brought up in a different school. Heedless of the unsuitability of both the occasion and the surroundings, he was gripped by an urgent impulse to throw himself at the girl's feet and offer to serve her as a true and loyal knight. Age, reason, and the very tangible fear that she would very probably laugh at such a maudlin gesture held him back and thankfully, he reflected later, the moment passed. They both became aware once more of the chill in the descending night air.

"It is late. I think we should go in now." Was there a chiding note in her voice? Silently and slightly bashfully Percevale nodded and, standing, offered her his arm. In the circumstances it seemed the least and most natural thing he could do.

12

After a modest lunch Mordred resumed his seat and continued to write. Sometimes it was a wearisome business. He was finding it so today. So far he had produced but a few dull pages.

A major difficulty facing the scholar who wishes to disentangle legend from historical fact is that the former often contains a grain of truth which, however small, is usually sufficient to establish its credence among those, unhappily still a majority, with neither the education nor the inclination to exercise fully their critical faculties.

So it is with the frequent tales of monsters and dragons that surround the Arthur myth. As legends they serve only to confuse and cloud our judgments of the era, but when one penetrates to the truth behind these charming tales we find, perhaps surprisingly, that they help us to perceive more clearly the true nature of Arthurianism.

The key to this particular aspect of the Arthur myth lies in a remote part of the

Welsh mountains. Within an isolated area of a few hundred square miles there lived, until recent times, a species of giant lizard. These creatures could not fly, as legend claims, nor could they breathe fire. Their diet was mostly vegetarian. Yet they were formidable animals, four times the length of a man, and could, if roused, kill or maim with ease.

When news of these creatures reached the court, it was already known among the local inhabitants that their numbers were fast declining. Only a score or so were thought to still reside in the area. Much of the region, as I have mentioned, was mountainous, but there were also several rich and fertile valleys that could not be cultivated so long as any dragons remained there.

A number of wealthy Welsh landowners therefore approached Arthur with a proposition. In return for his assistance against the dragons they would recognize him as their liege lord, paying him a yearly tribute and levying several hundred Welshmen for his wars.

The offer was too enticing to resist. Arthur needed men and money to defend his vulnerable northern frontier. Here was an opportunity to defend both and gain a valuable foothold in Wales at the same time. He agreed immediately and hurriedly dispatched a small force of knights and men-at-arms to the Cambrian mountains.

I did not attend the expedition, but I am told that the men enjoyed a good season's sport. One by one the dragons were hunted down and slaughtered. It is said that the smell of the burning carcasses caused neighboring dragons to cry long and loud in grief

for the loss of their kinsfolk. This, of course,
made the task of locating them much easier.

At the end of the summer the expedition
returned, bearing the heads of nineteen of
these pitiful yet once-majestic creatures, and
telling highly colored stories of their own
bravery.

The Welshmen thanked Arthur and went
away to begin cultivating their newly acquired
lands and a few more pages were added to
the Pendragon legend.

At this point Mordred paused and considered. Should
he end it there? There was a certain attraction in
a sudden, rather dramatic conclusion. On the other
hand, perhaps an extra paragraph or two were needed
in order to summarize the central argument. He would
read it tomorrow and decide then.

Next there was the question of the rogue manuscript. Had he perhaps been a little hasty there? For
all its gaudiness, it had made exciting reading in
places. And the period did have its attractive side, he
could not help but admit that. He might disapprove
now, but deep down he knew he had enjoyed the
tournament and had taken some pride in his not in-
considerable jousting skills. Of course he realized that
he had been young and relatively ignorant at the
time. Only later did he become aware of the tournament as an instrument of the ruling class; a useful
diversion to distract the peasants from thinking too
deeply about their social conditions—and a useful
means of weeding out the physically inferior members of the ruling class itself. Still, it had been fun at
times and he could not help but feel a residue of
vainglory at having once carried away the jousting
prize himself. As for those interminable quests, true
they were often futile—mostly they provided excuses
to escape from the oppressive atmosphere of the court,

the nagging wives and importunate mistresses. Nevertheless, it was surprising how many unexpected and unsought adventures were encountered by some of the knights—though, of course, one only had their word to rely on. Nor were all the knights devoid of integrity and a sense of fair play. There were those who had sincerely believed they had a duty to aid the poor and oppressed and who went to considerable lengths to satisfy these imperatives. Again, common sense and cool reflection told him that these occasional acts of decency, well intentioned though they no doubt were, served only to bolster the reputation of the ruling class, creating an illusion of justice and fairness that was just sufficient to disguise the iniquities that lay beneath.

In fact, he mused, were it not for that small band of decent fellows, Bors, Galahad, Gawaine, and a few others, the whole rotten edifice of Arthurianism must have fallen much earlier and with considerably less bloodshed and destruction.

Now, there was a fresh insight; perhaps a theme for a later chapter. The question of who was to blame for the final holocaust had always been a thorny one and Mordred had found none of the explanations he had so far devised entirely satisfactory. Here might be a new avenue of approach. He decided that it merited considerable attention and that he would spend the rest of the day thinking it over. With a sense of satisfaction as well as weariness he rose from the table. Yes, he decided, he had done the right thing. Still, it was a pity really; the raciness of the style made some of his other chapters seem quite pedestrian in comparison.

A noise outside made him go to the doorway and draw back the curtain.

The steady drip-drip of the rain sounded noisily on the roof of the hut and upon the ground outside, still wet from the recent downpour. At first he had welcomed it—in this part of the world crops needed all the help they could get. Now he found it tiresome and was disappointed that the day had not turned out as the morning had promised. Instead of taking the long and leisurely walk he had planned in order to ponder upon this latest idea, he would now be confined to his hut for the evening. But had there not been another sound, also measured but louder than the rain? He listened attentively for a moment, then with a resigned sigh he turned from the doorway and began to rummage through the miscellany that littered his shelves. After some thought he settled upon *The Oresteian Trilogy,* a relatively undemanding work, not a bad choice when one is confined indoors. He pushed up the straws on the bed, forming a makeshift but comfortable seat. It was dusk and so he lit a candle. It smelled a great deal but it was better than darkness. Mordred was no friend to the peasant rhythms of light and work, dark and rest. He sat down and began to read.

13

It was late and only those of the tribe who could hold their drink and stay the course remained by the fire. They were few in number. Most of the knights had by now dragged themselves wearily to their beds.

Clarivaus sat and stared blankly at the rhythmic, flickering warmth, almost oblivious to the occasional dark shapes that stirred nearer the fire—servants and sometimes slaves, whose constant task it was to replenish the hungry flames. He wished that he, too, were lying in bed like the more sensible of his followers, but he had a reputation to maintain. It simply would not do for him to leave before the last of his retainers. Sluggishly, he rocked his head from side to side and peered into the muttering shadows. Which of these, his loyal followers, would quickly seize upon the chance to make capital of some such momentary weakness?

With an effort he stirred himself in his chair and through the mental fog that seemed to blanket his mind he tried to disentangle some of the murmurings emanating from different parts of the circle.

"... Three months with child and she swore that no one had touched her; I ask you ..."

"... I will have the hilt carved and the pommel bound in silver—gold is wickedly expensive these days ..."

"... Drinkable enough I grant you, but no favor to speak of. Not like our northern brews ..."

The conversation, it was clear, was flagging. Something had to be done. It was time he made his own voice heard. He coughed loudly and spat hard in the direction of the fire. The murmurs stopped, the shadows shifted slightly, and though he could not see their owners, he could sense their attention, focused on him now from the blackness beyond the flames.

The respectful hush, interrupted only by the crackling of burning wood, continued for several seconds before he realized that he had no idea what to say next. Feebly, his somnolent brain groped for a subject arresting enough to justify his ill-considered intervention.

Now you have made matters worse, he scolded himself. Now they will think you an imbecile.

It was Tristram who came to the rescue before the situation became really embarrassing. Sensible, reliable Tristram, who had sat thoughtfully and quietly on the ground, on his lord's right hand. It gladdened him to see that his earlier intuition had been well founded.

"Some of the men, my lord, have expressed a wish for some sport. It is a long time since they last had the opportunity to truly exercise their skills."

To Tristram's knowledge no one had expressed any sentiment of the kind, but it was the best he could devise on the spur of the moment and the old fool obviously had no idea what to say himself. He should be grateful for such a timely intervention.

Indeed he was. "Yes, yes," he agreed, aware that he was slurring his words more than usual tonight and further realizing that being aware seemed only to make the problem worse. "We are in no real hurry, and our people have done no fighting to speak of since we left our homes."

Some of the assembled knights nodded in agreement. They, too, were bored.

Several days had passed since Sir Tristram had first found favor with the king. Now he was Clarivaus's chiefest councillor and in consequence greatly disliked by all. But, they had to admit, the young upstart did have some good ideas. They had sacked two more villages, but resistance had been weak and seemed to be growing feebler the farther west they went. They were beginning to feel the staleness that sets in after a long period of inactivity.

Others were not so sure.

"My lord, may we not be tempting fate in allowing our enemies time in which to prepare themselves against our onslaught? This settlement of which our scouts bring word, it is larger by far than any we have yet encountered. There may be strong resistance." Thus Sir Marhaus counseled prudence as usual. Why had he not revoked his title yet and sent him scuttling back to the ranks? Ah, yes, Tristram had advised against it. Marhaus is powerful, he said. He has many friends. It would be better to wait for a more opportune moment. And so Clarivaus had stayed his hand.

Now Tristram spoke to the assembled company. "If these people put up a fight, so much the better for us." The king turned and beamed proudly down at his protégé. It soon became clear on which side the weight of opinion lay. Marhaus and the rest of the dissenting minority lapsed into uneasy silence.

"No marching tomorrow," Clarivaus announced grandly. "Tomorrow we will have a tournament. All day." This settled, he turned his attention once more to the hypnotic dancing flames and let the effortless drowsy oblivion take hold of him again. Tristram smiled triumphantly across the wide circle and Marhaus glared back at him for a moment. Then the older man rose abruptly and stalked back to his tent. A few others hurried behind. Tristram watched them go, then turned to the king, almost asleep by now. You need someone to look after you, he thought. Now you've got me, you lucky man; I will look after you for as long as it suits my purpose. It occurred to him that he was taking on quite a burden—two old men together, the drunken king and the old hermit who had entertained him but a few days before. He had said some strange things, that old man with the staring eyes, and even stranger things after he had greedily swallowed the wine that Tristram, in his cunning, had offered. He, too, might prove useful in some as yet unspecified way, and so Tristram had spared him and they had parted in a friendship that was genuine on one side at least.

Am I not a merciful man? He addressed the gods, and laughed gently to himself at the thought.

In that same darkness Mordred slept. He was a light sleeper, for he lived in a dangerous place, and unwelcome intrusions, though not a regular occurrence, had nevertheless to be anticipated. But he slept well for all that. A further chapter had reached fruition and fresh ideas for the next were germinating already. Tomorrow, he believed, he would achieve much. And wonder of wonders, he had made a friend—no, not another mutant—a real, human friend. The man was a barbarian, admittedly, and his manner, initially, had been a trifle rough. But he could converse, and compared to the mutants, his was a towering intellect. In his sleep he considered these matters and a faint smile appeared on his tired face.

Not far away, a few days' ride merely, set in the

heart of an ancient wood, was the nemeton, the sacred grove of the Druids. Ever since men had possessed the capacity for fear, and long before the arrival
of the monks themselves, this place had been a place
of dread. A clearing, unaccountably barren, was surrounded by giant oaks that towered out of the gloom
like huge and silent sentinels. In such places as this
resided the magic of the earth; capricious, violent,
and uncontrollable—even by those most versed in
Druid lore. Here, at times, rain might be seen to fall
when there were no clouds in the sky and the rest of
the wood was bathed in sunlight. Sometimes, too, the
earth would heave and groan, seeming to emit sighs
and screams as if of desperate souls imprisoned deep
beneath. There were men living here too. They were
solid and corporeal and though they did indeed live
far below the ground, they were certainly not the sort
given to groans of despair. Nor were they greatly
troubled by such phenomena. Indeed, they welcomed
them, for they deterred the curious.

They were the last Druids of Albion and this was
their underground temple. No entrance was visible.
The only sign that this was a place inhabited by
mortals as well as the malevolent deities of nature
was a luminous skull that grinned with a pale light
from the shadows to further discourage the unwary.
It was coated in phosphorus and rested in a niche in
a heavy carved stone. It had been there for as long as
the Druids themselves and would no doubt have served
its purpose admirably enough had it been called upon
to do so. But the fact was that no sentient being had
had occasion to venture near for many years.

The only entrance to the temple was by means of a
long vertical shaft. To gain entrance one first had to
find and remove the cunningly constructed frame of
leaves that covered it. Steps and handholds were cut
into the sheer wall, but they were not immediately
visible, so a casual intruder might yet mistake it for a

ritual shaft or votive pit such as was often found near the holy places of the Celts.

There was no light in the shaft; only one person at a time might negotiate the precarious ladder. At the bottom, some one hundred and twenty feet below ground, there was a tunnel. It was too low to permit one to stand upright, but it was level and well supported by heavy stone pillars. Far down the tunnel there burned a steady light; the damp walls reverberated to the faraway activity of men. It might be night outside, but the Druids did not rest. They slept in shifts and the lights were kept constantly burning.

Following the tunnel and ignoring the many side passages, one eventually reached the source of the light and activity. It was truly quite astonishing and a first reaction might be that this was daylight and one was above ground again. It was an underground cavern, naturally formed and vast in diameter. Around its edge were the entrances to many tunnels and chambers, but only the one tunnel led to the surface. The others were all blocked. Not far above was the arched ceiling from which hung many hundreds of giant candles mounted in iron baskets. In their powerful glow the clusters of brown stalactites sparkled and glistened like huge decaying teeth in which jewels had been unfittingly set. Heavy chains mounted on pulleys connected the candle holders to a narrow gallery—also naturally formed. Every now and again there came the loud and fearful rattle of straining metal as unseen hands pulled one of the baskets into the gallery, replaced the exhausted candle, and wheeled the basket out again.

Far below, and reached by a staircase carved out of the rock, was the packed-earth floor of the cavern. It was a busy place, full of men in white robes, all deeply absorbed in their particular tasks. Some debated in groups; some stood alone, contemplating, perhaps, a puzzling set of figures they had devised or been given. Some sat at one of the many benches positioned around the wall of the cavern. On some of these were complex constructions of tubes and containers from which emanated a variety of odors, ranging from the mildly unpleasant to the unutterably foul. The occupants themselves were quite accustomed to the smell.

The most arresting sight was in the very center of the cavern floor. Here a wide and shallow pit was covered with a crystalline substance that was both thick and translucent so that the objects lying at the bottom of the pit seemed unclear and distorted, as if viewed through a swirling film of murky water. The substance was, in fact, a large and thick sheet of glass. Above it, suspended by a tripod, was a cauldron. Within this a fire burned, emitting a pale flame that wavered rhythmically, making no sound. It was difficult to tell whether the strange and eerie glow suffusing the immediate vicinity of the pit came from the cauldron above or the objects beneath; perhaps it was a combination of the two.

Situated quite near the edge was a dais upon which a figure stood. Unlike the robes of the others in the cavern, his was a dark shade of gray. He incanted gravely, in a low but clear voice, addressing himself sometimes to the cauldron and sometimes to the pit above which it hung, soundless and motionless. He spoke in a closely guarded tongue, a mixture of Celtic and earlier Iberian dialects. It was quite foreign to those around him and even he understood it only imperfectly. He recognized, for instance, the familiar references to Druid deities; Cernunnos of the stag antlers, Baco the boar-headed, Epona of the fire-flashing horse, and, of course, the god of the cauldron and of the pit, Urannos. He was aware, too, of the tenor of his words, placatory in intent. Most of the gods in the Druid pantheon were reasonable and relatively undemanding; as long as one made the necessary sacrifices and votive offerings, one was left well enough alone. But Urannos did not belong to this tradition; he was volatile and unstable and his anger was most terrible. That was why he had to be constantly appeased by the soothing propitiatory chant. That was why, when the chanter reached the end of his recital, he began again in the same drawn monotone. And when it was time for him to rest, he would be replaced by another.

As the gray garb signified, he was the only true Druid in the cavern proper. There were others; they were sleeping or resting in one of the many chambers around the cavern's edge. The men at work in the cavern enjoyed a status equal to that of the gray-clad priest, but they were members of the suborder of ovates. They were seers and diviners or, as some of them preferred to describe themselves, scientists. The other principal suborder, the Bardoi, was not represented. This was no place for the poetic muse.

Thus the incantation never ceased. If it did, the Druids believed, Urannos would once again burst forth and spew fire and destruction over the world. For the priest, standing for hours at a time with arms outstretched, it was a monotonous and uncomfortable task for which the only reward was a protracted and painful death. For even when dormant the god of cauldron and pit worked his fury with insidious slowness and stealth. While the Druids possessed some scant understanding of the causes of radiation sickness, they had no idea how to prevent it. And their numbers were diminishing far more rapidly than replacements could be found in a depopulated countryside.

These were serious problems, and sometimes desperate stratagems were required in order to overcome them. But the work went on and the god remained quiescent, venting his muted anger only upon those nearest to him.

Sometimes there seemed to be a stirring, ever so slight. Beneath the priest's partial gaze, through the green-tinged glass, the three black cylinders seemed to oscillate slightly like figures in a dream or shadows in a pond. He knew that this was an illusion only, an effect of the wavering flame. The handmaidens of Urannos had remained at rest for twenty years. They rested still. Of that he was certain. Almost.

14

Behind the town the ground rose steeply for a while before leveling out. From here Percevale could see the whole valley—the wood, sparse and gray in the strong early light, through which he had brought the damosel. He could see the road which their own had joined, winding its way downhill like a meandering notch cut into the landscape. Directly below him another road emerged from one of the town's four gateways. He followed it with his eyes until it vanished into the distance, out of the valley where, he surmised, it eventually faded, merging with the wilder country beyond.

But around him the landscape was genteel and well cultivated, the fields an elaborate arrangement of colored squares whose regularity almost made him dizzy. Across the valley a band of cloud was passing, its shadow advancing like a slow tide, bringing with it a chill in the air. It is hard to believe, he thought, listening to the comforting animal discord that drifted past his senses, that beyond these hills there lies an empty wilderness. No, not quite empty. He thought of the painted warriors who would shortly be coming along that same road, their swift progress attended by

clamorous yells and sudden death. I might have decided to stay anyway, he thought. The townsfolk and
their strangely ordered society annoyed and irritated
him, but he could not long resist the pull of common
humanity and he felt a sense of obligation to these
quarrelsome but seemingly well-intentioned folk. He
no longer felt such a strong urge to return to the
wilderness and his quest. Both could surely wait a
little while.

Behind him was the common, a two-mile-long stretch
of rough pasture with ponds and the occasional copse.
Here the townspeople were permitted to keep their
livestock. They were also allowed to gather dead wood
for fuel, though the felling of trees was expressly
forbidden. On the hilltop itself others were gathered
also, the mayor and physician, together with those
members of the council who had managed to leave
their beds at such an early hour. The sergeant-at-
arms and his complement of six were there. The
mayor turned to Percevale.

"This would be a good place to set up a permanent
watch, would it not, Sir Knight?" He beamed. Evidently, he was determined to put on a brave face in
spite of the debacle of the previous night, but his
apparent optimism did little to animate the spirits of
those around him.

"I just feel we ought to be here," Robert said to
Percevale. "We ought to be seen to be doing our bit."

"You are not very hopeful then?"

"I fear we did not make a very good impression last
night."

Percevale was about to reply, but he checked himself and turned away. Robert, watching him go, recalled the snatches of Percevale's discourse he had
overheard in the garden the previous evening. Of
course, the fellow is an outsider, he thought. He cannot be expected to understand. And all those years

spent alone or among barbarians. It is not to be wondered at that he is so out of touch.

Percevale walked across to what Robert had earlier told him was the green. This was a part of the common separate from the rest. Here no animals were permitted to graze and the trees and other plants were carefully tended. The grass was kept short. It was a trysting place for lovers, a picnic area for families. Sports and games were held here, some less innocent than others, for here, too, the young men of the town would regularly settle old scores and vent suppressed energies in bloody melees while their more genteel neighbors looked on in shocked disapproval and captivated horror. But today all was quiet and peaceful. Beneath an ancient sycamore a table and chair had been erected. One of the mayor's clerks sat here, arranging and rearranging a pile of papers, stopping occasionally to resharpen one of his quills. He smiled at the knight.

"You expect to be busy?" Percevale said without irony.

The clerk gazed thoughtfully in front of him, his attention momentarily distracted by a burst of shouting that seemed to emanate from the now-unseen councillors. He turned again to Percevale.

"His Worship requires that I take particulars of all recruits," he said. He chewed with thoughtful energy at the beard hairs that sprouted untidily beneath his lip. "Now I may think that a waste of time, especially as no one is coming, but who am I to say?" He added, as an afterthought, "Sir."

Percevale wondered briefly whether the man was impudent or merely ingenuous. Then his attention, too, was caught by the clamor behind him.

"Something's going on," the clerk offered, and leaving his table, he followed Percevale back to the vantage point above the town.

The councillors were conversing excitedly among

themselves, congratulating each other, and particularly the mayor. Oliver swung around a beaming gaze that encompassed both the knight and the physician. "You see, gentlemen, you are too easily disheartened."

Robert was shaking his head. "You are to be commended, Oliver. I was wrong." But his aspect bore a puzzled frown that betrayed both doubt and anxiety. "What has moved them so?" he muttered.

Percevale watched as the long black column of men left the town and began marching up the slope. As they drew nearer he could see that their bows were strung, their faces set.

Somebody turned to the mayor. "But where did they get those weapons?"

Oliver's smile quickly vanished as he realized that he should have noticed this first. He turned an angry gaze upon the sergeant-at-arms. The sergeant was a stocky man of unprepossessing build. His eyes shone with concealed amusement and he blinked innocently before replying.

"Frankly, sir, I thought you knew. I thought all you gentlemen knew." Seeing the blank incomprehension on the faces before him, he continued. "Nearly every workman in the town possesses a bow and a full quiver. They keep them under their beds. It's the woods, you see, sir. Beyond the fields. There's good sport to be had there."

The mayor made no attempt to conceal his displeasure.

"It's impossible! It's downright illegal! Do none of these people respect the law?"

"Not that law, sir." The sergeant seemed unmoved by his superior's darkening features. He had outlasted several mayors and would, gods willing, outlast several more. "It's their livelihood, you see."

"Is that why there is so little game these days?" Robert intervened. His amazement at the impudence of the lower classes was tempered with admiration for their cunning. How on earth had they managed to evade both the curfew and the rigorous laws forbidding the carrying of all weapons save cudgels? And if they could do that, what else could they do? It was an unsettling thought.

"That's right, sir. I expect you thought it was because of the war, but it's not that. A bit of night shooting is about the only pastime these people can afford—the price of ale being what it is. Small wonder that the supply of wildlife finds it hard to keep pace with the demand."

It was Percevale who finally intervened. "This is a piece of great good fortune. I had thought to train archers. That will no longer be necessary."

Oliver, recognizing the force of this argument, capitulated, contenting himself with a mild admonition only.

"Nevertheless, Sergeant, I do think that you could have enforced the ordinances of our community a little more rigorously." He turned and went to greet the townsmen who, having breasted the slope, were now forming into long, straggling lines.

"You are right, of course," said Robert as he and Percevale followed. "Still, it is rather worrying. Our laws are very strict about such matters."

Seeing the faces of the men from the town, Percevale was struck by their air of purposeful determination. This is a change from yesterday, he thought.

"How many of you are there?" he asked one of them.

"Seven hundred, give or take a few dozen. There are others who have yet to make up their minds. They will come later."

"This is splendid, splendid," said Oliver, stepping forward. But the grim-faced men only shuffled their feet restlessly in the wet grass and took no notice of him.

"What weapons do you have?" Percevale further inquired. "Besides those."

"A few of us carry knives, that is all."

"You will need swords." He turned to the mayor. "Have sufficient numbers been forged for these people?"

Oliver replied with a look of pained concern. When this failed to evince a response, he took the knight aside. "Surely it is not necessary for them to have swords as well?"

"We agreed that they should be properly armed." Percevale was in no mood for equivocation.

"Indeed we did," Oliver replied in a tone that seemed to suggest that this did not really matter. "But is it really necessary?"

"Yes."

Oliver sighed. Turning to his clerk, he issued the necessary instructions.

"But what about the papers, sir? I have them all ready."

"Never mind those. I shall see to that myself. Go on, Gareth, run along."

Percevale next spoke to the sergeant-at-arms. "Do any of these people have any experience?"

The sergeant appraised the lines thoughtfully. "There are about thirty here, sir, who have been trained as soldiers and nearly all of those have had combat experience."

"In the civil war?"

"Aye, sir."

"But that was years ago," Robert interrupted. "I know the men you speak of. They are none of them under forty and most are well over."

"But they'll make excellent instructors, sir. And leaders when the time comes."

Percevale nodded approvingly. Not only could this man stand up to the bluster of his superiors. He knew his job also. The sergeant returned the knight's gaze, silently acknowledging the unspoken tribute. It seemed they understood each other.

The mayor was determined not to be left out of

things. Giving the sergeant his due and just to show
Percevale that his community was not without its
own quota of heroes, he said expansively, "Of course
the sergeant himself commanded a whole company of
men-at-arms during that regrettable conflict. Did you
not, Sergeant?"

"On the other side, sir." The tone of the man's reply
suggested that he would rather the matter had not
been raised. Percevale merely shook his head lightly.
He had learned long ago that a man's essential
humanity bore little relation to the cause that he
espoused or the side on which he fought. The sergeant, with his honest face and steadfast eyes, was a
man in whom he could repose some measure of trust.
That was what really mattered.

"Of course, that was a long time ago," the mayor
breezily continued. "We have a common enemy now."

Do shut up, Oliver, thought the physician, but he
held his tongue.

Ignoring these unnecessary exhortations, the two
soldiers began to discuss tactics.

"I would like you to take these men to the level
ground behind us," said Percevale.

"The green?"

"Yes. Divide them into companies of twenty or so
and place a suitable fellow in charge of each company."

"They must be registered first," said Oliver in a
voice whose petulance only faintly disguised its
owner's sense of waning authority.

Percevale looked at him.

"What?"

"It is essential. There are details we need to know.
Occupation, skills, that sort of thing."

The knight turned on his heels and stalked off. The
sergeant, after a moment's hesitation, began to divide
the volunteers as instructed.

Though he saw no good reason why he should,
Robert took pity on his crestfallen colleague.

"There is so little time, Oliver," he said reasonably. "We have asked him to organize this business for us. We must give him leave to do it in his own way."

"But, Robert, giving them swords." The man's voice was thin and plaintive. "How in the names of the gods are we going to get them back?"

"I know," replied Robert in that same tone of concern he reserved for his more esteemed clients. He turned as one of the townsmen left the lines to speak with him.

"There is a patient for you. He arrived late last night. We took him to your surgery."

"It is not open today."

"This is a special case."

Robert wondered whether he should admonish the man for such a brazen lack of deference. Then he thought better of it and, making his excuses to his colleagues, he hurried off.

15

nne was waiting for him by the gateway.

"I told them there was no surgery today, that you were busy, but they would not listen. They absolutely insisted. They were almost rude about it."

"Who is he?"

"I've no idea. He is not from these parts, for it is an accent that I have not heard before. The poor man is in a bad state. He is absolutely filthy and his clothes are in rags." She was forced almost to run in order to keep up with his long, purposeful strides. "Robert, I really don't know what things are coming to. They really were quite rude, you know."

"I'll look into it, dear."

They reached the house. Drawing back the curtain, he stepped into the surgery. Anne remained in the doorway.

He went over to the pale, emaciated man who sat gazing disconsolately at the floor. Gently he touched his shoulder. The man did not start but only turned his face slowly upward, contemplating the doctor with a look of blank sorrow.

"My dear fellow—" Robert began in a voice full of genuine compassion.

"I offered him food," said his wife, "but he would not respond. As far as I can tell he is not injured."

"Are you hurt?"

The man shook his head.

"He would not answer me at all," Anne said.

"It is my bedside manner."

"He looks as if he could do with a bath. I shall instruct the servants."

"That is an excellent idea. Thank you." He took a stoneware bottle from a shelf and poured some of its contents into a small cup. "Drink this," he said.

The man drank a little and coughed.

"Slowly," said Robert.

The man emptied the cup.

"Better?" Robert asked after a while.

"Thank you, yes. What is that medicine called?"

"It is a distillation of mead. It is very strong." He drew up a chair and sat down opposite his patient. "Now then, perhaps you would care to tell me what brings you here and in such a state."

There was a short silence. Then, in a thin, rasping voice the man said, "They had to kill my horse, you know. The poor creature was all in."

Robert inclined his head sympathetically.

"I've been riding for days without food or water."

"You must be very tired."

"I did rest for a few hours last night. The people here, they have been very kind to me."

"Later we shall see about a hot bath for you."

"You are very kind." He looked beseechingly at the doctor. "I have told my story already."

"I have not heard it," said Robert. "I should like to hear it."

The man nodded, accepting the reasonableness of the request. He told his story in a halting sort of way. At times he would become quite incoherent; his eyes would fill with tears and he would break down. Then Robert would rest a steadying hand on his shoulder and say something soothing like, "There, my dear chap, take your time." And after a short rest the man would resume his tale.

He came, he said, from a small village some fifty miles to the east. The life there was hard and the people, like the land, which grudgingly bore their living, were poor. But mainly because of this they were exploited by no lord and so life was free of that oppressive burden at least. Then the painted demons from the north arrived, shattering their tolerable existence in a space of minutes. The first intimation the villagers had that they were abroad was when they came in a screeching ragged wave down the cultivated slope that led to their little settlement. Shrieking and yelling, their fierce weapons flashing in the dawn, they swiftly dispatched most of the men and women working in the fields almost before they had time to comprehend. Then they set upon the huts wherein the terrified survivors had foolishly, though understandably, fled. They scoured each one in turn, butchering the men and children first, the women a little later. Their faces were painted in fixed, inhuman snarls and they yelled like animals, so that all who beheld them quickly abandoned any thought of resistance or hope of mercy. Miserably, isolated in their little dwellings and paralyzed by fear, the villagers perished until none remained.

"But you survived," said Robert gently.

"Yes, I survived."

"No one else?"

The man shook his head.

In his desperation he had thrown himself into the village well. There, in the cold darkness, he had remained for many hours, treading water as softly as he dared; holding on, sometimes by fingernails alone, to the wet, slippery, and uneven stone. He listened as the cries of the dying gradually faded to be replaced by the shouts of the looters. They sounded disappointed, as well they might. There were few rich pickings to be had in such a place. Several times he was forced to immerse himself completely in order to escape detection; when they had drawn several bucketfuls to replenish their own water supply, he had very nearly drowned.

He waited until evening. Then, bending his body so that feet and back acted as alternating levers, he made the perilous ascent to the surface. By the time he climbed out of the well he was cold, exhausted, and hungry, but the sight of the devastation around him quickly banished all thought of discomfort from his mind.

He did not dwell on this, nor did Robert press him on the matter. It was clear to him that the man had lost family and friends and he could imagine well enough the sort of sight that must have greeted his eyes.

He found a horse. A broken nag. Though they slaughtered humans cheerfully and without compunction, the tribesmen simply left any livestock they did not need or which failed to meet their exacting standards. For days afterward he wandered around the countryside with no clear intention except, perhaps, to warn other settlements that might be in the area. The only people he did chance upon, however, were the barbarians themselves. He spotted their encampment before they saw him and was not followed. But his fear of them and his memory of their grim visitation were sufficient to keep him riding continuously until his sudden and alarming arrival in the town but a few hours previous.

"So you happened upon us by accident?" said Robert.

"The kind folk that brought me to you—it was they who found me and gave me food and rest."

"And you told them your story?"

"Yes. And many came and listened."

While we slept within our thick walls and heard nothing.

"I am very sorry for you," he said.

The man shook his head. "You have all shown me great kindness. I am most grateful."

Robert rose to go. "I must leave you now. There are others who should know of this."

"I should like some more of your medicine."

"Help yourself. My wife will look after you. Make sure you get plenty of rest." He turned and hurried out, almost stumbling into Anne.

"That is horrible," she muttered, "horrible."

"You should not have listened, dear. I would you had not heard."

"And these frightful people are coming here?"

"That is what we must ascertain. Can I leave the poor man in your charge?"

He returned to the common to find Percevale and the others standing around a large table upon which a hastily drawn map had been placed. From everywhere there came the sounds of an army in training, the sibilant hiss of flights of arrows, the ringing of distant swords, the feigned anger of bawling instructors. How ineffectual it all seems, Robert thought dejectedly. For a brief horrible moment he had a vision of the same field strewn with corpses, while a chill wind howled across a bleak and empty landscape, carrying wisps of smoke from the smoldering ruins below. Involuntarily he shivered, and, turning, saw his son. Like the others, he was poring over the symbols on the chart.

"Why are you not in the surgery?" he whispered fiercely. "Do you not know there is work to be done there?"

The young man looked up and smiled disarmingly.

"And when the time comes, Father," he said, "I shall return to it."

"Come now, Robert," said the mayor. "Your lad has proved a most efficient draftsman. It was he who drew the map for us."

Robert could see that his son was clearly enjoying his newfound status. His elders had admitted him to their counsels and he was flattered by it.

"I have just heard some disturbing news," he said.

There was silence among his audience as he recounted the fugitive's story, and it continued for a little while after he had finished. He looked at Simon, now thoughtful and apprehensive. Now will you return to your stocktaking? he thought.

"Did he say how long ago it was he last saw them?" Percevale asked. He, too, was concerned, though he was not yet thinking about defeat.

"No. On this point his memory was hazy and confused. However, if it is true that he rode without rest, then by his condition I would judge it was about two days ago. That is only the flimsiest of estimates, of course."

"Then they are closer than I thought," said Percevale. "It is vital that we ascertain their position and the direction from which they are approaching."

"And if they are indeed coming this way," added the physician hopefully.

"These people have an unfailing nose for plunder," said the knight. "You may be sure they will come this way. We must send out riders to observe their progress."

"I will go," said Simon hastily.

Robert's eyes widened in surprise and he gave an emphatic shake of his head. "I need him in the surgery," he said, and looked at the knight imploringly.

For a moment Percevale scrutinized both men. Then he spoke to Simon. "Good. Thank you."

"Should I leave immediately?" Simon asked, his voice less certain now.

"Yes. There is little time. Find someone to accompany you and head north and east. Travel normally for the first day, but after that you should ride only at night. Follow the road, but keep well clear of it. Good luck."

Still confused by the suddenness with which his unreflecting offer had been accepted, Simon stammered a hasty farewell to his father and went to saddle his horse. Robert watched him go with concern. "Will he be all right?" he asked.

"If he follows my advice," said Percevale, whose mind was already on other matters.

He does not see, thought Robert gloomily. There will be a terrible slaughter, even if we win, which I doubt. But all he sees is a good scrap. He knew he was being unfair to the knight, but that did not greatly alter the way he felt. He wanted to speak out but knew he would not. He felt a sudden desperate urge to pack a few necessities and flee, but he knew he would not do that either.

He looked up. Percevale was holding the stick of charcoal with which Simon had drawn the crude map. "Now then, gentlemen," he was saying, "here is what I plan for us to do."

16

At midday they stopped and women from the town brought lunch for their menfolk. Elaine came too. Percevale watched her as she approached, her white gown trailing soundlessly in the grass. Over her arm she carried a basket.

"Your father is not here," he said.

"He has gone back to the surgery," she replied. "I met him on the way. He is not hungry, but it would be a shame to waste all this food, would it not?"

They found a quiet spot on the edge of the green and Elaine looked with approval at the folk who gathered, eating and pleasantly conversing, the children playing noisily. In spite of the warlike preparations in which the men, until a few minutes before, had been busily engaged, the atmosphere was one almost of festivity.

"I've never seen so many people here before," she remarked optimistically. "It almost feels as if we are a real community."

He thought this was a bit of an exaggeration. The gentry and their families occupied one corner of the field while the townsmen and their families occupied the rest. Nevertheless, he did feel that here a new sense of unity was being forged. For how long? he wondered.

She had heard the story of the nocturnal visitor. "Do you know, the poor man hid in a well while those savages murdered his family?"

Percevale nodded.

"He must be feeling terrible now."

"You do not think he should have done otherwise," he suggested. "Stood by them, for instance?"

"What do you mean?" Her cheeks reddened as she prepared to argue fiercely the case of a man she had not yet met. "That's just the point," she said. "Had circumstances been different—had his son, if he had a son, been standing by him, or had there been more time for reflection—then perhaps he would have behaved differently, chosen what you clearly regard as the more honorable course."

"But instead he yielded to blind, instinctive terror?"

"Yes, and will no doubt despise himself for the rest of his life." Her tone softened measurably as she realized that she was, perhaps, a little overstating her case.

"Some people believe that it is unreflective actions that are the truest guide to character," Percevale observed.

"Then he is on the side of life," she said, changing her tack. "Hooray for life."

"Hear, hear."

"Do you censure him too?" There was a note of concern in her voice, as if the answer he would give mattered very much.

"No, I do not. Had not that well been so providentially provided, we would be short of some very useful information." Seeing her cheeks redden again, he added less flippantly, "And yes, I have seen how fear can sever the strongest bonds."

She seemed satisfied with this and proceeded to the next topic.

"I spoke to Simon before I came here."

"Oh. Has he gone now?"

"Yes," she replied. A little coldly, he thought. "He has gone."

"He did volunteer," Percevale said. "No one pressed him. Has he taken a companion?"

"A man named Gareth. He works for the mayor. What you just said, about there being no pressure brought to bear. That is not the impression I received."

"He offered to go. Your father attempted to dissuade him but I thought he really wanted to be off. Perhaps I misread the situation. I am sorry if I did."

She did not reply but lowered her head and in silence contemplated her hand resting on the grass. Percevale watched it too. It is so pale, he thought. So delicate. With a deliberation almost painful and unmindful of whether others were looking (they were not), he placed his own hand on hers. Her alarm was immediately evident, though he did not think it was her sense of propriety that was shocked. Anyway, it did not deter him. Suddenly conscious of the many years that stretched behind him and the fewer years that lay ahead, he felt consumed by a feverish urgency. So his hand remained while he spoke.

"He will be safe enough, I am sure of it. As long as he observes a few elementary precautions, he will be all right."

"Yes. You do understand, don't you?"

Percevale withdrew his hand. "I quite understand. If he has not returned by tomorrow morning, I will fetch him myself."

"Thank you. Poor Simon. His head is full of romantic longings, yet he lacks the physical courage to put them into effect."

"He showed courage enough today, I thought."

"That was before he had time to reflect. He does not want to be a doctor," she added.

"That cannot please your father greatly."

"I don't think Father would mind so very much if only Simon had proposed a sound alternative. He says that he wishes to be a scholar. He wants to study and teach."

"Study what?"

"I don't think he has decided yet. The real difficulty is that there is simply no provision in a small community like ours for that sort of thing. We have a school where the young may learn some useful skills, but we cannot afford to support people who want to spend their whole lives reading books."

Percevale wondered if perhaps on this point he understood the girl's brother better than she did. Inventive and vigorous though her people undoubtedly were, he had so far seen no evidence of cultural activity. The physician's taste for antiques was an exception and even here it was difficult to disentangle the acquisitive and aesthetic impulses that were at work. The printing press was always busy and produced a constant stream of information ranging from tracts on animal husbandry to tax demands but little that could be described as edifying or uplifting. There was no library and no theater. Arthur's court, he reflected with some degree of self-satisfaction, had possessed both—in the latter the comedies and tragedies of the Greeks had been most popular, but the king had also been an enthusiastic patron of the indigenous bardic tradition of poetry and folklore. In those days there would have been some outlet for the creative energies of such as Simon—the universities, for example, with their large communities of disputatious scholars. And for those of a more austere and rigorous cast of mind there had been the Druid order, an intellectual elite which took its members from all classes of society. But no, he told himself, that would be no life for one of swift and generous impulses. Only those sufficiently devoted to the pursuit of learning within a closed, totalitarian society bothered to apply. And the Druids did not accept just anybody.

The universities, he knew, had been destroyed long ago and the Druids, he presumed, had also ceased to exist. Nothing had risen in their stead. Percevale was no intellectual, but he did possess a certain deferential regard for culture and it occasioned him some sadness to think that so much had vanished without trace.

"I am sorry if mine seems a rather stuffy view," said the girl, "but it is the way things are here." She changed the subject then, asking Percevale about his plans for the defense of the settlement. "Father is quite impressed."

"Good. He struck me as being a little downcast this morning."

"Well, he thinks it is a good plan," she replied, familiarity having blinded her to such observations. "He said it was simple but ingenious."

"The ingenuity is not mine, alas, and it is far from simple, for it requires much precision and closeness of timing."

He was no longer surprised at her interest in what he had always presumed to be exclusively masculine affairs. Now it seemed perfectly natural to him that she should be privy to such matters. He led her to the table and explained to her the various symbols on the map. He showed her the dispositions of the archers and the places where they were to be concealed until the moment when they would spring from hiding and take the enemy in the rear.

"But they will turn and attack the archers. What then?"

"There will be two lines of bowmen," he replied, impressed with the speed with which she had grasped his strategy. It had taken longer to explain it to the council. "Hopefully, this will confuse the enemy and for those few moments they will not know which line to attack. While they are procrastinating, our own horsemen will make a sally from the town."

"But the townsmen do not possess horses."

"Your people do."

This surprised her. "I don't suppose they took to that idea with much enthusiasm."

They had not. A long silence had followed Percevale's explanation of this part of his plan.

"None of us here have ever fought this sort of battle," someone had said eventually.

"Nor indeed have most of these people here," answered the knight. "They seem willing enough nevertheless."

"But their lives are conditioned by violence," argued the mayor. "Ours are not. Why, you know, every weekend the apprentices come to this very spot and—"

"Yes, I have heard about that," Percevale replied a little more sharply than he had intended. He did not greatly blame them for being afraid. He thought they would come around, if tardily. Softening his tone, he said, "You hunt boar with spears, do you not?"

"In the woods, yes," the mayor replied. "That is hardly the same thing."

"Indeed no. It is easier with a man. He is a bigger target and moves with considerably less agility. On the other hand, of course, he has more imagination and so may try and fight back. That is why you need to practice, gentlemen." He concluded with the sort of look that effectively forestalled further objections. "Now then, how many fit riders are there among you?"

There had followed another lengthy pause, after which Robert spoke.

"Sir Percevale is right. We must be seen to be doing our fair share."

"But we are doing our fair share, dammit," said the treasurer, who felt sure he would be placed in the front line. "The burden of administration is enormous.

I haven't had a proper night's sleep since this affair began."

"It's all right for you to talk like that, Robert," said the mayor. "You'll be safe behind the lines, tending the wounded."

"That is a mean-spirited remark, Oliver. Might I remind you that my son—"

At which point Percevale had lost his temper and shouted at them. After that they had slowly come around.

"Sixty or seventy," offered the mayor sullenly. "Depending on whether you include all of us here."

"I do. The physician, as you astutely observed, will have to be excused. He will be needed elsewhere. The rest of you may need some exercise, but you are otherwise fit enough, I think."

After the mayor and his secretary had repaired to the town to muster the able-bodied gentry, Percevale told the sergeant-at-arms to find fifty volunteers to act as human targets for his unwilling cavalrymen.

"The riders will use the blunt ends of their spears. Your men may defend themselves with staves and there will be a pot of ale for every man unhorsed."

The sergeant had grinned wickedly first at the knight, then at the unhappy group around the table.

"Are you not being rather hard on them?" said Elaine. "Poor Oliver, they will unseat him easily, then beat him with their sticks, for he is an unpopular fellow."

Percevale agreed. "But there is no time to tutor them in more leisurely fashion."

"I suppose not. You're really beginning to enjoy this, aren't you?"

This took him a little aback. Yet he had to own there was some truth in what she said. He had not sought this fight but he knew also that he could have outwitted them and fled ere now had he really wanted to. He could have discovered where they had hidden his horses and his weapons—the girl would have done that for him, he was sure—and left in the night.

"It is a task worthy of my mettle," he answered noncommittally.

"But is it because ours is a good cause or is it simply that you love fighting?"

"I do not know," he said. He looked at her, and as he did so, he thought of the years spent in bootless quest, hunting an old dotard in order to avenge a deed that the rest of the world had long forgotten. Moving amid the desolation and horrors of the barren lands or the uncivil and war-mongering kingdoms of the north. Futile, futile! he thought, and a look of pain crossed his face. Quenching it quickly, he said, "Perhaps a little of both."

"And you think we have a chance?"

"Oh, more than just a chance. Much more than that."

He rose then, for he saw that the young men of the gentry were coming with their horses and weapons. One of them was leading Fleet, for Percevale had demanded that his own accoutrements be restored to him. His spirits rose at the sight of the destrier's comforting gray bulk towering above the men around him, its gentle head nodding in slow and amiable rhythm in time to its measured strides.

"And Mordred," she said as he went over to meet them. "What of him?"

Percevale walked on, pretending not to have heard.

17

Despite another late night, Clarivaus's men rose early. Most of them were up at dawn and without bothering to eat (last night's meal had been an ample one) they began to strike their tents and load their wagons. From a small copse that stood atop a conveniently situated spot of high ground, Simon and his companion watched as their enemies prepared to continue their journey.

They had chanced upon the glow of their campfires shortly after midnight on the first day and had camped at what they thought to be a safe distance. Now, as the sun rose behind them, casting a healthy glow upon the land, they saw how illusory the darkness had been. They were far too close, only a short walk from the edge of the encampment, where already herdsmen were beginning to drive the livestock into some order preparatory to departure. It only needs a few of those animals to stray up here, thought Simon, and someone to come after them. Neither of them carried weapons.

From behind the noisy, milling livestock, other sounds could be discerned moving across the air's morning stillness—a man's shouted command, the in-

sistent yell of a hungry child, the clamor of hollow
iron as uncleaned cooking utensils were loaded uncer-
emoniously onto wagons.

Watching all this from their insecure hiding place,
Simon could not control the intense nervous excitement that gradually built up within him. It expressed
itself first in a violent trembling that seized his legs.
Then it spread to the rest of his body so that he
wondered that the very ground did not vibrate in
response. It was not simply terror at the thought of
discovery. He felt also a strange and unaccountable
thrill of pleasure when he considered the awful risk
they were taking. They were within hailing distance
of a fierce and merciless foe, close enough even to see
a man urinate over the remains of a fire and sense, if
not quite hear, the sizzle among the ashes.

His companion did not share his excitement. He
fidgeted nervously and expressed his fear that the
enemy might hear the ponies.

"Tether them a little farther off then, Gareth,"
Simon said without taking his eyes off the scene before them.

At one point a herdsman passed within a few feet
of him, scarcely more than a spear's length. He was
driving before him a huddle of protesting, errant sheep,
and as Simon slid quickly behind the low ridge, he
took with him a fleeting impression of a slight, lean
figure, his face largely obscured by a mass of facial
hair, his body ill-clothed and unkempt. He does not
seem a particularly daunting specimen, he thought as
he lay with his face pressed close to the damp earth.
Why, he even uses the same curses and imprecations
that our own workers use. Perhaps, though, their
warriors are made of sterner stuff. Nevertheless,
he kept his head well down and his belly close to
the ground when he judged it safe to crawl forward
again.

By the time Gareth returned, their leading horsemen were already beginning to move off. They did not seem to be in any great hurry, but spent several minutes jostling rancorously for favorable positions in the column. Places at the front seemed to be the most popular. Here there were several gaudy banners and pennants bearing crudely executed devices. When all was at last ready, they began to head off in a leisurely fashion along the ill-defined track that eventually became the road through the forest. They were taking little trouble to keep together, and soon an appreciable gap existed between the receding mass of horsemen and the slower footsoldiers who were also beginning to arrange themselves into a semblance of order together with the wagons and the livestock.

For a long time the two young men lay still, watching the slow motley procession of animals and men. By the time they judged it safe to move, the sun was warm on their backs and the grass beneath them was drying fast. They got up, their limbs stiff and uncomfortable, their clothing damp and clinging. Simon gazed thoughtfully at the distant line of figures, now melting slowly into the distance. He turned and looked at the remains of the enemy's presence—a space of flattened and slightly discolored ground, a few wisps of smoke from still-smoldering campfires rising falteringly and quickly dispersing.

"Come, Gareth," he said, remembering the urgency of their errand. "We must hurry if we are to circle around them and reach the forest road before they do."

"Would it not be wiser to stay well clear and go around the forest altogether?" Gareth suggested. He felt that they had taken enough risks already.

"It would take too long. What if our comrades send someone to meet us?"

To this Gareth reluctantly agreed. "I will go and fetch the ponies."

A few minutes later they mounted and, spurring their ponies, rode off in haste in the direction which Simon had indicated. From his place at the head of the mounted column Sir Tristram, fancying that he saw some slight movement, turned quickly and scrutinized the distant horizon.

"Something amiss?" Clarivaus asked.

"Nay, sire," answered the favorite, and he relaxed again. It was, he felt, a glorious day, one of those rare occasions when he felt his senses to be at their highest pitch. His mind could exult in the most trifling things: the cleanness of the air, for instance, the almost tactile blue of the sky, and the overbearing presence of the surrounding landscape, with its wide flat spaces near the road, the gentle wooded undulations a little farther off, and, in the dim distance, a line of broken-backed hills. He was acutely aware, too, of more immediate sensations, of how the horse beneath him felt like a perfect and natural extension of himself. He felt its hooves pounding rhythmically on the soft, springy turf and felt as if he were a part of that also. Looking back, he saw a flash of silver, the sun striking fire off the helmets of the infantry. Why, I might be a king already! he thought. His ambition was waxing dangerous now, his confidence high, his plans well advanced. He felt unassailable, and when he noted Sir Marhaus a little way behind him and looking much out of countenance, he could not resist the temptation to attempt some devastating and elegant wit against the man. Making his excuses to the king, he rode to the side of the road and waited until the other knight had drawn level. Then, approaching with an affected bow, he said, "Greetings, Sir Marhaus."

The other knight was deep in conversation with his companions. He was sufficiently taken aback by the unexpected intrusion to fire a brief glance of angry disdain at Tristram before turning away.

But the high-spirited protégé was in sportive mood. He smiled as he rode his own horse alongside.

"Sir Marhaus," he said again. Marhaus turned, and Tristram was delighted to see that a cold fury burned in his eyes. "It is said," he continued, "that unlike the men you are following, you do not paint yourself in martial colors before going into battle. I pray you, why is that?"

For a moment he thought that Marhaus was going to explode with rage. Good, he thought with swift calculation. I shall kill him in single combat, then proclaim him a traitor. It shall be yet another service for my beloved master.

But to his surprise the older knight suddenly changed his demeanor. He was actually smiling. After a brief pause he said, almost in a whisper, "It is said, Sir Tristram, that there is a canker in the king's mind that will not out. It blinds him to his enemies and makes him deaf to the counsel of his friends." He turned to his fellows, all of whom were eyeing Tristram with undisguised malevolence, their hands resting menacingly on their sword grips. "My companions and I are preparing a physic, but, alas, it is a most desperate one." Here he slapped his own pommel with a suddenness that made Tristram almost jump in the saddle. "Now then, lad"—and his large white teeth gleamed—"I wonder if you can perhaps suggest a gentler remedy." He turned to his companions who broke into broad grins.

Maintaining with some effort an appearance of indifference, Tristram turned his horse and rode forward to join the king, his cheeks burning from the gentle laughter that followed him.

"There goes a dangerous man," said Marhaus as he watched him go. "And he will become more dangerous still, now that he knows of our designs against him." His companions swiftly checked their laughter; in their hearts they were far from glad. Six of their number were dead from wounds received at yesterday's tournament. Sir Tristram had much to answer for.

"We cannot move against him," said one suggestively. "Not unless we move against the king."

"Nay," said Marhaus, who still felt the pull of loyalty though he scarcely knew why. "We will not do that. We shall just have to be patient."

For a little while they rode on in silence. Then another of his friends broached a question that had been troubling him for several minutes.

"Tell me, Marhaus," he said hesitantly. The knight turned. "If it is not too personal a question—"

"Yes?"

"Why is it that you do not paint yourself before battle? Everyone else does."

Marhaus frowned. There was a note of heavy irony in his voice when he eventually spoke. "I do not need to paint myself when I make war on children," he said. "I rely upon my sword arm, not yells and a fearful visage. Besides," he added almost plaintively, "the stuff gets in my hair and my beard. It's frightful. It takes me hours to clean it off."

> The kings and petty lordlings who have hitherto ruled the land of Albion have ruled it only for themselves. It is true that many of them deluded themselves into the belief that they were acting on higher impulses. Arthur was particularly adept at this form of self-deception and considered his authority to be a form of trust exercised in the interests of all the people. I believe that in this he was sincere—

It was the evening of the following day and Mordred was hard at work on the lengthy final chapter of his testament. No, he had not finished; he was not yet halfway through the massive work, but he felt the need for a change. He had, he felt, spent long enough merely documenting events. It was time he gave a little thought to critical analysis, for this was one of the main purposes of his work. He was not merely seeking to vindicate his own damaged reputation; he wished also to develop in these pages a coherent and workable alternative to both the well-meaning despotism of Arthur and the formless chaos that the last two decades had loosed upon the world.

So you are not cheating, he told himself, pausing briefly to rest his aching hand. This is the most important chapter of all, the justification for all that has gone before. The arguments contained here would have to be formulated carefully and revised thoroughly before they could be considered fit for posterity, so it was as well to begin contemplating them now. He dipped the quill, struck out the last phrase he had written, and continued.

> In this he may well have been sincere; nevertheless, the record is disappointing. A few well-meant efforts by a few knights to curb some of the excesses of the more brutal of the king's vassals do not add up to a convincing social policy. In spite of the patina of glamour and the oft-repeated sentiments about defending the poor and the helpless, the code of noblesse oblige was in reality but a hypocritical rationalization of the greed of the nobility. In return for the minimal protection needed to preserve a cheap and expendable unit of production, the noble might with a clear conscience consume the choicest products of the peasants' labor, while the peasants themselves, robbed of human dignity and self-respect, must root like pigs in the wood for what remains. In this fundamental re-

spect the life of the typical peasant in Arthur's time was much the same desperate and uncertain struggle as it had been during the reigns of his less colorful predecessors.

Clearly, if the future is to have any meaning at all, it must sever its links with such a gaudy and disreputable past. Something more solid than the mere rhetoric of justice must be found to fire the hearts of a generation grown justifiably skeptical. Of course, there are those who will disparage such ideals as illusory and unattainable. They pour scorn upon the advocates of more equitable social arrangements, citing human nature as their evidence for so doing. Naturally, as one would expect from people who are defending the indefensible, their evidence is selective, their logic flawed. A brief glance at a few historical and geographical facts will show this.

The literature of the Greeks makes many references to societies which were in form broadly egalitarian. Hesiod, for example, speaks of a golden age where all men possessed a nobility of purpose and of visage (gold here, of course, refers to the quality of the people, not their metal technology). Would such a poet, one privy to the subtlest truths of man's existence, be capable of constructing a falsehood? Our answer to such a question must surely be an unhesitating "no." Later, Herodotus, that most excellent of historians, tells us of the Argippaei, a tribe who live to the north of Scythia. They do not eat meat and have no concept of war or weapons. Most significant of all are the noble Hyperboreans who dwell in the north of Albion, in a land veiled by mists. I have many times visited and conversed with the people of this favored land and have seen for myself how no man calls another master but each counts himself as one of noble blood. No man wants for the essentials of life and in mind and spirit there is a total harmony and community of interest.

These examples are, of course, of primitive, static communities. Yet their stability, their very existence even, is sufficient to demonstrate to the most stubborn reactionary the possibility of a new and revolutionary ordering of society.

Here Mordred paused again, this time to light the tallow candle, for it was growing dark.

Having established that a fairer, more equal social system is not outside the realms of possibility, we must then proceed to the question, how is the just society of the future to be organized? Here it will be sufficient to delineate broad contours. Readers interested in more detailed and specific questions such as defense, the gathering of revenue, and patronage of the arts are referred to my prewar pamphlet "Feudalism—and After?" (Pendragon Press).

Clearly, it is not enough to simply reproduce the idyllic and utopian societies of the Argippaei and the Hyperboreans; attractive though they may be to those of quiescent humor, they are also stagnant and unprogressive, ill-suited to the dynamic and purposeful age which is to come. They are signposts, not destinations. Our task is to find a way of welding the concepts of justice and prosperity, order and change.

At which point Mordred stopped. It was late and he had worked almost without respite all day. He knew from experience that to continue now, when his powers were at an ebb, would only necessitate much revision in the morning. Tomorrow there would be time to formulate the next stage of the argument. He glanced quickly over what he had written so far and thought he detected a wayward, rambling quality about the prose. This did not worry him greatly. For all its pristine clumsiness, he saw in his text the authentic voice of the future. The age to come, the age to which he addressed himself, would not, he believed, be greatly impressed by heady declamations but by the granite hardness of impeccable logic.

His reverie was interrupted by an unfamiliar sound from outside. Quickly, for though age had sapped his strength it had done little to slow his responses to the approach of danger, he discarded the pen and took up the sword that he always kept close by. Swiftly and stealthily he slid out of the chair and bent his ear to the source of the disturbance. He was sure that footsteps were approaching out of the hostile darkness. Three visitors in two weeks, he thought. I must be the most popular recluse in the district.

He took no chances but went quietly over to the doorway. The footsteps were very close now; no doubt their owner fancied he was treading carefully and the ground beneath was soft and wet enough to absorb most sounds. But Mordred's hearing had grown acute after so many years of near solitude; every step seemed like the pounding of a hammer.

When he judged the moment to be right, he raised the sword, took careful hold of the edge of the curtain, and, with a violent tug, pulled it open.

18

He had thought there might be a minor setback; in view of the size of the operation and its complexity, it was only to be expected. But not on such a scale, not such a disaster as this.

Clarivaus sat disconsolate in his pavilion while a wary retainer tried to attend to his wounds. Tried to, because every time he happened upon a sore spot (and there were many though none serious), the king would give a mighty roar and strike the unfortunate fellow for his clumsiness.

Everything had begun so promisingly. They had attacked shortly after dawn, a yelling mass of soldiery, sweeping like a dark and swift tide along the road and spilling into the valley. His suspicions, he realized later, should have been aroused much sooner, but he had assumed that the huts that they passed were empty because the inhabitants had somehow received advance warning and had fled behind their flimsy defenses.

Then there had been the half-dozen or so peasants who had taken to their heels the moment the warriors emerged from the wood. They were dressed like women but they had been exceptionally well built and had reacted so swiftly that they might almost have been waiting for a signal.

But his euphoria, as always on such occasions, was too great and so, when the enemy's bowmen emerged from the trees and hedgerows on either side of them, and began forming into ranks with a calm and ordered precision, he was taken completely by surprise.

The flap of the pavilion opened and a bearded warrior, his face scarred and filthy, his right shoulder wrapped in a makeshift dressing, stepped inside.

"How does my lord, the king?" he asked.

"Well enough, I thank you, Marhaus," Clarivaus stiffly replied as he watched with a baleful and apprehensive eye the frightened servant gingerly tie yet another bandage.

With a significant flourish of his left arm Marhaus produced a piece of paper from his belt. It was well known that he was one of the few among the tribe who could read and write.

"I have numbered our dead and wounded, sire," he said.

"And written it down too, I see," replied the king sourly. "Most commendable of you, Marhaus. Most efficient. I shall see you get a mention in the annals. Oh," he added, as if the oversight had not been intended, "but you write those, too, don't you?"

"Aye, my lord, I do."

Clarivaus was weary. He did not wish to know how many of his noble-hearted followers had met their deaths that day. He did not want to give the defeatists—like Marhaus—any more leverage.

Yet Marhaus had saved the army. It rankled to do so, but he had to admit that much.

The first volley fell among them before they even knew what was happening. The second followed quickly after. A great cloud of raining death, it caused havoc among the packed and angry mass of warriors. Horses reared and screamed as their riders struggled frantically to bring them under control; footsoldiers cowered beneath their shields in a helpless fury that shortly turned to fear as their confined space became thick with the dead and the dying.

Clarivaus, uncertain and irresolute, wheeled his horse desperately in all directions, shouting pointless commands which no one heeded, while dismay gripped his army and massacre seemed certain.

Then Marhaus was at his side. He called above the din. "Sire, we may not stay here! Let me give the order to attack!"

Clarivaus, his mind responding instinctively to this hint of remedy, nodded dumbly and Marhaus, acting with a decisiveness and sense of command that temporarily stemmed the confusion, quickly organized counterattacks against the bowmen—the cavalry against one flank, the infantry against the other.

But now the gates of the town opened and a new danger issued forth. It was a strange sight, for the enemy's cavalry seemed at first an ill-assorted and unprepossessing crew and their sheepish battle cry sounded thin and distinctly lacking in enthusiasm. But it was a warrior who galloped at their head, a shining apparition whose silver mail gleamed in the sun, mounted on a great warhorse whose hooves thundered and shook the convulsing earth.

This motley band fell upon Clarivaus's infantry (for they knew better than to try and engage his horsemen) and wielded their long, sharp spears with deadly effect. When they discovered how easy it was to dispatch an enemy who is too overcome by panic and confusion to think of anything but flight, they rapidly warmed to their task, slaughtering with gusto the demoralized footsoldiers.

"Don't tell me that, Marhaus," pleaded the king despondently, his eyelids heavy beneath their weight of pain, guilt, and drowsiness. "I don't want to know that. Tell me instead how many we slew of the enemy."

"It is a trifling enough figure when set against our own grievous losses, sire," said Marhaus. And of course he went on to give all the details.

It could have been worse, Clarivaus supposed. It comforted him little to think so now, but it could have been a complete rout, ending in annihilation.

Marhaus, quickly recognizing the futility of men on horseback attacking archers who fled behind an impenetrable thicket of vegetation, turned and counterattacked. His cavalry was now much reduced in number, but they pressed home their advance with ferocity and determination and the horsemen from the town soon lost their eagerness and fled in disarray.

All save their champion. He did not flee but stayed the field, dominating it with his solid, immovable presence and his swift, merciless sword. Many of the king's bravest knights rode against him. All were overthrown with a savage energy that was breathtaking to watch.

Clarivaus could not for long stand idly by and watch this happening. Though far from confident of his chances against such a redoubtable adversary, his sense of noblesse oblige and his simple love of a good scrap were impulses that simply could not be resisted. As another headless body fell to the dust, he brandished his sword above his head and, yelling his most colorful invectives, hurtled straight for his enemy.

"Well, there are still many of us left," he murmured not very convincingly.

"Aye, my lord, it could have been a complete massacre."

Marhaus was right to sound bitter, he realized. Six hundred men, half their number, had been left on that bloody field and many of those who had hobbled to safety would not fight again.

But what of Tristram? For if Marhaus had saved the army, or what was left of it, leading the scattered remnants away as the archers began to re-form and their horsemen steeled themselves for a renewed onslaught, it was Tristram who had saved the king.

With a seemingly effortless sweep of his left arm the enemy knight struck Clarivaus squarely beneath the chin with the edge of his shield. For a split second everything seemed to freeze, then the king found himself flying earthward at great speed, landing with a jar that made his teeth rattle and his body crack in several places. Turning, he looked up through a veil of pain and saw his opponent, dark and forbidding, towering above him like a huge statue. For a moment longer the figure remained, silent and silhouetted against the sky. Then the knight turned and rode slowly away. No one challenged him.

It was Tristram then who rode forward. Strangely, for there was no enemy nearby, he seemed to hesitate. Then, without dismounting, he reached down and with a powerful arm drew Clarivaus up and behind him.

And so they had fled, ignominiously, disordered and discomfited, with the taunts of their surprised and delighted enemies loud in their ears.

It was that which depressed him more than the size of the defeat. As it was, in spite of their great loss, they were still a formidable force. They would have to be more careful in the future, but otherwise he saw no reason why the expedition should not continue. For those who remained, there was the far from negligible compensation of a larger share of booty.

Yes, he admitted, it is a grave setback, but that is

no cause for us to scurry back home with our tails between our legs.

"We have been humiliated today, Marhaus," he said as another bandage was tied around his head. "We must avenge our shame."

Marhaus frowned. "Sire, we cannot hope to overcome them now. They know that some of us have escaped and so will not relax their vigilance."

Clarivaus shook his head. "I do not intend to hazard the lives of any more of our brave men—if I can help it." Fending off the servant, for he felt that his body was swathed enough now, he added, "I have sent Sir Tristram on an errand which, if successful, will yield the town to us without so much as a sword being raised."

In fact, he had no idea where Tristram was or what he was up to. He had merely nodded vaguely when the knight had made his hurried departure, speaking cryptically of returning with a vast power that would confound their enemies and make them a great and feared power in the land.

"That is just as well for me then," quipped Marhaus with uncharacteristic wit. But his face showed that he was unconvinced.

Marhaus left the king's pavilion and stood for a moment listening to the muted keening of the mourning women and gazing at the darkening sky. Why is it always like that after a great battle? he wondered. He wondered, too, as he made his way slowly to his own tent, which would prove the more dangerous, the king's incorrigible optimism or Tristram's rising ambition. One or both of them, he was sure, would get them all into big trouble.

The Moot Hall had been hurriedly converted into a makeshift infirmary. The council debating chamber on the ground floor was now crowded with beds, not because the wounded had been many but because it was not a large room.

Percevale, his helm beneath his arm, made his way gingerly between the narrow rows. Sometimes he stopped to exchange a few words of comfort or a forced smile.

He should, he realized, be in better spirits than this. They had gotten off surprisingly lightly. Most of these men would be on their feet in time. Nor were there many dead, less than a tenth of what the enemy had suffered, he calculated. Yet the atmosphere was heavy with sadness, as if the grief of the luckless few had touched them all. The prevailing gloom infected him, too, though he could not help feeling annoyed at the townspeople's too delicate sensitivity. He felt that it was not unreasonable to expect some gratitude for the help he had rendered. Such grieving, he reflected petulantly, is excessive and self-indulgent.

Of course, there were those who had cause to make great dole.

He came to a far corner of the room. Here the physician was attending to one of the more badly wounded. True to the advice he often gave to others when bereaved, he was attempting to drown his own grief in ceaseless labor and concentrated effort. Standing at a discreet distance, Percevale watched the struggle taking place behind the red eyes and the drawn features. Outside, the light was fading and ladies in plain garments slightly spotted with blood held oil lamps aloft, moving them at the physician's whispered directions.

This dismal little scene, with its silent attendants, the shifting patterns of yellow light and brown shadow, the mellow glint of the knife, worked now with a mechanical dexterity, was one of unutterable pathos, and Percevale felt a helpless pity for the small and now-broken man before him. He felt also a little ashamed of his earlier uncharitable thoughts concerning the townsfolk.

At the edge of this sad little tableau—outside it really—stood Elaine. She was cutting some lengths of bandage—rather inexpertly, for she was not possessed of that temperament that finds fulfillment in tending wounded soldiers or warming their hearts with her gentle presence. Duty and concern for her father had brought her here, and she was almost relieved when Percevale touched her gently on the arm and motioned her outside. The movement caused Robert to look up, but at the sight of his worn and empty face Percevale turned quickly away and the physician, as if mindful that his own grief should not intrude upon the repose of others, bent once again to his task.

Outside, there was little more comfort. The sky was leaden and the air humid. Elaine, looking up, wondered briefly why it should be. There had been a brilliant dawn.

"He takes it hard, your father," Percevale said. They walked slowly together along the empty street.

"We all do," she replied simply. "But Father the most. Simon, you see, was his favorite. They had their differences. If you had witnessed one of their real arguments—and there were many—you'd look even more surprised. Father had great hopes for Simon. Blancheflor and myself he regards as a dutiful parent should, but in Simon he believed he saw an extension of himself. Naturally, this has quite defeated him. He tries to hide it, but, as you see, he cannot."

Her voice was dry as she spoke and he could tell that she was having difficulty holding back the tears.

"I am sorry," he said. She looked at him with a puzzled expression. "I might have saved him," he explained.

There was a moment's pause, as if she were considering her reply. "You are not to blame," she said. "You have delivered us from our enemies. It was a great victory, was it not?"

If there was irony in the remark, Percevale could not detect it. He agreed that it was. He could have wished that they had pursued the enemy with more vigor instead of allowing so many to escape, but he did not speak of this, nor of the disquiet it caused him.

"They will not come again?" she asked.

He thought not. "They will seek easier victories elsewhere if they have any sense. But"—and here he paused significantly—"these people do have a certain pride which sometimes overrules considerations of common prudence. No," he decided, dismissing this possibility, "they could not be so stupid. I do not think they will come again."

They turned and retraced their steps in silence. When they reached the doorway again, she looked at him the way she had looked in her father's garden some evenings before. Again Percevale felt like an embarrassed adolescent, inadequate and uncertain, and he was almost relieved when she eventually broke the silence.

"You are tired," she said. "You should rest. I shall rejoin Father. I am quite hopeless, as you see, but I feel I should keep an eye on him." She stayed a moment longer, as if expecting some response, then she turned abruptly and walked away.

Watching her go, Percevale felt his petulance return, though this time it was directed principally at himself.

There were many reasons why he should have seized the opportunity that had just presented itself, many reasons why he should have taken her to him and made avowal of his love. There were also reasons to the contrary. His was a life governed by violence, and though he would, if pressed, deny it, he derived a strange and savage pleasure from the whole bloody business. That morning's work had been hard but exhilarating. Afterward it appalled him, but at the time he had enjoyed himself as he slaughtered all comers, had felt a cold ecstasy course through him as with rhythmical efficiency he dispatched one eager adversary after another. Had they come against him all at once, it would have been a different story, but there would have been no glory for them in that, and so they had not. She is better off out of it, he thought. She has cherished in me an image of romance and manageable dangers. Today perhaps she has caught a glimpse of the reality behind the bright carapace.

Yet, though he tried to persuade himself that these contrary reasons were much the more pressing and unselfish, it was with a profound sense of dissatisfaction that he crossed the street and directed his steps to the physician's house. He could not avoid the uncomfortable fact that in rejecting her thus he was bringing some dishonor upon her and possible unhappiness to them both.

Ah, well, he thought with little conviction, they would both get over it in time. Certainly there could be no future for the two of them, not as things stood. He could not change now and adopt some other way of life. This is the only thing I am good at, he thought.

19

This is indeed excellent. I haven't tasted wine
like this since—since—"

"My last visit?" prompted Tristram, and he
smiled good-naturedly from the best chair, the one
Mordred reserved for his rare guests.

"Ah, but before that," said Mordred, "it was many
years. You are not drinking yourself?"

In answer, Tristram proffered his empty cup but
quickly withdrew it when it was half full. He suspected that it would be a little while yet before his
host's tongue was sufficiently loose to let slip what he
wanted to know.

Mordred drank some more. Somewhere at the back
of his mind a voice struggled to be heard. It was
warning him, telling him to be on his guard against
this smiling visitor who had ridden many miles in the
night simply to exchange reminiscences. But the warm
red liquid was softly infusing his body, eroding his
better judgment, and he did not hear the voice.

"I admire your people," he said, his voice already
slightly slurred and louder than necessary.

"Thank you."

"Yes. You have vigor and energy. You will inherit

179

the future." He stopped and turned, fumbling in the candlelight for the scattered parts of his manuscript. "Here," he said, and thrust some sheets of parchment into Tristram's hand. "This is addressed to the future, to people like yourself, my friend. Read it."

The young man felt the waxy material between his fingers and stared uncomprehendingly at the scrawled symbols. "It looks most interesting," he said diplomatically, "but I cannot read very well in this poor light. Perhaps you could tell me something of it in your own words."

Too intoxicated by wine and enthusiasm to notice this clumsy evasion, Mordred responded eagerly to the invitation. Even through the thickening alcoholic haze he was still aware that his was a relatively unsophisticated audience, albeit a remarkably attentive one, and he would therefore need to simplify his thesis. "It is about power and responsibility," he began haltingly. "How felicity may be assured when the two are conjoined and how disaster is inevitable when they are not."

Tristram knew nothing of responsibility. It was not in his language. But the mention of power made him sit forward with interest.

"Arthur, my father, the king"—Mordred looked uncertainly at his guest who nodded quickly. Yes, he had heard of King Arthur—"he had a great and even burdensome sense of responsibility. When he came to the throne, he wanted to do so much—free the slaves, relieve the poor, educate the masses—but he was reluctant to exercise the power that is required to do such things. His conscience was too delicate; it could not bear the prospect of a ruinous civil war. The great lords of Albion would not have stood for such things, you see. They wanted to keep their power and their wealth and Arthur's projected reforms threatened both. So he postponed them and sought to win over the lords by reason. Meanwhile, and partly in order to

secure their goodwill, he humored their urgent clam-
orings for self-aggrandizing and expensive military
adventures such as the expeditions to Brittany and
Rome. It was then, alas, that he discovered his weakness. He found that he enjoyed it—shaving the Bret-
on king's beard in public view of the poor man's court;
dictating terms outside the walls of Rome while the
senators, the finest of their race, so they say, groveled
submissively in his pavilion. Do you know, the Romans were so ashamed at the humiliating defeat which
Arthur inflicted on them that they forbade mention
of it in their annals? It is not recorded anywhere save
in the libraries of Albion and I suppose there must be
precious few of those.

"I think they will one day get their own back. They
are not the sort of people who can easily forget such a
defeat. Perhaps they are even now planning their revenge—that fellow who is giving our friends in Gaul
such a bad time; he sounds very formidable. One of
the coming men among the Latins." He waved a knowing finger. "Oh, yes, I have my sources; I keep abreast
of the momentous events of the day. Mind you, you
would not think that anyone with a name like Julius
could put the wind up the Gauls, would you?"

"If any foreigners dare to venture north, they will
meet a bloody reception indeed," Tristram snapped.
His lip quivered with belligerence. This story of ancient heroism, though strangely told, had already fired
his imagination. Why aspire merely to be king of an
obscure realm of mist-shrouded hills and damp forests? Somebody someday would unite the legendary
and lost kingdom of Albion. Why should it not be he?
If he could learn what he had come to learn . . .

He felt a sudden surge of self-confidence. And something else, something akin to patriotism, though that
was another concept foreign to him.

Unaware of the widening future his guest was laying
out for himself, Mordred said, "Do not underestimate

the Latins, my friend. They are not easily deterred by
defeat. No matter how many battles they lose, they
always seem to win the war." He paused for a moment
to consider where he might fit this pleasing little
epigram in his memoirs before returning to his theme.

"Yes, Arthur came to relish this more and more, the
glory and the acclaim. He found that he possessed a
real talent for strategy. He grew hungry for more, and
as his appetite for power developed, so he lost interest in such mundane issues as rising prices and popular discontent, preferring to leave them in the hands
of intellectuals like myself.

"Now, you see, he exercised power without responsibility and this time he was willing to accept discord
and eventual civil war in order to retain it."

Mordred was pleased with the symmetry of his
account, pleased also that his guest showed no sign of
waning interest, seemed eager, indeed, for more.

"I think that toward the end he realized this, that
he had betrayed himself and so brought his country
to oblivion. His, and the kingdom's, tragedy is that he
realized too late." The wine had loosened Mordred's
inhibitions as well as his tongue, and he found himself, to his surprise, stifling a sob or two. "If only he'd
listened, for I warned him many times of the state of
the nation. But he'd lost interest, you see—"

"As I see it, your desire, then, is for order," Tristram
interrupted suddenly as enlightenment dawned.

Mordred blinked and rubbed a moist eye. "Yes," he
replied, rather confused, for now both his train of
thought and his emotional calm had been disturbed.

"I see," said Tristram with a note of satisfaction. He
nodded thoughtfully. "These are indeed distempered
times and order is called for; one who can bring order
and unity to our troubled land is called for." He spoke
in careful, measured tones, anxious that the old man,
who was by now quite drunk, should hear every word
of his painfully constructed argument, anxious also lest

his own mounting excitement betray him. For he was certain that he was on the verge of discovering what he had almost ridden his horse to death for, the old man's secret, one which he was sure neither bribery nor the threat of death could squeeze from him. On Tristram's first visit—he had not been so drunk then— Mordred had only intimated darkly the existence of a great and terrible weapon that none could resist. Tristram, though impressed by the old man's commanding stature, had done no more than store this mildly intriguing claim for possible future use.

Then had come the disastrous battle and the humiliating defeat which should never have happened; and as he rode furiously the many miles, retracing through the lengthening day and the gathering night the path trod by the once-confident, now-shattered army, so his conviction grew that this eccentric anchorite did know something. And whatever it was, it held the key to his, Tristram's, destiny. Why else had he spared him thus far?

And Mordred? Alas, this time he did hear the warning voice, for it was shrill and clear and insistent. But his tongue was loosed beyond his control and it would have its way. Yes, yes, he agreed, nodding stupidly as Tristram spoke softly and smoothly of their shared concerns. Yes, he agreed, if the Romans came, they might prove difficult to stop. Yes, only if the country were united could it withstand such a disciplined assault. And how was this to be done? How could even the most determined ruler manage to keep such a quarrelsome people together? What power could he wield that would command the loyalty of his countrymen and the awe of his enemies?

And so it went on. And as Mordred let slip one tiny revelation, so it became easier to let slip another slightly larger one. And Tristram smiled indulgently all the while, listening most carefully and prompting where required.

And soon it was done, and Tristram had all the information he wanted, far more than he could properly assimilate, in fact. Mordred even told him how to find the entrance to the Druid temple. To such a benefactor how could he be other than merciful? As he rose to leave, he gently patted his host on the back, saying, "I will take my leave of you now, old man, and will not kill you as habit and prudence command. You have done great service, perhaps greater than you know. In time, you may even have occasion to thank me for releasing you from your burden." He looked for a moment more at the gray-haired figure, now slumped and silent in its chair. Then he turned and strode quickly away into the night, sprightly and exultant, and doubly dangerous now, for he was emboldened no longer by mere personal ambition but by a sense of mission.

Mordred felt ill. Also he felt a vague sense of shame and remorse. He did not know why this should be, but he quickly drank some more wine.

He did not wish to become sober yet.

20

I had not expected anything like this," marveled Clarivaus, his eyes widening in disbelief. "It is truly magnificent. There must be much plunder here."

Tristram nodded, pleased with the response. The two of them were standing in the semidarkness at the top of the stairway that led to the cavern floor. Behind them in the tunnel flickered the torches of the rest of the king's party.

Again Clarivaus drew his breath sharply between his teeth. "Was this place fashioned by giants? Surely mortal men could not build thus."

"Neither men nor giants, sire." Tristram pointed upward. "It is a natural cavern. See."

For a moment the king gazed thoughtfully at the barbed stalactites glinting balefully in the light of many candles. "Ah, yes," he said.

Thus far, they had escaped detection. The unsuspecting Druid guards at the head of the tunnel had not heard their stealthy killers descend the narrow shaft, and their screams had been muted and short. No further resistance had been encountered. And it is unlikely that we shall meet with any down there,

Clarivaus thought as he contemplated the diminutive figures milling about below him.

Now the time for stealth was over. Making no further attempt to conceal his presence, he began to descend noisily the long flight of steps, his footsteps ringing on the dark stones, the upraised swords of his followers flashing with an evil gleam through the soft light of the cavern.

Pale faces turned toward them and, seeing their approach, uttered cries of alarm that spread and echoed, bouncing back and forth across the great chamber and sounding long afterward like a continuous and urgent whisper. In that place any noise of appreciable volume was magnified and extended. Stools fell noisily backward as their occupants leaped from their benches and the sound of their hollow falls came like distant explosions. The hushed workshop atmosphere became suddenly one of confusion and clamor. Some of the Druids rushed to the foot of the stairs, where they were swiftly and brutally cut down. The rest, seeing this, gathered anxiously around the only sanctuary they knew, the dais in the center of the cavern and its tall priest who, with one eye directed uncertainly on these rough intruders, continued to recite his soft incantation.

Clarivaus stepped over the small heap of bodies and began cautiously to inspect his latest conquest. Passing by the benches with their assortment of vessels, his nose wrinkled in distaste, but mindful of Tristram's advice he did not touch or examine them closely. He directed his steps instead to the mass of huddled figures sheltering about the dais. He eyed them first with scorn, then perplexity, and finally with some unease.

"Their faces," he whispered to Tristram. "What has happened to disfigure them so?" But Tristram could explain neither the ugly red weals that scarred the faces of the cowering Druids nor the deeper glow that

issued from somewhere behind them. He knew only
that he had a sudden and impelling desire to be above
ground once more.

"Where is your king?" Clarivaus demanded. He, too,
was impatient to be gone. "Answer quickly that your
lives may be spared." The wall of cadaverous faces
stared blankly back at him. Why should they care for
such a threat, thought Tristram, when they seem half
dead already?

"Come on," said the king. "Who is it that you serve?
Show me that I may speak with him. Put down your
swords," he added, turning to his men.

Dawning comprehension appeared on some of the
faces. There were nods and murmurs of inquiry and
assent. One of the ovates then stepped forward and
the rest drew aside to make a pathway that led directly to the high cauldron, its single flame pulsing
silently in the damp air.

Confronting the northern king with a toothless smile,
the young man inclined his head slightly and said,
"Here is whom we serve. Come."

He led Clarivaus and Tristram through the parted
ranks of now-deferential Druids and to the edge of the
pit. Bending down, Tristram peered through the green-
tinged translucent haze at the dim shapes below.

"We did not know who you were, that you are indeed the ones spoken of. Please forgive us and our
poor welcome." He stepped back a little. "Please.
Speak with Urannos."

Though the Druid was a good head shorter, still
Clarivaus could barely repress the shudder that ran
through him. The man had no eyebrows, and, like the
others, he wore his headgear tightly bound to conceal
his baldness. The thin smile that creased his gaunt
and skeletal face showed no mirth. "I felt as if I were
conversing with a dead man," he confided later.

Shaking off these disturbing thoughts but keeping

his eyes firmly on the Druid nonetheless, he whispered to Tristram, "Is that it?"

"Aye, my lord, this is what the old man spoke of. I am sure of it."

By now the other priests who attended the shrine had been wakened from their dormitories and were approaching the scene with worried haste. Three walked behind and one, their chief, walked at their head and seemed, to Clarivaus, even more forbidding and sinister in appearance than the rest.

"What do you want?" he demanded in a voice whose cracked sibilance made him sound older than his years. "Why have you come here with such violent intent?"

For a moment Clarivaus could not speak but stared in mute horror at the man's ravaged face. Unlike the others, it bore none of the livid red streaks. Instead, the bones that protruded like clearly defined ridges beneath the dry and tightly drawn skin emitted a pale-yellowish glow that reminded him of the grinning skull that stood sentinel above, his unexpected discovery of which had nearly imperiled their whole mission. Mordred had neglected to mention that.

Behind him he heard the uncertain shuffling of feet as his men moved sheepishly back. Reminding himself of his position—Oh, how burdensome his responsibility was!—he asserted himself.

"We will do you no harm if you cross us not," he announced stiffly. "We come for the—the—"

"Urannos," Tristram prompted him.

"That is so. And you will assist us. It would be healthier for you if you did."

For the moment the eyelids of the chief Druid flickered as if he had caught the unintended irony of the remark. The ovate who had earlier spoken approached him. "Father, are not these the men for whom we have waited, the ones who will release us from our burden?"

The priest rested a bony hand on the man's shoulder and gazed pensively at Clarivaus for several moments. This was a disturbing experience for the king; propriety demanded that he flinch not from the red-rimmed eyes that bored with such concentration into his own. But the habit of command was in him deeply ingrained and was not to be easily shaken. They are hideous, he told himself, but they are also mortal. If they hesitate, I will kill a few, and if they hesitate still, a few more. . . .

"No, my boy," answered the priest, and he removed his hand from the younger man's shoulder. Both Tristram and Clarivaus saw the flakes of skin that fell away as he did so, and both closed their eyes.

"No," the priest said again, "I do not think these are the men. But yes"—and he turned to Clarivaus, who opened his eyes to see the younger Druid lightly brush from his shoulder the little heap of human detritus— "you may take the devices. With our permission if not our blessing."

"I want neither. I want to know how to use these monsters."

The ovates who heard this gasped in horror and dismay. The priest shook his head tolerantly. "Your disrespect to Urannos is doubtless due to your ignorance. Perhaps he will forgive your sacrilege." Before Clarivaus could respond to this stinging condescension, he quickly added, "We will show you how to make use of the handmaidens." Turning to the priest, who all this time had unceasingly, if a little hesitantly, continued his whispered ritual, he said gently, "It's all right, old fellow, you can stop now. For the moment anyway." He contemplated for a moment the wide-eyed and gruesome faces of the other Druids and sighed gently. "We can all stop now."

He gave a signal and two of them went obediently over to the pit. Kneeling on the edge, they pressed their palms heavily against the thick glass and began to push forward. Slowly, and with a nerve-jarring screech, the canopy began to slide open. Moving to opposite sides of the pit, the two men grasped its now-exposed edge and with the additional leverage thus obtained pushed harder. When about three-quarters of the glass had vanished into its stony recess, they stopped, for now the objects that lay at the bottom of the shallow pit were quite accessible.

Clarivaus went forward and looked down at the three bronze cylinders, each about the height and thickness of a man, each lying in its own carefully fashioned niche, unstirring, gleaming with a purposeful menace in the cauldron's glow.

"They don't look much, do they?" he said to Tristram. Yet he found their appearance curiously unsettling. Or was that just the surroundings? He shrugged and turned again to the chief Druid.

"I need only one of these at present. For the rest, they shall remain here, as will my men, to guard them." The Druid nodded submissively, though from the ranks of the warriors there escaped a low moan. Clarivaus rounded on them angrily. "I will see that you are reinforced quickly and relieved soon. Oh, my brothers," he added in a more conciliatory tone, "do I not look after you always?" Before any of them could answer, he turned to Tristram, who had already climbed into the pit and was crouching next to one of the cylinders, examining its surface closely.

"What are you doing?"

"There are symbols scratched into the metal, sire. I know not what they signify nor what language they represent. It is not ours." Though illiterate, Tristram was bright enough to recognize what he could not read.

"They are in code," the priest explained. "I will read them to you if you wish, but they are lengthy and you will require a good memory."

"We can read," the king replied hotly. "Only write plainly, that is all."

The priest nodded gravely. "Good. Do not keep the device for too long. Whatever your purpose is, use it quickly. For your own well-being you should do this."

Clarivaus looked at the deathly faces around him and apprehended his meaning. While the Druid went to his chamber to write the necessary instructions, he ordered his men to bind ropes around one of the cylinders and lift it from the pit. The warriors were strong and no strangers to heavy burdens. Even so, it took six of them to carry it, staggering and cursing, up the long flight of steps.

"You must be very careful," said the priest as he returned and handed Clarivaus a scroll. "The hand-maiden is in two parts and they should not be separated until the time comes for their use. Thus you must not drag it or drop it or in any way strike it sharply."

"Do not worry." He indicated the unhappy trio of soldiers whom Tristram had selected to stay behind. "These men will remain to protect you and the devices."

"We are most grateful," said the Druid.

"Do not try to leave or take anything with you," said Clarivaus, hinting darkly.

The Druid raised a shrewd, hairless eyebrow. "Where do you think we would go?" he inquired gently.

Clarivaus grunted. "I may shortly return for those other two, though it is quite likely that we shall have no need of them."

Do not wager on that, Tristram thought. He, too, had been greatly overawed by these gloomy surroundings, had felt his courage falter at the sight of the loathsome beings who ministered so resignedly to their own slow destruction. But now, as he contemplated the vast power that lay within his grasp, his spirits rose again. He followed the king up the echoing stairway, his mind busy with fresh calculations.

The Druids and their reluctant custodians watched them go.

"Do you think they know what they are doing, Father?"

"No more than we did all those years ago, my son."

"Then a surprise awaits them, does it not?"

The lusterless eyes of the chief Druid burned briefly in their huge sockets, intensifying the eerie glow that suffused his lifeless features. From deep in the tunnel he could still hear the low, muttered curses of the bearers and, above them, the shouted imprecations of their king as they stumbled through the darkness. His thin, parched lips extended into the merest hint of a smile.

"Indeed it does, my son. A very great surprise."

21

(From the *Boke of Mordred,* Chapter 46)

... That final winter of the war was harsher than I have ever experienced before or since. For the people's army it was a time of great adversity. Arthur and his allies, flagrantly contravening hallowed customs of warfare, continued to harry our gallant but sorely tried forces, even though the campaigning season was long over. Towns which had embraced us and the justice of our cause barred their gates to us for fear of reprisals. The necessity for candor obliges me to admit that our forces were ill-equipped to meet such unforeseen conditions as these, and in their makeshift camps in the snow the soldiers endured much hardship. The surprise attacks of our cunning and unscrupulous enemy killed many of them, but the snow and the bitter cold killed many more.

Thus did Arthur deploy his most valuable weapon, the weather; thus, too, was our position when I first learned about mine.

The first reports I received were neither greatly illuminating nor very encouraging. From one of my spies, operating deep behind enemy lines in the inaccessible southwestern peninsula of Albion, there came word of a hitherto unknown substance possessed, it seemed, of singular properties. Its existence, the report said, was a closely guarded secret; not even Arthur, within the heart of whose territory the deposits lay, knew aught of it. Such quantities as had been so far discovered were in the possession of a small and quite insignificant coastal tribe.

Receipt of this news excited great interest among those of the Druid community who shared in my counsels, and they pressed urgently for further information and, if possible, samples of the new mineral. I was not at first greatly disposed to acquiesce—I lacked, after all, that celebrated Druid prescience and I still remembered the occasion, only a few months previous, when a similar degree of excitement had been generated over the discovery of the mineral now known as "the northerner." Many inflated claims had been made about its strategic value, many hopes raised. Yet apart from helping troops to find their way in unfamiliar territory when other means of navigation were unavailable, it had since been found to be of little worth.

I had not lavished my favors and my protection upon the eastern Druids for such trinkets as these, and I was unwilling to further indulge their passion for the novel and the merely curious, especially as this latest request involved the putting at risk of a loyal and useful spy.

But the Druid establishment then, if not

now, was a powerful body, and its influence
was extensive. I stood to lose more by offending than by humoring it and so, contenting
myself with a few mild protests and the expressed hope that the outcome would justify
the risks, I dispatched the necessary orders.

The tale of how my intrepid spy, through
bribery and guile, obtained from its jealous
guardians a substantial quantity of the mineral that was afterward named in honor of
him, how he brought it under the walls of
that most strongly guarded of all Arthur's
fortifications, grim Camelot itself, and passed,
mortally wounded, through the enemy's lines,
expiring only when he had reached the safety
of our own, is best left to one more skilled in
the bardic arts than I. Suffice to say that his
mission was a success though I little deemed
it at the time.

At any rate, the Druids were satisfied and
in a spirit of gleeful expectancy they set out,
in their underground laboratories, to unlock
the secret of this latest discovery.

For myself, I had more pressing concerns
and soon lost interest in the unprepossessing
black rocks. Regular reports reached my head-
quarters, but the Druid mind, even when it
expresses itself in plain Celtic, is quite impenetrable, and I found their accounts of
lengthy and it seemed largely fruitless exper-
iments both wearisome and incomprehensible. I gleaned this much: The substance might
contain the ingredients of a new and powerful weapon. In its natural state, Urannos—as
it came to be known—was both harmless
and useless. However, once it had undergone
a laborious and arcane process of purifica-
tion, it became awesome and deadly. If two

small pieces of the purified mineral were merely to touch each other, they would release a slow, invisible poison, bringing upon all nearby a painful, wasting disease. If the same two pieces were brought together with sufficiently calamitous force, they would create destruction on such a scale as would dwarf even the sulphur weapons with which Merlin's Druids were reputedly experimenting.

Yet there was a drawback: We did not know the secret of transmutation. Oh, there were many qualified alchemists among my Druids. They could transform base metals into gold—albeit at a staggering and uneconomical cost—but they could not break the secret of Urannos.

Initially I had been skeptical about the whole thing, but the Druids were very persuasive and they pressed me constantly. Think, they counseled, what power I could command if only they possessed the ritual of transmutation.

I did not want to rule the world, but I did want to win the war. I was desperate; I was prepared to chance anything.

A new expedition was mounted to the southwest. I could not risk the lives of any more good men—I had so few left—and so, leaving Agravaine in charge of the army, I took a few ovates and my bodyguard and went to discover for myself the magic that confounded even the Druids.

We traveled by sea, keeping out of sight of land and of Arthur's watchtowers. It was a terrifying voyage, deserving of a chapter in itself. I had great trouble concealing my own fear in order to calm that of my fellows, but the sailors were a hardy crew and they assured me that we were many miles from the edge of the world.

We braved many storms which made us all very ill. But at least the bad weather kept the sea monsters away and at length, and with much relief, we came to rest on an unguarded part of the Cornish seashore and thence proceeded inland. Our guides and maps proved to be of excellent worth, and within a day we reached the village of the magicians—though I scarce could believe it at the time. It was such a filthy place—a few wattle huts at the foot of a hillside into which several tunnels had been bored. And the people themselves were ragged and uncouth. Whatever they were, they were certainly not Druids. Their ragged garments were the strangest of any priesthood that I have encountered. They treated my ovates with fearless contempt and laughed when I told them I had known Merlin; they called him a charlatan. Though they enjoyed the protection of the West, they favored neither side in the war, preferring to hold both in equal disregard. Yet they unsettled me, these old men, as they capered before me, half starved, their clothes in shreds, believing themselves lords of the earth. The Druids were frightened of them, too, I could see that. They tried not to show it and looked down their noses at these ignoble savages, but they were clearly rattled.

I do not think they were native to the region. There were no women or children among them, and how they fed themselves I do not know, for there were no signs of crops or livestock. They spoke Celtic after a fashion, but many other languages also, and it was difficult to hold discourse with them when sense and apparent gibberish mingled so confusedly in their speech. They had no gods; all their allegiance, their sole purpose, revolved about the black rock that they mined from deep within the earth. Strangely enough, for something so central to their existence, they had no name for it. They were quite pleased with ours, though, and I was greatly flattered when they asked if they could adopt the name themselves.

Their leader was a hollow-eyed scarecrow of a man who in younger days and newer clothes might have cut quite an impressive figure. Embroidered on his shoulder was a strange and faded cosmological device, the significance of which I never was able to divine. His manner was as odd, but his language was more lucid than his companions' and to my surprise he seemed quite willing to relinquish his secrets to my eager Druids. He even offered us some of his apparatus. "It is worn and old and too dangerous for us to use," he said. "But it would be interesting to see what you do with it."

He demanded payment, of course, but was not greatly interested in the vast horde of synthesized gold my men had brought with them. He asked, instead, for comparatively worthless trinkets—weapons, jewelry, items of clothing—"to take back with us," he explained.

As I have said, their words made little sense.

But I think what gave them more pleasure than our swords and brooches was the praise and flattery of the Druids whom they took with them into their hillside. I declined their invitation, choosing instead to wait outside.

When, two days later, they reemerged laden with the parchments on which they had recorded the many complex spells and the apparatus with which to weave them, they were quite awestruck.

"My lord, such marvels," said my chief ovate, then shook his head in dumb wonder.

I was not so easily impressed by the iron boxes they carried with much labor and care. "If they are so clever, why don't they look after themselves properly?" But he only shook his head again. It was something to see my chief Druid at a loss for words, and it gave me even greater pleasure to see him and his companions abase themselves before such primitive fellows.

For the Druids were such terrible snobs.

We left shortly afterward, for we all felt uneasy about the place and its inhabitants, and, despite unfavorable winds and yet more storms, we returned without mishap. I was very pleased with myself. Not only had I penetrated the enemy's lines, taking from him a treasure that he did not even know he possessed, I had also undertaken a truly pioneering sea voyage. When I returned, I expected cheering crowds and a chapter in the annals. Instead, I was greeted with news of an attack against my capital and of the death of my dearest friend.

A company of knights and men-at-arms, led by Bedivere, I later discovered, had sailed up the river Colne, surprising and almost taking Colchester. Agravaine had seen them off but was mortally wounded in doing so; he died a few days before my return.

I was mortified. It gave me a little consolation to learn that the attackers had been

driven off with heavy losses. Only the complete destruction of my enemy could console
me, and in my grief and rage I drove and
harried my poor Druids harder than they
had ever driven themselves.

Still, it was several months, well into the
spring, before the first explosion occurred.

I did not myself witness the results of this
calamity, but those who arrived on the scene
sometime afterward brought back reports of
destruction on a truly awesome scale.

Of the laboratory itself and its personnel,
no trace could be found. Nor did anything
remain of the sacred wood below which the
laboratory had been sited. Where both had
been was now a vast and jagged chasm, wider
than twenty men, so the report said, and so
deep that its bottom was lost to darkness.

Of course there could be little doubt as to
the cause of so great and unsought a catastro-
phe, and while the loss of so many selfless
and dedicated scientists was a matter for som-
ber reflection, there was surely consolation
to be found in the knowledge that their final
experiment, though fatal to them, had been
wholly successful.

Fortunately, the Druids had communicated
sufficient information to their colleagues elsewhere to enable them to reconstruct the complex sequence of events that had produced
such earthshaking results. It is greatly to be
regretted that two more laboratories were ac-
cidentally destroyed before the Urannos was
brought satisfactorily under control, but progress is never easily won and I had far more
Druids than I really needed.

Those who were left—and there were many
—were understandably ecstatic. Only one

thing remained. The device had yet to be tested under battlefield conditions.

By now it was late spring and our forces were poised for the summer offensive, a gigantic pincer movement that would, if successful, win for us the key enemy stronghold of Glastonbury, the capital of the West, and with it the approaches to the whole southern half of Arthur's territory. Most strongly did the Druids urge me to make use of their wondrous discovery in the coming campaign, yet for some while I resisted their pleas. I had not forgotten poor Agravaine, or those many others, but I had misgivings. Was not the use of such a weapon, I asked myself, an offense against humanity? It seemed likely, judging from the reports I had received, that if even one of the four devices now in existence were used on the field of battle, it would destroy a goodly portion of the enemy's forces, perhaps as much as a quarter if the conditions were right. Was it not unmanly to kill so many of our fellows in such a craven manner? Then I considered the advantages. A swift and telling victory, though costly in the short term, might save many lives in the future.

These were grave and weighty matters and long hours were spent in consideration of them. At length I resolved thus: A single Urannos device would be deployed during the forthcoming offensive if at any point defeat seemed inevitable. Even in so extreme a circumstance, moreover, its use was to be confined to the periphery of the battle, where its powers might be suitably demonstrated without causing excessive casualties.

Thus it was that an awesome and hideous

power came into the hands of men who comprehended its vastness too late. Perhaps you who read this, you of the future age to whom this testament is addressed, are of a more rational and scientific temper. Perhaps you are already using Urannos wisely and in the service of peace and justice. I believe in progress and I am sure that this is so. At any rate, you will surely pay little heed to those credulous and superstitious folk who tell you that Urannos was brought out of darkness by the dreaded war goddess Morrigan in order to lure men to their destruction. This version, and its many regional variants, has an undeniable poetic appeal, but like most folktales it is but a clumsy attempt at rationalization and deserves no credence whatsoever.

It was not my intention to bring my testament to such a precipitate conclusion. Crucial events deserving of several chapters have been hastily and perforce compressed into a few pages. It is as unsatisfactory to me as it must be disappointing to you, the reader. But there. Recent events have shown me that I am no longer a critical observer of the past but an unwilling participant in its momentous sequel.

22

Are you ready yet?"

Marhaus sighed. "Almost, sire," he called. Beside him the line of sweating men heaved and strained at the thick coarse rope as slowly, with short jerks, the huge stone came into view. When they could pull no farther, the rope was made fast and the men collapsed exhausted on the stony ground.

Marhaus stood back and contemplated his device. It was primitive in construction but in its way ingenious. It consisted of an angled tree trunk supported by two crossbeams at one end and firmly embedded into the hard earth at the other. The raised end, beneath which the suspended rock slowly turned, projected over the edge of a deep and narrow chasm. Directly beneath and far below, two diminutive figures laboriously manhandled a similar-size rock into position.

Despite his misgivings over the king's latest venture, Marhaus felt justly proud of his handiwork. He had accepted the commission with the utmost reluctance, yet to everyone's surprise, not least his own, had succeeded. Of course it was rather simple and, he was forced to admit, not wholly original, but for a man of his background and unsophisticated outlook it was an achievement. Any fool today, he reasoned, can fashion an arrowhead, but the first to do so must have been a true genius, however crude his first efforts.

There had been logistical as well as creative problems. They were in the very heart of the wasteland. Not far from this spot legendary Glastonbury had once stood. It was a fitting enough location for devilry but one entirely barren of suitable vegetation. The wood had had to be transported many miles.

For a few moments the trunk creaked and bent with the weight and the heavy rock, secure in its hempen cradle, spun gracefully in the dry still air.

"Get on with it, man!"

Marhaus turned to the king with a brief apologetic nod, then gave the signal. A soldier stepped forward and with a swift blow of his sword slashed through the thick bundle of twisted strands. There was a sharp whistle of displaced air as the stone plummeted, and Marhaus, following its rapid progress, saw the two men at the bottom of the chasm, now fleeing for their lives, and realized he had forgotten to warn them.

Far above though they were, the men at the top heard clearly the satisfying crack as the rocks met and broke, hurling a barrage of stony shards in all directions.

Clarivaus looked over the edge. He watched without interest the two small figures pick themselves up and mouth inaudibly to their comrades above.

"Very good," he said. "That's three times now, isn't it?"

"Yes, sire." Marhaus was feeling well pleased with himself.

"And such a collision as you hope to engineer with this contrivance of yours will suffice to waken the monster?"

"It is no monster, sire." Once more Marhaus re-

moved the scroll from his belt. "It is a god—and goddess. Urannos, if the text speaks true, is a twin deity.
That is why the cylinder is in two parts and why
both male and female parts of the deity must be
brought convulsively together, with great force, for
the whole being to manifest itself."

Standing beside the king, Tristram smirked undis-
guisedly at his rival's unwitting innuendo.

"I see," said Clarivaus, little the wiser. Fancying he
saw a flaw in the argument, he said, "Why then is it
called a handmaiden?"

Marhaus shrugged wearily. He had endured much
lately of the king's needless and niggling pedantry. "It
is in the text, sire. I cannot vouch for its verity or its
meaning." He paused. "Perhaps the handmaiden is
merely the container and not the deity which dwells
unseen within."

Clarivaus snorted. "It sounds like a lot of foreign
nonsense to me. We have gods and we have goddesses.
What's wrong with that, I ask?" Marhaus shrugged
again. "Well, you'd better set it up then." His eyes
narrowed warily. "There's no danger of anything going
wrong, is there?"

"My apparatus will do its part," Marhaus confi-
dently replied, "so long as your man does his." He
indicated the slave who, standing a little way off, was
watching events with mild interest. Seeing the three
men looking at him, he rose quickly to his feet, smiling nervously.

"Of course he will," Clarivaus hissed, and smiled
briefly at the slave. "I have given the fool money and
promised him his freedom. He thinks he is taking a
small risk only."

Marhaus nodded and turned to go. Clarivaus stopped
him. "You are perhaps a little skeptical about the
power of our weapon?"

But the other man readily detected the king's sly

irony. "Not so much as to ignore the precautions advised here, sire." And he tapped the scroll.

"A pity," the king whispered when he had gone. "Else I might have persuaded him to remain. I'd rather have him do the job than that idiot. You can never be sure with servants these days."

Tristram nodded sympathetically. "Aye, my lord. The monster could then deal with all our enemies together."

"It is not a monster, Tristram. It is a deity. You should not speak disrespectfully of the gods, even if they are foreigners."

It was not until late afternoon that everything was ready. The tribesmen felt nervous in the wasteland, so different from the fertile country that lay around it. They looked with disquiet upon the pale-yellow landscape, naked and sickly hued and glowing faintly in the heavy sun's fading light; they looked on the twisting structures of rock, potent with hidden menace, and felt primordial terrors stir within their normally phlegmatic breasts. They were not to know that every mutant for miles around had fled at first sight of the shaggy, wild-looking strangers.

The man they left behind shared none of these fears; he was not by nature superstitious and was anyway too preoccupied with his sudden and unexpected good fortune to worry about unseen and fabled denizens.

He was not stupid either. He knew there was a danger involved in what he was doing; why entrust the task to a slave else? But he also believed that chance was in his favor; an optimistic view for a slave. He saw a chance, a slim one, of returning to his family; perhaps his wife would remember him still, though the children would have grown up long ago. Yes, he thought as he contemplated the rope he might not sever for several hours yet, when you consider the alternatives, there is not so much at hazard. A quick death may be preferable to several more years of toil under harsh masters.

For a moment he considered cutting short his tedious wait and, picking up the sword they had left him, absently stroked the rope, paring away a few loose strands.

But a promise was a promise, even if it did mean waiting until morning. And besides, they might find out and come looking for him—as they would if he were simply to leave the device and go. He had thought of that too.

But if he did as he was told, and their threats and inducements told him that he must, how was he to maximize his own chances of survival? He had discreetly overheard snatches of the conversations that had passed between the king and his counsellors. He had heard them speak of a "blinding flash" and a "deafening roar." His eyes carefully searched the immediate vicinity, alighting on, not far away, one of the many curious rock structures that dotted the landscape. This one had once been the core of a substantial hill; now it was little more than man-high, smoothed almost to a perfect oval and tilting precariously yet securely enough upon its tiny base. Could he reach it in time? He had watched the tribesmen as with futile extravagance they smashed boulders on the chasm's floor and he had counted the seconds it took each one to fall. He got up and paced the distance, converting the paces into seconds, as near as he could. Then he tried a practice sprint. Yes, he concluded breathlessly, for he was really too old for these exertions, I should be able to make it, just.

Then, safely in the shelter of the rock, he would shut his eyes and stop up his ears. Whether all this would prove sufficient he could not tell, but in the circumstances it was the best he could devise. He hoped it would work, if only to discomfit his masters.

He would so enjoy the thought of them returning, expecting to find him dead for a fool, and so reclaim the purse they had given him, only to discover that instead he had vanished completely.

23

Percevale woke early from an uneasy sleep and, raising himself, peered through the almost opaque window. Seeing that it was not yet full daylight, he lay down again, but though he dozed fitfully for another hour or so, he did not sleep. The regret he had felt yesterday had turned into an aching sense of loss. He could feel the onset of that harmful and debilitating melancholy that sometimes assailed and troubled his solitary moments. Normally he was able to master these occasional bouts of self-pity, but this time it went deeper. He could see with an unfamiliar and unsettling clarity the dismal and futile road to which he was seemingly bound, could see also the alternative which had been briefly offered and which he had foolishly spurned.

So for a few years more he would be Sir Percevale, Knight of the White Gryphon, and the world, or that small part of it that cared about such things, would marvel at his feats of arms until age and slowing reflexes finally proved the making of some younger man.

And he would continue his quest, for though it now seemed to him obsessive and without point, he knew

that without it his life, which for so many years had
been devoted to little else, would cease to have
meaning.

This will not do, he sternly admonished himself.
Such morbid reflections will prove your downfall
sooner than any young barbarian on the make.

Deciding that a brisk walk, perhaps a ride, in the
fresh air might do something to restore his spirits and
his sense of proportion, he rose and quietly dressed.

The town was just beginning to awaken. Along the
narrow pavements there were few people about, though
a detachment of militia, lately much swollen in
numbers, crossed the street which ran at right angles
to his own, their bootheels striking hard upon the
shining cobblestones.

Approaching the square, he saw a figure he recognized.

"I have lost my job with the mayor," explained a
disconsolate and worried Gareth. "Someone told him
it was I who disrupted the meeting." His eyes widened, lending convincing emphasis to his protestation
of innocence. "Now, why should I do a thing like that,
a man in my position? And who would take such a
story to the mayor?"

Percevale was solicitous. "What will you do?"

The young man shrugged. "I shall bide here and ask
for work. That is what people do. Perhaps by the end
of the morning I will be fixed up, perhaps not. Good
jobs are hard to come by at the moment. Thank you,
sir." He pocketed the proffered coin. "I have little in
reserve. I shall be in trouble when it finally runs out."

"Could you not go elsewhere, beyond the town?"

Gareth looked puzzled. "Where would that be?
No, no, that would not do. I have to support my
mother as well as myself, you see. She is too old to
work and her health is not good. Which reminds me,
it is time for her medicine. I must go now. I shall be
back later."

"I am sorry to hear of your plight," Percevale said.

Gareth tucked his thumbs into his belt and bit his tongue thoughtfully for a moment. "I don't suppose you will, sir," he began hesitantly, as if he had not already said the same to a dozen others that morning, "but if you do hear of anything that might suit—"

"Of course." Percevale then watched as with swift energetic strides his small figure strode away, disappearing eventually behind the huddle of tall buildings that crowded the narrow street where he lived. As he began to make his own way back to Robert's house, his thoughts turned to the mingled circumstances which, like subtle and interlocking threads, had conspired to draw him to and keep him in this place.

It had started, he remembered, with the itinerant tinker who had fancied himself also a swordsmith. It was their chance meeting that had first alerted Percevale to the peril from the north. He had been a frightened man in a hurry, for despite the lethal stock he carried, his own skill with a weapon was negligible.

Then there had been the encounter with the ogre and its fair captive. There was no reason why he should have chosen the route he did. There were few tracks across the wasteland, and with no particular destination in mind, one direction was as good as another.

Even then he might not have found her, for she had not cried out during the attempted ambush and the short struggle that had followed. Only chance and a certain morbid curiosity on his part had led him to that musty alcove in the rocks.

And there were smaller, subsidiary, but far from inconsequential threads, such as the wretched physician and his wife—still a partial enigma. It was a mesh of human concerns which left him, a creature of open spaces and few commitments, confused, bewildered, and dreadfully conscious of his inadequacy.

My task here is completed, he told himself. I can serve no purpose by staying further.

He stopped at the infirmary. He did not like to intrude upon the physician's grief, but he did feel that Robert should be the first to learn of his decision.

"I quite understand, naturally." Robert cleaned his bloody hands in a bowl of tepid water. His composure seemed somewhat restored, but his voice sounded heavy and weary and on his face there were more lines than had been there yesterday. "We have kept you from your own business for long enough. We are most grateful for your counsel and your assistance."

It was very quiet in the infirmary. Most of the patients were still asleep, their low, hushed breathing barely audible. Robert laid down the towel he was holding and stood for a while in still contemplation. There had been something he had been meaning to say to the knight for some time; his wife had several times urged him to broach the subject, but he had been reluctant. And so many things had pushed it aside. The battle, poor Simon. Thankfully, it would not be necessary now.

From somewhere among the ranks of tightly packed beds there came a low, anonymous moan as some-body's nightmare fleetingly surfaced, shaking Robert from his reverie. "I'm sorry," he quickly said. "I have been very busy these last few days and have had little time for sleep. Where will you go?"

"I may follow the enemy for some while; it is not yet certain that they will return from whence they came. I would advise you to be on your guard these next few weeks at least."

"We shall heed that advice." Another brief silence followed. "Sir Percevale, you may have discerned in my manner toward you of late some hint of reproach."

"Indeed, no—"

The doctor raised a hand. "It is true. I have in some

measure blamed you for Simon's death. It was quite wrong of me, of course."

"Perhaps I could have saved him."

"You were nowhere near. No, it is I who am to blame and I apologize unreservedly. I hope you will understand the irrational response of a bereaved parent."

"Of course."

"Without you we should all have certainly perished." Percevale bowed.

"And when do you intend to leave?"

"Directly I have made my farewells to your family. I think it best that I do not linger."

"I will send someone to fetch your horses."

Sensing a lightening of the physician's spirits, Percevale decided to make just one parting request.

"There is a young man who works for the mayor. A friend of your son, I believe?"

"Gareth, yes. I have heard of this affair. It is a bad business, I agree. Oliver has become insufferable lately. This victory has quite gone to his head. You are right to raise the matter with me. It is a minor affair, but an injustice nonetheless. I shall see what can be done."

"Thank you."

"I daresay you will not be sorry to be quit of such trifling—good Gods! What is that?"

Both men instinctively closed their eyes as the intense light filled the room, blanketing all else within. As Percevale struggled for an answer, he became aware of screams from outside, some of simple terror, a few of agony, as eyes injudiciously turned toward the fireball were blinded and seared. With a growing sense of foreboding he turned to the window, shielding his eyes from the still-painful glare.

At first he could see nothing. Then out of the glaring whiteness there emerged pale and insubstantial figures. Dimly they swam into view, groping their

way in a brilliant mist, their human cries mingling
with the shrieks of horses.

Comprehension dawning, he turned from the window with a cry of despair, cursing the madness of the
world and the continuing perfidy of his ancient enemy. During the brief seconds that followed, as he
searched blindly for the fragile security of a chair,
many visions flickered through his dazed conscious-
ness. He saw, once again, Arthur, silver and ghostly,
wordlessly mouthing his astonishment as the horses
bucked frantically in their urge to escape the earth
that roared and baked beneath them.

Another sound, distant at first, then clearer and
more insistent, penetrated the turmoil in his mind.

"What is it? What is happening?" Robert's pale and
frightened face peered closely into his own. "Is it the
end of the world?"

"I do not know," Percevale answered vaguely. The
last time this had happened a world had ended, a fine
world, too. Slowly he rose and went outside.

The first thing he noticed was an uncomfortable tin-
gling sensation as a rush of warm air brushed and
prickled his skin. Then he heard a roar as of distant
thunder. It is farther away than before, he thought.
There is that much comfort at least. Looking about
him, he saw that most of those who had been outside
had escaped relatively unscathed and as they realized
this, so their panic began to subside, though many
wandered about still, crying aloud and incoherently.
He saw Elaine on the other side of the street, standing in the doorway of her father's house. She did not
see him. Like most others, she was transfixed, locked
in contemplation of the writhing horror that had risen
in the sky.

"It is the end of the world," Robert whispered behind him in a tone of horrified awe.

It is as before, Percevale thought. After the light
comes the darkness. He watched as the shadowy col-

umn billowed and plumed until it hung high above the earth like a sinister gray flower, a foul bloom that mocked nature from the top of its unsightly stalk.

"It is an abomination," Robert whispered again.

Percevale, with an effort of will, tore his eyes away. "The gates are opened and unmanned," he said. "They must be closed immediately."

But Robert gave no sign of hearing him.

"Physician, bestir thyself! It is not yet the end of the world, though it may seem so. The gates must be closed."

Robert looked at him in disbelief, then turned away. "He speaks of closing gates against such as this," he muttered. With an impatient sigh Percevale went to see to the task himself.

24

In the event, it was not until the afternoon that Clarivaus, with Marhaus, Tristram, and a small escort, arrived at the walls to present their demands. The king was in a rare good humor, quite recovered now from the doubts that had earlier beset him. When the black cloud had first risen, his army had quailed at the sight; many of his bravest knights had flung themselves in terror to the ground. He himself had trembled inwardly and for a while had listened with shaking conviction to Marhaus and his plea that they end this insanity forthwith and return to their homes.

But that had been several hours ago; uncertainty was behind him now. He looked into the sky and though it was still unnaturally dark, the gaunt cloud with its haunting images was gone. He could see instead his enemies, cowering ineffectually behind their flimsy battlements.

This is no time for wavering, he chided himself. In the circumstances, he might be prepared to be magnanimous. He was certainly not repentant.

"Greetings, gentlemen," he called. "As you may have guessed, we come to parley."

Percevale, too, looked at the sky before replying. The cloud had not vanished but merely dispersed, spreading like a malignant growth across the horizon, blanketing the sun and extinguishing life and hope. Looking down at his adversary, he felt his powers of reason and anger dwindle, become puny and worthless. It is like dealing with a child, he thought hopelessly.

Nor did there seem much point in trying to reason with his younger companion, who sat in silent, impassive triumph. Only the rearmost of the three leading riders seemed to him to possess any conception whatever of the immensity of the forces they had invoked. His face showed clearly his disapproval and anxiety—and his powerlessness.

"How did you get hold of that?" Percevale said eventually, fully conscious of the feebleness of his response.

"It is—a little something we found on our way here." Clarivaus gave a short laugh and turned, smiling, to his companions. "And there is more where that came from."

"How far away is it?"

"Oh, you are quite safe, I assure you. We know what we are doing."

"It is about a day's ride away," interposed Marhaus. "I think we are safe enough."

"You are fools to avail yourselves of such an instrument for the sake of mere plunder and revenge," Percevale said, his indignation slowly returning.

"I am Clarivaus and no fool but a king and the son of a king!" His tone dropped to one of gentle menace. "I think you should adopt a more respectful attitude in the circumstances."

"Then, King Clarivaus, I must fear you are out of your depth and repent me of the mercy I lately showed you."

Clarivaus seemed pleased with the tone of the rebuke.

"Come, Sir Knight," he said, "we know what we are doing. We do not seek plunder. Nor even revenge."

Percevale frowned warily. He opened his mouth to speak.

"No," Clarivaus continued. A purposeful gleam appeared in his eyes as he repeated the vision that had been lately unfolded to him. "We have set ourselves a nobler task: that of reuniting and reawakening this sorely afflicted land. The marvel you have seen but presages another and a greater." His face glowed with enthusiasm, his voice grew soft and importuning. "Now, listen. With your help we can build a new Albion. It can be done, believe me. It shall be greater than the old and this shall be its capital. From here we shall first subdue the south. After we shall move against my misguided and recalcitrant brethren in the north."

Percevale shook his head wearily. Conquest and subjugation. True, Arthur had used them, but as a means, not as an end. "And after that?" he asked.

"Who knows? The world perhaps. There is so much to conquer. What say you, Sir Knight, is it not a worthy task I have set myself?"

"You require that we acknowledge you as king and master," Percevale said. "Where is the worthiness in that? I see only common ambition."

"Then you have no vision!" It was an unfair rebuke, as he had only lately been vouchsafed some himself. "You will serve me as loyal subjects, naturally. Someone has to organize things. But you will be subjects, not slaves. You, of all people I would have expected to respond better. This is a generous offer."

"I think you should have kept to plunder and simple brigandage," Percevale replied. "This is subtle mischief you purpose and I much fear you are out of your depth." He could not be sure, but he thought he saw the rearmost horseman give a nod of assent. "Look," he added, "here are my terms. Let the issue be decided by single combat between the two of us. You may choose the weapons."

Clarivaus, as if he had been expecting something like this, merely smiled. "Now, you know that is against the rules, Sir Knight, challenging a man you have already beaten." He rubbed his jaw with a genial ruefulness. "I do not hold that against you, though, not at all."

"Then select a champion to fight in your stead."

But Clarivaus shook his head. "After your performance the other day? I think not." He reclined a little in the saddle. "I have had enough of this temporizing. One more offer will I make you. Join me and I will make you chief among my warriors. We need someone with a good sword arm and a flair for strategy. Think on that."

Percevale did. He noticed how the jaw of the king's hitherto thin-lipped companion had suddenly fallen in disbelief. At length he replied, "I should need time to consider such an offer."

"You have three days."

"It is not enough."

"I have been indulgent enough," said Clarivaus briskly. "Very well, four days. If we have not heard from you by then, we shall work more of our magic. It will be closer next time." He wheeled his horse to go and his followers did likewise.

"How do I find you?" Percevale asked.

"Follow the road through the wood. You will find us. Do not think of mounting an attack against us. It will not help you, for our devices are far from here and in safer hands than ours." He raised a languid arm to signal to his escort, then stopped.

A line of archers had taken up positions along the parapet, their bows drawn in grim readiness. Beside them stood the sergeant-at-arms, waiting for orders.

The confidence vanished from Clarivaus's face and a note of anxiety entered his voice as he spoke.

"You will not hinder our departure, I hope?"

"Now, that would be against the rules, wouldn't it?" Percevale smiled. He pursed his lips thoughtfully for a moment, relishing this momentary advantage. "You may go," he said at length. "There would be little point in stopping them," he explained to the sergeant as the sound of the horsemen's rapid departure faded into the distance. "They have, I am sure, laid plans for such an eventuality."

The sergeant-at-arms merely shrugged as he dismissed the bowmen. "In that case, I hope our patrols do not discover them, sir."

"They came by a circuitous route and your men are searching for an army. I think we need not worry about that."

They were joined by Robert and the mayor.

"Who was that? What is happening here?" Oliver demanded. He was breathless and agitated, his normally sanguine manner greatly disturbed by the morning's events.

Percevale told them.

"But that is preposterous!" Oliver cried. "We have already beaten them fair and square."

"They have Druid magic," said Percevale. "Against that no mortal power can avail."

The mayor considered this. "I suppose we cannot buy them off?"

"I do not think so. They have become idealists now."

"I thought the tales of Druid magic were fanciful legends," said Robert. It had grown visibly darker now. The sun, a milky disc, shone wanly through the smoky gray haze that covered most of the sky.

"As you see," Percevale replied, "they are not."

"Many people are cowering in their houses and refusing to come out. They say it is Morrigan the war goddess, come to destroy us all."

"Yes," said Percevale. "That is one answer." He began to walk back to the physician's house and the others followed him.

"And what is your answer?" Robert asked. "What do you counsel?"

"Surely that is clear enough. The source of this magic must be found and destroyed."

Oliver breathed in sharply and turned on him, his round, slightly sunken eyes wide with sudden consternation. "Do not act hastily, sir. This is a situation that demands utmost caution. Yes, caution."

Already his shrewd mind was busily sifting the information it had so far received, searching for signs of possible compromise, perhaps even of advantage. Four days was a long time in politics. He leaned forward and the knight tried not to wince at the slightly stale breath that warmed his face. "Be careful, sir, be careful."

Percevale turned to the doctor. "You had better pray that the wind does not change," he said simply.

25

He went to the stables next and made ready the horses. First he loaded the sumpter horse, then he saddled Fleet. He led them outside and saw a figure standing in the gray light.

"Who would do such a thing?" Elaine's brow was furrowed with concern. Her father had already told her, but she asked anyway.

Percevale did not immediately reply. He was wondering if the mayor would try to stop him from leaving. Perhaps the guards at the gate had already received orders. Perhaps they had taken his sword which, together with others of his belongings, lay in the physician's spare room still.

"Was it something like this that ended the war?" she asked, falling into step beside him.

"It is almost in the same place."

"And you believe it to be Mordred?"

He turned to her. "He does seem to be the most likely candidate."

"That is your true reason for going." There was a note of fretfulness in her voice. "It cannot be for our sakes. No one here wants to jeopardize their lives as much as you seem to. Mordred must be an old man now, older than you are."

"Old perhaps, but no dotard." He tied the horses to a post outside the house. Looking along the street, he saw that the nearest gate was closed and guarded, but then, it had been since the morning. Oliver was nowhere to be seen.

He was impatient to be gone. He had so little time and such a wide area to cover—and only the most meager of clues which the enemy king had incautiously dropped.

But she was speaking to him, perhaps for the last time, and he had treated her, he felt, rather badly. So he stayed and reasoned.

"I do not seek Mordred now for revenge but because he must be found. It is Mordred who was first responsible for loosing this terrible evil upon the world. It is he who is behind all this, of that I am sure."

"And where will you look? You have not found Mordred these twenty years. Father tells me you have four days."

"At least I know which direction I must follow."

She shrugged as she stroked the destrier's warm flank. "You know best your own plans. At any rate, I am glad that you do not forsake us, in spite of what others are saying. I have heard of the offer their king made you. It must have been a tempting one."

"I used it to buy time, that is all."

"And I am keeping you unnecessarily. What a fine creature is this. Gentle and powerful. You must be very fond of him."

"Yes." He looked at her. "Yes, I am."

She turned, returning his gaze. "If you are successful, will you return?"

He did not answer.

"I should like you to return," she said frankly.

For a moment he wondered if he had heard correctly. She spoke in such a low voice. "Pardon . . ."

She raised her hand as someone hurried by. That brief respite must have strengthened her resolve, for her voice when she spoke again had an edge of determination, almost of anger.

"You cannot be so blind to my feelings," she said. "You have toyed with my regard. Tell me, was not that evilly done?"

"I—"

"This has not been easy for me, you know; entering your room that first morning—it took me the best part of the night to gather sufficient courage for that." Her arms in their flowing sleeves rose and fell in their helplessness and frustration. "Oh, this is not right," she wailed. "You have the words, not I. I should not have to say these things. It is not fair."

But I do not have the words, Percevale thought miserably. Ah, Gawaine! You were a great fighter but a poor suitor, and here am I most ill-equipped.

And yet, though his mind was in turmoil, though the world was falling about their ears, it slowly dawned upon him the course he must take. There was no time for reflection or for consideration of hard practicalities. Nor was there need. He looked into her tear-filled eyes and saw once more his image there, distant and gleaming. His suspicions hardened into certainty. He knew now her true parentage and he knew also where his duty lay. Here was not only a second chance for him but a fitting conclusion to the quest and all his travails. In a way, he thought, it will bring things full circle.

And so haltingly, with the bashfulness of a schoolboy, he made his tender avowal.

"Know, lady, that I love thee as ever knight loved lady. I will honor and cherish thee and will forever be your true and faithful knight."

It was her turn to be caught off guard, and an embarrassed silence fell between them as she slowly digested the measure of his words. Then she reached

up and kissed him lightly and chastely so that Percevale
felt a great joy which for the moment quite overshad-
owed their other perils.

"Alas, we may not continue this pleasant dalliance,"
he said eventually, suppressing his ardor. "For though I
would rather stay, yet must I seek out and destroy the
enemy and his awesome power."

She did not demur. She realized that she had a hold
over him now, that she could make him stay if she
wanted. It gave her a sense half of elation, half of
guilt. But she was determined not to use her new
power. She would not be like those damosels who,
once they have won their knight, seek to entice him
from the path of chivalry, robbing him of his manhood
and integrity. She feared for him desperately, yet she
was determined to put a brave face on matters. She
smiled as she kissed him yet again.

"May the gods speed you in your quest; may it
succeed."

They stood facing each other for a little while longer.
She was the first to pull away. "Goodness," she exclaimed with a feigned lightness, "I shouldn't be here,
I have patients to attend to." And she added in a
hushed voice, "Come back to me soon." Then she turned
with set expression to the infirmary and her lonely
duties there.

"I will," said Percevale to himself before going into
the house to collect his belongings.

His sword and his clothing were still on the bed
where he had left them earlier. As he took them up
and turned to leave, he caught sight of his reflection
in the mirror. It was an image to which he was by
now accustomed; nonetheless, the sight of those streaks
of gray among the dark hairs of his beard and head
did occasion him a momentary doubt.

Are you not too old for this romantic foolishness?
he asked himself.

No, came the swift and decisive reply, and he left

the room and hurried downstairs with a feeling of confidence and lightness of heart that he could not remember having experienced for a long time. The problems and dangers that lay ahead, the prospect of failure, all these had quite suddenly dwindled into insignificance. The Druids might bury their magic beneath a mountain and set an army to guard it. He would find a way.

"Sir Percevale."

He stopped. For a moment his confidence wavered, but it was a moment only. The Lady Anne, her face partly in shadow, moved aside as he came to the bottom of the staircase. He bowed.

"A word, Sir Percevale, if you please." She beckoned him into a small room, one which he had not noticed before.

I will never get away from here, he thought despairingly.

There was but one chair in the room and in this she sat.

"You are leaving us now?" There was a look of polite interest on her face.

"For the present, yes, lady."

"My husband has told me of your intentions. I wish you good fortune."

"Thank you."

"But that is not what I wish to discuss with you." She paused, scrutinizing him closely as she folded her hands, slender fingers absently laced. "It has not escaped my attention—or my husband's—that you and Elaine have spent much time in each other's company. Though our minds have of late been preoccupied with other matters, we have noticed this also."

Percevale was silent. If she wished to know something then she must ask.

"What are your intentions concerning my daughter?"

Had she asked him that a few hours before, he might have blushed and fidgeted as he sought to evade her dreadful directness. Instead, he felt a great sense of relief. *At last, there is no more innuendo, no more of those impenetrable glances. It is all quite out in the open now.*

"Lady, I assure you they are entirely honorable. It is my firm intention at the first opportunity to—"

"Of course," she said flatly. Her eyes narrowed and there appeared on her face a humorless, faintly triumphant smile. It might have been the smile of one who has practiced a long and successful deception on another. Only in this case, as he realized later, it was he who had deceived himself.

"No doubt," she continued, "you have noticed the total absence of any resemblance between Elaine and the rest of my children. Or, for that matter, between Elaine and her father."

Percevale did not know what to say. Like most people in those times, he took a tolerant view of illegitimacy, a phenomenon too common to attract real censure.

Nevertheless, one did not usually advertise the fact. She went on. "No doubt you have sometimes wondered about those features which my daughter does not share with me."

"I—"

"The Pendragon forehead, or the color of the eyes."

"I had formed no such conjectures," he hurriedly lied.

"Of course you have." Her manner was openly scornful now. "It has more than once crossed your mind that she is Arthur's natural child."

"Even if that were so, it would not change my convictions," Percevale said.

"Oh, well, that may be, that may be."

She relented a little. *Perhaps he is as principled as his words imply,* she thought. She had good reason to hold chivalry and all its foolish pretensions in low regard, but reason and fairness also told her that there must have been substance to create the shadow. Perhaps here was some of that substance.

However, it was too late to turn back now.

"She is not Arthur's child." She looked at Percevale, but if he was disappointed, he did not show it.

"Arthur had eyes for one woman only, and when she betrayed him for that Gallic poseur Lancelot, he lost interest altogether. He certainly would never have cared for a simple lady's maid."

"Then I do not—" Percevale began in a faltering voice.

"Mordred, now, he cared."

Her face gradually softened, assuming a reflective and wistful appearance as she recalled that distant glorious week when she had been Mordred's lover.

It had happened during the last campaign of the war. The rightful king, at the head of his people's army and fresh from a victory over one of Arthur's lords, was staying at the castle, the home of one of his allies. There he had become smitten with her beauty.

"I will make you my queen," he had declared to her one night.

She had, of course, protested, reminding him gently of the vast social gulf that separated them, the sheer impossibility of such a match. But he had shaken his head with an emphatic violence. Then he had thrilled her with his powerful invective against rank and class and how he would destroy all such artificial barriers to human happiness and self-realization.

"But before I can wed," he added, staring up at the tapestried ceiling with its scenes of frozen elegance, "I must win this war, for though I never sought it yet the civilization of Albion depends upon our victory."

His forces had taken Glastonbury but now his father, the corrupt king, with a huge army, was laying siege to his own capital. "Starving his own people," Mordred said. Many of Mordred's friends were trapped within, and as Arthur was directing the siege in person, so must he, Mordred, go in person to raise it. "But I shall not be long." This was on their final night together. "This will be the decisive battle, the final reckoning." In the gloom of the bedroom she fancied she could see already the light of anticipated victory in his dark, gleaming eyes. "Then I shall return to claim both my kingdom and my queen in the name of the people of Albion."

"Of course," she said to Percevale, "I do not blame you for his death in that terrible battle. I daresay you were too young even to have taken part. I don't blame anyone really. Robert has been very good about it, he never held it against me, never tried to take advantage. And you, you seem a kind enough fellow really. If my—" She looked up and stopped.

The knight was no longer there. Instead, her husband stood in the doorway.

"Has he gone?" she asked innocently.

"Yes." He stepped into the room. "He looked very upset as he left. He would not say good-bye or anything. What did you say to him?"

"I?"

"Yes. I saw you speaking together."

"Robert, your face is getting red. You know that is bad for you. You don't want to start another of your awful headaches."

"Did you tell him about Elaine?"

"I did, as a matter of fact. I thought he had a right to know." She raised an ingenuous eyebrow. "Do you not think he has a right to know?"

"I think you have done a mischief here," said Robert, turning his back on her. "And I think you know it too. Oliver and some of the others seem to think they can negotiate with these scoundrels. I just hope they don't try to stop him from leaving, that's all."

Later, when he was able to think more clearly, Percevale saw that it was his own presumption and pride that were really to blame. He could have loved the girl for herself alone; assuredly she so loved him. Instead, he had loved her for quite the wrong reasons and so deserved his downfall. He tried to tell himself that it did not matter, that whoever her father was it was no fault of hers.

And every time I look into her eyes I shall be reminded of my mortal enemy whom I now, more than ever, am pledged to destroy.

It was a poor basis for a permanent relationship.

But he had promised himself to her. They had exchanged vows. Honor bound him and now only death could release him.

All the rest of that day he rode, skirting round the edge of the wood to avoid the enemy, and picking up their trail again when he reached the wide plain. Through much of the night he rode also, stopping only when the horses had clearly had enough.

I shall not find it, he thought dismally as he rose next morning and saddled the horses. The magic could be anywhere, safely buried in the barbarians' own camp even. This quest is even more futile than my last. It is simply something to do.

And then, quite unexpectedly, his luck seemed to change. Toward noon he came to the edge of a dark wood. Here beside a pathway a figure stood, clad in a gray cloak that concealed his face, and carrying a staff that he did not need, for his body was straight and healthy. Percevale shook his head, wondering if this was an illusion brought on by a largely sleepless night. In the old days forests and woods were strange places, redolent with magic and the promise of adventure. Then it had been well-nigh impossible for a knight to pass through a wood without spending some time in an enchanted castle or meeting with a dwarf or a silent horseman jealously guarding the pathway. But all that was long ago. Mordred's magic, wholly evil and wholly human, had destroyed that world of genteel enchantment.

Yet here he was, face to face with a hermit at the edge of a wood. His spirits almost lightened. When such encounters had taken place in the past, the outcome had almost always been a satisfactory one.

The hermit stepped forward and raised his staff. Percevale halted.

"Whither ride you, Sir Knight?" he asked.

"I seek the place," replied Percevale, "whence comes the evil that has blighted and wasted this land."

"Ah," said the hermit, "I know what it is you seek and where it lies, but it will not avail you knowing that without also ye have my counsel."

"But what is thy name?" Percevale leaned forward, his eyes trying vainly to penetrate the shadows within the hermit's cowl.

"At this time," came the reply, "I will not tell it thee."

"It is hard to see that thou art a true man if thou wilt not tell thy name," said Percevale.

"As for that, be it as it may. Wilt thou be ruled by my counsel?"

Percevale paused but only for propriety's sake.

"Lead on, sir," he said, dismounting. "And I will follow on foot."

26

When evening came, they halted and the hermit built a fire. Watching him stoop over the small pile of gathered kindling, sheltering his small flame from the breeze that had somehow managed to penetrate even this far into the forest, Percevale suddenly remembered that he had brought no provisions for the journey.

"I have no food," he announced apologetically. There was a resonant crackle as the fire leaped into life and the hermit gave a satisfied snort.

"No matter," he said without turning and, taking his small sack, he tossed it to the knight. "It was caught but this morning and will be quite fresh."

Percevale removed the cony, a fine specimen and already skinned, and together they fashioned a spit and roasted it over the flames.

As they ate, the old man questioned Percevale.

"I know what it is you seek, of course. But tell me, what do you know of it?"

"It is the doom of the world," Percevale said.

"But how does it work?" The hermit's eyes gleamed in the firelight. "Can you tell me that?"

To Percevale the question seemed irrelevant. What

did it matter how it worked? It worked, that was enough. "I have visited the place whence it came."

"Oh?" His companion's interest quickened.

"It is to the southwest and not far from the sea. Perhaps a week's ride from here."

The old man nodded. "Yes, it would be about that. And when you reached this place, what did you find?"

"Nothing."

"Nothing? What of the madmen who claim to be magicians yet dress themselves in rags?"

"I found the remains of some huts, all of them burned. I found the earth for many yards around scorched and black and still warm. That is all."

"Well, well, I knew there was something odd about those folk." He looked at Percevale. "Whatever possessed you to go there?"

"My search for Mordred."

Percevale's companion paused. He had already, by degrees, pulled back his cowl so that much of his face, red and warm in the fire's glow, stood revealed. Still he had not been recognized. Ah, the ravages of age! he thought, though he well remembered the knight from his device.

This made him bolder. "Ah, yes, I have heard of Mordred. In my opinion he has been greatly and undeservedly maligned."

"Oh?" said Percevale, and arched an eyebrow.

"He is no monster, you know. Even Mordred had feelings." Removing a piece of gristle from his mouth, he flung it into the darkness behind him. "Even Mordred could love."

"Be careful what you say, old man. In other matters I shall be ruled by you but not in this."

Mordred shrugged but, sensing that his companion was unsettled and disturbed by these remarks, he could not keep silent for long.

"He is not the only guilty one, you know."

Percevale shot him a hostile glance but said nothing.

"Merlin, for instance. As Arthur's chief Druid he was preparing even worse weapons and much earlier."

"Do not talk nonsense. Merlin died long ere."

"And do you know how he died?"

"Everyone knows. He fell into the clutches of the wicked fay Nimue and was imprisoned by her within a stone."

"Yes, that is a pretty story and in some respects it is a fitting allegory—it is just the sort of ending that smooth-talking elliptical scoundrel would devise for himself. but it is not the truth."

Mordred paused for a moment, wondering if it was safe to continue. There was a dangerous frown on the knight's face, but also curiosity. "Merlin's weapon was plague, a plague so virulent that it would have destroyed half the inhabitants of the Eastern Kingdom within a few days. After this it would quickly become harmless and a western army would be able to enter and occupy the territory without danger to themselves. That was the plan, anyway. Fortunately something went wrong and Merlin became its first and, happily, only victim."

"This cannot be," Percevale said. "Merlin died long ere war broke out between the two kingdoms."

"That is correct," said Mordred.

"It is preposterous," Percevale insisted with faltering indignation. "I do not believe you. Why should I believe what you say?"

"Because I am hermit of the woods and therefore wise in such matters," Mordred replied cunningly.

Percevale turned away, but pain and doubt as well as anger were written on his face.

The next morning they reached the clearing. A light damp mist hung in the air. Around its perimeter there was no birdsong or hint of life. Only a preternatural stillness and an atmosphere of latent menace.

"This is an unwholesome place," Percevale observed.

"It is one of the last outposts of the old magic," Mordred whispered. "Older even than man himself. Men did not fashion this clearing or the cavern beneath, though men reside there now."

"But the trees about its edge, they form a perfect circle."

"Men did not make it so." He indicated the two guards who sat near the temple entrance. "Either their confidence is unbounded or they are completely devoid of imagination. No sensible person would linger in such a place." He turned to Percevale. "Do you feel it?"

"I feel a chill and a vague unpleasantness, but what it is I cannot say."

"Yes, yes." Mordred nodded. "Different people are affected in different ways. But the magic is dormant at present and so I think we are safe."

He looked again at the guards. Though clearly not expecting trouble, they were well armed and had a clear view on all sides. "But they are a problem."

"There is no time for stealth," said Percevale. "If the devices are here—"

"Oh, they are here," Mordred assured him.

"Then the enemy may come for them at any moment."

"Well, you'd better hurry."

Percevale unsheathed his sword, feeling as always a half-guilty thrill at the soft friction of the metal as it left the scabbard. He knew he should call upon them to surrender first. The letter of chivalry did not extend this privilege to varlets, but Gawaine had instilled in him his own belief that mercy was indivisible and not to be apportioned by rank.

But there was no time for such refinements and they might try to escape and warn their comrades, and anyway, he did not think they would surrender. He tried to tell himself that it was on such calculations and not his rising excitement that his decision was based. Silently he ran forward.

Surprised though they were, the sentries sprang quickly to their feet, uttering cries of alarm which they must have known would be inaudible to their companions deep underground. Yet, though they recognized the knight and knew well his prowess, they were no cowards and did not attempt to flee. Drawing their weapons, they ran to meet him.

It was quickly over and at the end of it Percevale was not even breathing hard as he wiped his sword and returned it to its scabbard. You have come a long way, Sir Knight, since our last meeting, thought Mordred with rueful admiration.

"Which way now?"

Mordred bent and lifted the framework of twigs and leaves that covered the entrance to the shaft.

"I shall go down first," he said. "You follow close behind. Do not worry," he added as Percevale looked first at him, then at the darkness below. "I am fitter than I look and I know this entrance well. It is you who must take care. There are places for your hands and feet, but the shaft is old and some of them may be loose." He lowered himself into the black circle and Percevale followed.

The niches and handholds, he quickly discovered, were neither large nor plentiful, and they had to be felt for carefully by hand and foot. Several times he dislodged crumbling shards of stone and it seemed to him a long time before he heard the dull, far-off thud of their impact.

Then, when he thought he was nearing the end of his precarious descent, the footholds ran out. Immediately below him was a shape, slightly darker than the surrounding gloom. The old man's head was approximately level with his own feet.

"Jump!" a voice urged.

Percevale did so, landing noisily on rough stone. Small, crabbed hands helped him to his feet. Then Mordred pointed to the small circle of light that marked the distant end of the tunnel. "Keep your head down," he said and, turning, led the way.

Percevale inquired about the many side tunnels that he dimly discerned as they passed.

"They serve no purpose for us," said Mordred.

They came to the stairway and the cavern proper, though both were careful to remain in the shadows.

There was considerably less illumination than usual, also less activity. It was as if the Druids, sensing that their presence no longer fulfilled any purpose, had withdrawn into lassitude, exhibiting a superficial industry only.

Percevale, gazing upon the scene, felt an impatient tug at his arm.

"Yes, it is an impressive structure, I know, but we have not come to admire it." Mordred, forgetful or overconfident, or perhaps both, pressed his face close to Percevale's. Looking down at those feverishly glinting eyes, the knight felt a momentary confusion as something blurred and indistinct tugged at his memory. Then the face turned quickly away and his brief unease quickly vanished beneath the weight of more pressing concerns.

His gaze moved, was drawn rather, toward the cauldron with its silent flame, the pit below with its two shining cylinders of bronze, and the small solitary figure of the beseeching Druid uttering his meaningless and inaudible rhythms. He turned to Mordred.

"This is it?"

"You sound disappointed," Mordred said. "You were expecting something more obviously sinister perhaps—chanting figures around dark flames and unspeakable rituals, that sort of thing? People know so little about the Druid mind." He wrinkled his nose in distaste as something wafted upward on the slow-moving air.

"Nothing to worry about," he said. "Just one of their nasty little concoctions." He was silent for a while, gazing reflectively at the scene below him. "That is the evil you seek. Unprepossessing little things, are they not?"

"And the man who stands before them?"

"He is not part of the magic, though many of the Druids believe he is essential to it."

"How are we to destroy such a place?" So far Percevale had given little thought to this.

"Ah," said Mordred. "It is lucky for you that I was nigh." Stooping, he opened his small sack. When he straightened again he was holding a black metal sphere. "It's all right," he said, "take it."

It was small and rested easily in one hand, though heavy. A long cord protruded from a hole in the surface.

"One of the Druids' better ideas," Mordred explained, taking it back again. "They call it firepowder: it is a mixture of saltpeter, charcoal, and brimstone."

"What does it do?"

"A great deal more than its appearance suggests. It explodes with considerable effect. No," he added hastily as the knight frowned, "it is a tiny explosion compared to what those things can do. But if we are lucky, it will start a fire—there are substances down there that should burn very well given the chance—and a fire, if it spreads far enough, will destroy your magic. Over there." He pointed to a group of dark openings at the far end of the cavern. "One of those contains enough firepowder to bury this place forever. That is what you want, I suppose?"

Before Percevale could puzzle over this unexpected note of entreaty, Mordred began again searching through his sack. At length and with an impatient sigh he looked up. "Have you a light? I seem to have mislaid mine."

"It is lucky for you that I was nigh," replied Percevale, handing over his flint.

"We shall have to go closer," Mordred said.

"We may not do so unobserved. If there are risks involved here, then it is I who should take them and not you."

"Be still, Sir Knight, this is no time to be quarreling. You will have your chance. Now, do you see the guards?"

There were six of them and they were at the far side of the cavern. Not far enough, thought Percevale.

"I cannot handle so many," he said in response to Mordred's inquiring glance.

Mordred shrugged. "Then we must trust to surprise and good fortune." Striking the flint, he set it to the cord. Percevale saw a spark and a thin wisp of smoke drifting upward. Then the small flame began to travel slowly the length of the fuse, leaving behind it a trail of blackened hemp. As Mordred stood erect and began to move forward, Percevale grabbed him by the arm.

"Keep you behind my shield!" he hissed angrily. "And wait until I give the word!"

But already they were discovered. One of the guards, more alert than his fellows, had seen the flame leap out of the darkness and the sudden movement where none should be. He called out and pointed.

"Come on!"

Percevale and Mordred began their swift descent of the steps. Small faces, twisted and distorted by the light, or something worse—Percevale could not tell—turned at their approach, registering alarm and disbelief.

Then, halfway down, Mordred stopped. For a moment he held the glowing ball aloft, an eerie figure, his face illuminated by the burning cord, the rest of him shrouded in shadow. Then he flung it from him.

Everyone, even the cautiously advancing guards, halted in their tracks and watched entranced as the flaming sphere described a long and graceful arc through the air, landed noisily and with almost perfect accuracy beneath one of the benches—

—and went out.

Percevale turned in surprise as his companion uttered a stream of irreverent oaths. "Was that the only one?" he asked in dismay. Below, their adversaries were quickly bestirring themselves. A spear struck a nearby step and bounced noisily to the ground.

"Yes, it was!" Mordred shouted and swore again.

"Then follow me!" said Percevale, and lifting his shield he plunged headlong down the remaining steps and into the waiting line of soldiers. He gave them no time to recover from the suddenness of this onslaught but quickly turned and attacked again, wielding his sword with an undisciplined ferocity, for speed and surprise, not accuracy, were his object.

Twice they attempted to encircle him and twice he broke their unsteady and ill-prepared line, for he knew that as long as he could prevent them from acting in concert, then the initiative was his. But precious seconds were slipping away and he was tiring rapidly. He wondered where the hermit was, if he had evaded the guards and the Druids. There was noise and great confusion behind him, but there was no time to look.

A heavy blow sent him reeling forward. The steel hoops of his hauberk, bent and twisted, but mercifully not broken, dug painfully into his back. With a cry of anger he turned and brought his sword down upon something white that flashed briefly before him. There was a scream, and the white blur became splashed with crimson, but already he had turned again, darting first one way, then another, keeping his enemies guessing and, above all, apart.

But the loss of one of their number had made them even more wary. They were keeping their distance now and using their spears to force the knight to keep his while they formed a new line. Then, when they

were ready, they began advancing, slowly and deter-
minedly, pushing him back with quick jabbing move-
ments of their long spears. This time, he knew, there
would be no breaking through. They were going to
encircle him, then finish him. Somewhere behind he
sensed the closeness of a wall. If he could get his back
to that, then at least they would not be able to take
him from behind and he could take some more with
him.

But they had seen the wall too. From their anonymous, snarling faces, there emerged a chilling chorus
of hate and then they were upon him. He felt a dull
shiver against his arm as one spear glanced off his
upraised shield, and the pain as another entered his
side, tearing through his mail coat. Blindly he struck
in all directions—sometimes he hit something, more
often he did not. Another spearhead pierced him.
Hard and cold it felt, then excruciatingly painful as it
was pulled free.

This is a terrible way to die, he realized with a
clarity that was almost as painful as his wounds. This
slow, wearing butchery, it is not noble at all. A cold
numbness began to spread through him as he felt
himself slowly sink beneath the blows that rained
down upon his shield and his body. He began to feel
that strange and quiet euphoria that often attends the
dying. The shouts all around him, the swords, the
bloody spears, they all seemed quite distant now,
quite unconnected with him. Even when the shouts
changed to something quite different and the blows
suddenly stopped, he remained for a while detached
and unconcerned. It was only when Mordred pulled
him to his feet, jolting him into pain and reality, that
he became aware of the smoke and the rolling echo of
an explosion.

Mordred guided him to the stairway. Around them
a sheet of flame was etching its tall, powerful image
on the walls of the cavern. Small shadowy figures

rushed about in noisy confusion. Percevale's enemies, distracted for the moment from their bloody task, were helping the Druids tackle the fire, though their vessels of water seemed of small avail against such a blaze.

Mordred pulled him, gasping, up the stairway. It seemed impossibly steep now. "We must hurry. Can you climb?"

"I think so." He shook his head to clear the blurred images that danced before him.

"You must try." Mordred's face glowed in the flickering glare. His eyes burned with grim delight. He looked back toward the flames, now spreading quickly, devouring eagerly the pools of combustible material that his grenade had strewn around the floor. He smiled at the efforts of the firefighters. "They'll not put that out." He turned Percevale, now in front and laboring heavily. "Go on, man! We must hurry now!"

Percevale, weak and breathless, reached the top of the stairs and wondered how he was going to negotiate the far more difficult passage of the shaft. He turned to his guide, but the hermit was no longer there.

Mordred lay a few steps before him, a spearhead embedded deeply in his back. They had not been pursued. It was merely bad luck, a parting shot, delivered by its owner in haste.

"No," he whispered as Percevale bent down and attempted to lift him, "the wound is too deep."

"Let me at least try." He doubted whether he had the strength to help himself, let alone the hermit also.

Mordred shook his head. Then he raised it a little, and Percevale placed a hand beneath it in support. Below him, the flames grew higher and the shouts louder and the fire, quite out of control now, moved inexorably toward the far wall.

"You must get away," Mordred said. "As far as you

can. When the firepowder explodes, it will tear the earth asunder."

I will not have another old man die because of my carelessness, thought Percevale. Slipping his hands beneath his shoulders, he began to pull him upright. Mordred gave a cry of pain and rage.

"It hurts too much!" he shouted. "Don't you understand? Now go!" Percevale, weakened by the effort, lowered him gently. "No, wait," Mordred added in a fading voice. "There is something I must tell you first."

Percevale nodded. He placed his head close to Mordred's ear. The words were very faint now.

"Something very important . . ." His head dropped limply to one side and a thin trickle of saliva gathered at a corner of his open mouth and flowed slowly downward.

Percevale laid his head upon the cold stone and closed the glazed dead eyes. With a final backward glance he rose to his feet and staggered up the remaining few steps to the tunnel, now illumined by the reflection of the flames below.

I never did learn the poor fellow's name, he thought guiltily.

27

He stumbled until he reached the bottom of the shaft. No one followed. Then he began the slow, agonizing ascent.

It was a journey in which every movement seemed more painful than the last and none brought him any nearer his destination. Every foothold seemed to tear his wounds open a little more. It was not fear that drove him on. He had been quite prepared to meet death in the cavern and was sorely tempted to hasten its approach even now. The circle of daylight above him seemed so small; it would be so much easier simply to let go and fall into the insubstantial dark below his feet; so much less painful.

But he did not let go. Even when, at one point, his foothold gave way entirely and his legs were suddenly swinging through emptiness, he willed himself to hang on as if a great deal more than mere survival depended on it, heaving himself painfully up by arms alone until his frantically searching feet found and gripped a further niche in the crumbling stonework.

The circle of light, at last, began to loom larger, and eventually his hands clutched at grass and soft earth and he pulled himself, breathless and with tears of exhaustion, to the surface.

For a few moments he lay there, savoring the air and listening to the muffled roar that vibrated through the ground below.

But the longer he rested the more difficult it would be to rise and he could not stop yet. Reluctantly he got up and limped over to where the horses were tethered.

"Now then, Fleet," he said softly as he untied the destrier, "I must trust in your speed and in the good-will of the gods." An unusual invocation, as he was not by nature a religious person.

Taking the reins of the sumpter horse in one hand, he lifted himself carefully into the saddle.

They had only reached the edge of the clearing when the earth seemed to shift slightly. A series of loud cracks sounded from behind, and, turning, Percevale saw the forest slowly raise itself into the air. The massive gray trunks pulled themselves effortlessly from the ground, exposing their thick roots amid a cascade of noise and flying earth and rock. He had only a brief moment in which to wonder if this was indeed the work of the Druid's firepowder or whether the spirits of the wood also were combining in their own destruction before something hard and searing-hot propelled him from the saddle and into an oblivion that was almost welcome.

It was dark when he finally awoke. A bright moon silhouetted the broken trees around him and he saw, beneath one of them, the still, cold form of Fleet.

He raised himself. The pain was still there, and it was still considerable, but for the moment it was eclipsed by a great sense of loss. He had loved all his destriers, and of them all Fleet had been the bravest and the best. Only Grimalkin had held an equal place in his affections and that because he had previously belonged to Gawaine. His eyes moistened as he lightly stroked the cold mane and whispered a valedictory farewell.

"Good-bye, old friend. Your race are few in number now. I do not know where I may find your like again."

The packhorse had survived and, being a creature of limited imagination, had not strayed far. Percevale strolled carefully toward it, extending his hand and muttering soothing noises, and it came to him without protest or demur.

Of the clearing there was little to be seen save a deep indentation filled with rocks and loosened soil. He went closer in order to confirm that no clues remained as to what lay buried beneath. None did save an overpowering warmth that prompted him to step back quickly, sensing danger even while he could not identify its exact nature. He fancied too that he had seen a dull glow pulsing through the gloom but his senses were in a confused state and he could not be sure.

He removed all his baggage from the sumpter horse, his helm, his spare armor and weaponry, the accumulated flotsam of a lifetime's weary errantry, and hauled himself onto the creature's back. The horse stirred a little beneath the unfamiliar load, but its spirit had already been broken by the sights it had lately witnessed and it did not resist.

He took the reins and guided the horse gently through the trees. The pathway, he hoped, was somewhere nearby.

Of the days that followed he knew little. He knew that he should tend to his wounds, at least ascertain their seriousness. But he did not, and after a while they ceased to pain him. He was aware that he was following a rough track across open countryside but in which direction it was taking him he neither knew nor cared. Occasionally he stopped. When weariness assailed him, he would sleep for a while; when he was hungry, there were the cold remains of the poor hermit's cony, which had providentially found its way into one of his saddlebags. For the most part he left the reins slack, leaving the horse to follow its own inclination. He was in no great hurry.

Then one morning the animal stopped in its tracks. Percevale raised his head and saw in the distance in front of him the dust of an approaching column. They were far away still, but he did not think he could outrun them upon such a mount, even had he energy to try. A small group detached itself from the front of the column. No point in trying to run now, thought Percevale. He sat and waited for them.

A familiar figure rode at their head. Percevale felt very tired now. Nevertheless, there were forms to be observed. He pulled himself erect and drew his sword. The leading rider slowed his mount and pulled it to a halt a few feet in front of him.

"Nay, Sir Knight," said Sir Marhaus in a voice that was tinged with compassion and not a little admiration. "I'll not fight with thee, though I had wondered if our paths were destined to cross again. Put up your sword, please."

Thankfully, Percevale did so. Marhaus scrutinized him carefully. "I fear you are gravely wounded," he said at length.

"I'll manage," Percevale whispered hoarsely.

Marhaus thought otherwise, but he merely nodded.

"Where is your king?" asked Percevale.

"He is dead."

"Has there been another battle?"

"Nay, rest easy," replied Marhaus, seeing the look of faint alarm that crossed the knight's languishing features. "The only battle of late has been among ourselves, a quarrel between the king and one of his favorites."

"I see." Percevale sensed that the northerner wished to tell him more, but he was tired and in truth not greatly interested. "So where are you going?" he asked.

"Some of us are going home, some to the southeast."
Again he caught the look of concern on the knight's
face. "Nay, not to plunder but to fight. Perhaps you
have not heard?"

Percevale looked at him.

"A Roman army has landed," said Marhaus. "In Kent.
A great army, thousands of men. It is led by one of
their greatest generals, the one who defeated the
French so soundly a few years back. Now, it seems,
he is administering similar medicine to the southern
tribes."

Percevale was saddened at the news but not greatly
surprised. It was inevitable that the Latins should
one day seek revenge for their ancient humiliation.
The surprise was that they had not come sooner.
"They will prove tough adversaries," he said. "I do
not think they will be beaten this time."

"Nor I. Though they may, could we but avail ourselves of the Druid magic," said Marhaus. "That's
what the lads think anyway."

"They are right. The Latins could be destroyed by
the Druid magic."

Marhaus studied him thoughtfully for a moment.
"No," he decided, "killing an enemy is one thing, but
those weapons—they are not right. No, I do not agree
with the Druid magic. It is best that it should be
destroyed. It has been destroyed, has it?"

"Completely."

"All this talk of uniting tribes," said Marhaus, "making the land strong and whole—dangerous nonsense
really. It doesn't work." He shook his head dismissively.

"It did once," Percevale said.

"King Arthur, yes." A wistful look stole into his face.
"Great Albion we were then."

"That's right."

"The Scourge of the West, they called us." He
shrugged, shaking away the past. "But it did not last,
did it?"

"No," Percevale agreed, "it did not last."

"I do not think we are meant for nationhood," said Marhaus, fingers clawing absently through the forest of his beard. "It is a mold to which we are ill-suited. It isn't in our nature to get on well with our neighbors. There is too little land and too many people, that is the trouble."

"I suppose so," answered the knight, a little surprised that his erstwhile adversary should be given to robust philosophizing. I have always thought all barbarians were alike, he mused.

"Some of the lads are going to try their luck against the Romans. I do not know if they are fools or heroes, but I know they are not patriots. They are not going to defend their shores from the foreigner, they are going for a good fight."

"You are not going with them?"

"No. The rest of us are going home. Frankly, we've had enough. The plunder has been very poor this season and we want to see our families again. The way I see it, things are going to change mightily. Whether it will be for better or for worse I do not know, but this land will never be the same again. And you, what will you do?"

"I do not think I shall be fighting any Romans," Percevale answered weakly. "As far as I am concerned, they are welcome to this land. They can surely do no worse to it than our countrymen have done."

"So long as they leave folks like us alone, eh?" said Marhaus with a slightly forced joviality.

"That's right."

Marhaus turned briefly to the silent knot of riders who waited just out of earshot. Behind them the vanguard of the army was now clearly visible. A scattered array of garish pennants fluttered hopefully in the breeze. He lowered his voice. "Look, I should like to have some of those wounds seen to, but the lads might object. You are the enemy still, I suppose."

"I understand."

Then Marhaus leaned forward in his saddle and extended his right hand. The wound was quite healed now. "If we may not be entirely reconciled, at least let us part not as enemies."

Percevale took the hand.

"I should get off the road if I were you," Marhaus added as he turned to go. "Until we've passed, that is. My position among the men is not very strong, you understand?"

Percevale nodded and steered his ungainly mount off the rough track.

"Good fortune attend you," said Marhaus as they parted. Percevale raised a hand in brief acknowledgment. When he was almost beyond earshot, Marhaus called to him across the flat expanse: "Remember, Sir Knight. Things will not be the same again. Take what peace and happiness you can. Cherish it. I intend to."

And so they parted.

He was not followed. No one from that shrunken and demoralized army was interested in the sagging figure on his pathetic mount, and he rejoined the road farther on—or was it a different road? Toward dusk it brought him to the edge of another wood—or was it the same wood? He did not greatly care. He was dying and such things were of little consequence. He wished he could have seen the girl again, that was all. It did not matter who she was or where she came from. To his shame, he realized that now. It did not matter about Mordred. Love mattered more than all of these things, he believed now. It mattered more than life. Even more than honor. It was too late now, of course.

He had dreamed about her much of late, in his sleep and sometimes in his waking moments too. He was dreaming about her now as she emerged from the trees in front of him. As through a mist she came toward him, her pale face illuminated by the fleeting daubs of light that fell through the branches above.

I am really very lucky, he thought as he slumped exhausted over the horse's neck. So very lucky to have been vouchsafed this final, blessed illusion. There was a strange smile on his face as he slid gracelessly from the saddle. He did not hear Elaine as she cried out in pity and terror, nor did he feel anything when with outstretched arms she dashed forward, catching him as he fell and lowering him gently and with white-faced apprehension to the ground.

28

Elaine did not let him die. Mustering a strength she hardly knew she possessed, she half-carried, half-dragged his near-senseless body to the abandoned cowherd's hut she had found nearby. There, for several days and in a state of mounting apprehension, she nursed him and watched over him.

Her knowledge of the healing arts was scanty. This was a deficiency of her own making; her father had many times offered to teach her some of his skills, but she had not proved a willing or an attentive pupil. Now, as with anguished perplexity she struggled with the different salves and potions she had brought with her, she cursed those lost opportunities.

But care and common sense did in some measure compensate for her inexperience. She cleaned and bandaged his wounds, changing the dressings daily as she had observed her father do. She could do nothing about the ugly orange weals that so fearfully scarred and disfigured his back, but she did apply generous quantities of an ointment, and this seemed to help him sleep more comfortably.

The first two days proved the most critical. As his fever mounted he became increasingly delirious, uttering much that was to her incoherent. He sweated so profusely as to cause her to wonder where so much fluid came from.

Then, quite suddenly on the third day, the fever broke and he slept soundly for the first time since the flight from the cavern.

Elaine, too, exhausted by her ceaseless ministrations, allowed herself some few hours of rest.

When she awoke, splintered shafts of brilliant sunlight were lancing the many cracks in the roof and walls. When she saw Percevale, his face turned toward hers, the merest of smiles on his gaunt, ravaged features, she could barely restrain her joy.

Later he was able to sit up in bed and though his appetite was far from strong yet he suffered himself to be fed by her.

"We are on the edge of that same forest through which you first brought me," she informed him as she held another spoonful to his reluctant lips. "It seems so long ago now, doesn't it?"

As he smiled in agreement she thrust the spoon deftly into his mouth. "You may not think so now, but it is good for you," she said as he choked and swallowed the warm mixture.

"Are we far from your home?" His voice was thin and pitifully weak. Like an old man's, she thought.

"Not far."

"I thought I was going to die," he said.

Elaine thought of the troubled hours spent in lonely vigil and silent entreaty, clasping his wasted body close to hers and willing him to live. "So did I." She put the bowl down on the floor. "Many times."

"You have saved my life." With a contented sigh he lay back and almost immediately fell asleep.

She carefully rearranged his blanket, tucking it under his chin and over his shoulders. "You are worth the trouble," she murmured.

The next time he awoke, his condition was much

improved and they conversed longer. "I am feeling much better," he said. "You have done a good job on me." She laughed at that.

She did not question him about his absence, thinking that the subject might be a painful one for him. For his part, Percevale did not volunteer anything in case she might disapprove. All those deaths. He did tell her about Fleet, and she was greatly saddened, for she had loved the gentle destrier that had once so quietly borne them into this strange adventure.

Then he asked her how she had chanced upon the hut, for it was an isolated dwelling, set back from the road and screened by trees. She blushed before replying, as if she had feared such a question.

"It was Ralph who found it," she said guardedly, "Not I."

"I see." A silence followed. Then, as if resolved, she sat stiffly upright, her fine lips tightening.

"There is much that I have not told you about that sorry affair."

"There is no need." Percevale's voice betrayed his sudden anxiety. He did not want events now in the past to disturb his present repose. He feared the strength of his prejudices and did not want them aroused.

"That is kind of you," she said, "but others have no doubt given you their verdict on the matter. It is as well I gave you mine." She looked at him intently, dark eyes blazing with a now familiar determination. "I want to tell you," she added.

Wearily, Percevale assented.

She had not been in love with Ralph; she insisted on that. Nor had there been a planned elopement. One night she had overheard her parents arguing fiercely. Such rancor was a rare thing in her household and, unforgivably, she had eavesdropped. Tempers had broken and indiscretions were committed on both sides. It was a brief, if bitter, exchange, as these things generally are. At the end of it Elaine had returned to her bed stunned and incredulous and, she judged, amply repaid for her foolish curiosity. No names had been mentioned, but she had learned enough to realize that the man to whom she had paid her filial respects for so many years was not her father.

She was not, she happily admitted, morally offended by this. Rather, it was in a spirit of injured pride, a feeling that she had been unjustly and unnecessarily duped, that she approached her parents the following morning.

"I simply wanted to know who my real father was. Do you not think that was a reasonable request?"

"Of course." But not in this case, he thought.

"They would not tell me anything. Refused point-blank. That was very wrong of them, wasn't it?"

Again Percevale agreed while secretly he offered thanks for their obduracy.

"So you see now why I ran away."

Percevale did not fully. But he did not wish to seem deficient in understanding. He raised his head gravely.

"Out of spite really," she added helpfully.

"And the young man?"

"Poor Ralph, yes." She sighed. "He had his own reasons for wanting to leave. He was an ambitious boy. Father thought he had ideas above his station. I think his trouble was simply that he had more brains than most people gave him credit for but was still not as clever as he thought he was. Also he believed himself infatuated with me. I should not in honor have gone with him, but the world beyond the town was full of so many unknown dreads. I felt I needed a companion. We were not lovers."

"It does not matter." He was surprised to find himself voicing such a sentiment, but it was true. It did not matter.

"Oh, but it does," she insisted, "for it is the truth. There was nothing between us. Do you believe that?"

Percevale, astonished and not a little offended that such a question should be asked of him, looked at her sharply. "Of course I believe you," he replied.

They stayed in the hut for a fortnight altogether. Each day Percevale would exercise his slowly repairing body by taking short walks in the forest, sometimes with Elaine to support and accompany him, sometimes alone. At the end of this time she said to him, "I am sure my father can take better care of you than I can. If you are fit to ride."

Percevale had not yet fully recovered his strength. He was beginning to wonder if he ever would. "You are my doctor and my nurse," he said. "You must decide for me now."

And so they set off. Elaine upon the sprightly jennet she had taken from her father's stable and he upon the acquiescent sumpter horse, trailing at times yards behind her yet content enough to do so.

But when they returned to the town in the valley, her father was no longer there and the streets, when they entered them, had a changed and gloomy aspect. There should have been a market that day, but the roads and pathways were strangely unpeopled.

"I do not understand," Elaine said. "When I left, the place was swarming with Oliver's militia. I remember they kept asking people silly questions, even those they knew well."

They could tell the house was empty as soon as they pulled the horses to a halt outside. Most of the houses in the street had the same cold, untenanted look.

"But we should check just to make sure," Percevale said in reply to her look of dismay and disbelief.

The house had been thoroughly and efficiently stripped of all its possessions, though whether by the occupants or by others, there was no telling.

While waiting for her to finish her search of the upstairs rooms, Percevale found his attention drawn once more to the now bare patch of wall where the physician's tapestry had once hung. It had been a fine piece, and he regretted that he would not now be able to study its mysteries further.

Soft footsteps descended the stairs then and entered the room behind him. "There is nothing," she said, eyes brimming. "No clues, nothing. What would drive them away without leaving word?"

Perhaps the belief that you would no longer wish to join them now that you have established new loyalties and new priorities, Percevale thought, but he kept this to himself.

They tried the infirmary, but that, too, seemed at first deserted. The beds had been dismantled and taken away. In one of the rooms behind the main hall they found Gareth. He was seated at the mayor's desk, an untidy pile of papers before him. When they entered, he rose and greeted them with surprise and a genuine warmth.

"I had not thought to see you again," he said to Percevale.

"What have you heard then?" inquired the knight.

"That there was a great upheaval, that it devastated many miles. That the magic was destroyed." Eagerly, he added, "Was it?"

"It is buried. No one will find it and anyone who ventures near will surely die."

Gareth shrugged as if that would have to do.

"Where is my father?" Elaine asked him.

"I am sorry, I really don't know. They have all gone." He sat down again. "Save for myself and a few others, a hundred at most. They did not believe that you could save them a second time, Sir Knight. The mayor, he tried to negotiate with the enemy, but when their king learned of your mission, he became angry and would not bargain. So they left."

"They should have had more faith, Gareth. Like you," Elaine said.

"I? I stayed because I have a bedridden mother." He gestured to the laden desk. "Now, look at what has to be done." There was a note of peevishness as he added, "Why could you not have left us to mend matters ourselves? We could have done so."

"I acted for the best," Percevale replied, unmoved. "Your people should have stayed. A day or two at most, that is all that was required of them."

Gareth shrugged. His small outburst was quickly over. Gloomily, he said, "That may be, but what of those of us who are left? What are we to do?"

To this Percevale had no reply.

"Did my father leave a message?" Elaine asked again.

"Not with me, I'm sorry."

When he saw that Percevale would not be persuaded to stay, he invited him to take his pick of the few horses that remained. "It is the least I can do," he said without irony as he brushed aside the knight's proffered thanks. "It is because of your efforts that the mayor was persuaded to give me back my job."

"Poor Gareth," Elaine said later. "Do you know, that Oliver, before he fled, took with him some vital parts of the manuscript machine. They cannot get it to work now."

"It was his machine. They can have no use for it now."

"It was a spiteful and malicious act," she said, ignoring this. Turning to him, she added, "Do they have a chance—of keeping things going, I mean?"

He thought of the empty streets, the air of neglect which had so quickly taken hold of the once thriving community. "I fear not."

"Yet you would not stay to help?"

"My presence would not be long considered a welcome one," he said. This was probably true, though there were more pressing reasons. He felt a dutiful sympathy for the young man who with undisguised reluctance had taken up his arduous burden, but he could not stay. Where his destiny lay now he had little idea, but he was certain that it was no longer in such a place.

"Had it not been for you," she said quietly, "they might have stayed."

He was not surprised at her remark, but he was a little hurt. "You should not blame me that your people are infirm of purpose," he said. "I acted only in their best interests."

"I hope you will not always think like that." There was a quaver of petulance in her voice.

"Like what?"

"That you always know best. It will not bode well for our future together if you do."

He waited for her to elaborate, but she did not, and so their first quarrel ended in a protracted and sullen silence.

The town and the cultivated valley they had long left behind them. To their left was the edge of the forest, growing more sparse with every mile that passed. To their right and stretching far away was a trackless wilderness of yellow gorse and green shrubland, its heavy scents released by the hot July sun that burned overhead. Before them ran the long straight track, quite devoid of traffic, dipping and rising again in its progress across the silent landscape.

And somewhere beyond these diminishing hills lay the sea. It would be a long time yet before they would reach it or even sense its proximity. But already he could envision the place. And in perfect detail, though he had only been there once before. He could picture still the flanking gray buttresses of foam-lashed rock and between them the tiny sheltered cove where the water lapped smoothly over the small pebbles, grinding them unhurriedly in its gentle swirling motion.

There, on a day very like today, twenty years before, a boat had waited. Those who manned it waited
many days for their expected passenger. When he did
not arrive, the vessel slipped its moorings and sailed
away into the night while those on board quietly
grieved, mourning the passing of a great king and
bewailing the cruelty of the magic that had so violently superseded their own.

All this Percevale had learned much later, and
though he had then removed Arthur's shrouded body
from its makeshift tomb in the courtyard at Cadras,
and though he had waited many days on the shore
while the cold sea had played around them both, yet
the vessel had not returned. The faeries of Avalon
could heal the dying and cure the sick at heart, but
they could not raise the dead.

Elaine spoke again. "I am sorry they could find no
destrier for you."

"They are a rare breed. I did not expect to find one."

"But without a warhorse a knight is—"

"—obsolete. Quite. No matter. I have this fine palfrey. And"—he turned to the sumpter horse trudging
stolidly behind—"patient Griseld there." He smiled.
"And of course I have you."

It was, as she knew well enough, a forced cheerful-
ness on his part. But it was not the lack of a suitable
mount or his responsibility to her that caused him to
think as he did.

At first it had been merely a passing dread. The
thought, during those long, slow days when he had
lain abed or later, promenading through the woods
and resting gratefully on her arms, that he might
never fully recover. Then later, finding that the simple act of mounting a horse required great effort—
more still when others were around and the pain had
to be disguised—his suspicions had turned to certainty, and the sad realization finally dawned that he
would not be a knight again. Something had happened

to him during that terrible ordeal at the cavern. Something that had sapped forever a part of the strength and health he had expended on that day.

It was hard to accept, but accept it he must. They were the last of a kind, Fleet and he. Their passing was long overdue and would not be greatly mourned. The Latins were the future now. It would, he suspected, be a long time before they penetrated this far, perhaps a century or more, but come they eventually would, bringing with them a quite different civilization—stern, efficient, amoral. The Celts might resist at first, but superior organization would subdue them. In a little while they would even come to accept the Romans and their future—so full of promise. Then they would forget their own noble past or, worse still, turn it into fanciful legend. It was a heartbreaking thought. He could not bear that. With eyes that were almost moist he turned to her.

"I am glad you are with me."

She smiled and, reaching over, briefly squeezed his shoulder.

He knew he could not live in such a future, however distant. Was it that which had turned his thoughts to the little cove and the silent vessel that had long ago anchored there? Would it be there for him? To think that it might was doubtless an arrogant conceit. And yet that strange image had sprung unbidden to his thoughts and was even now directing his paces.

In his dreams he had gone aboard and been made welcome.

"What ails thee, Sir Knight?"

"A weariness assails my spirit, lady, and a dark brooding malignancy lies within me"—he pointed to the pit of his stomach—"here."

"Then come with us to a place where no such cares will rise to trouble thee."

She was so like Elaine, the lady who stood on the vessel's graceful prow. Yet clad in white samite of unbelievable purity and richness.

Were they dreams only or was it more? A final
demonstration, perhaps, of the dying magic of the
former time?

"Where are we going?" It was the first time Elaine
had asked him that question.

Would she come with him? Would they permit it?
She must. They must. He realized he was presuming
again.

"I would come with you anywhere." Her brow was
furrowed with concern. "I mean that."

"But there is your family—"

"They are lost to me and I to them."

"I cannot say for certain where we are going. Simply bear with me for a while." She nodded and for
several hours after they exchanged little in conversation, content merely to be in each other's company.
Then toward dusk, after they had ridden many miles
and the track had long disappeared, she again turned
to him. "There is something different in the air. Do
you notice it?"

Percevale did, and as he apprehended it, so his
spirits rose a little. He quickened his horse's pace and
Elaine, stifling her mounting curiosity, followed.

Farewell, Mordred, he thought. And wherever thou
art, rest in peace. Whatever waits for me, hope or
disappointment, my quest is surely ended and I will
trouble thee not.

"Look!"

Quickly, he wheeled. She had stopped and was
pointing skyward, where white shapes circled end-
lessly. From nowhere a wind had sprung, freshening
and invigorating their tired and travel-stained faces.

To Percevale the shrieks of the gulls sounded harsh
and mournful, yet they seemed to carry also a message of eventual release. To Elaine, who had never
before seen birds so large or so white, they were a
source of wonder. She felt now that they were nearing their destination and was a little fearful, for he

had told her so little and she had not pressed. But she also felt a certain calm, a readiness to accept whatever awaited them. She called to him to wait, but her words were scattered upon the wind. Eagerly, she dug her heels into the jennet's flanks and sped after him. Down the slope. To the sea.

EPILOGUE

My dear Cornelius,

Greetings from this far-flung and benighted corner of the empire. Also apologies. Your letter requesting further information was, like all recent dispatches to and from this corner of Britannia, delayed by yet another Catevullanian uprising—the natives in these parts seem to be forever restless!

However, this latest local difficulty partially resolved at last, I can now set quill to parchment and tell you as much as I know.

It is not much, my friend. Historians—real ones like yourself—are rather thin on the ground in our provincial backwater and the conjectures of a mere amateur like myself must seem of poor worth to the author of *The Germanicus*. However:

The skeleton in which you showed so much interest is that of a young male of some seventeen or eighteen, years, short of stature but unusually broad. He is not a typical native of the region. Indeed, the poor fellow is so badly deformed that in life he must have been a walking nightmare. The skull is asymmetrical and the spine cruelly twisted and bent. All this you can examine for yourself, for I am having the remains shipped to Rome as you requested—even the commander of a forgotten garrison town can exert some pull, you see!

Strangely enough, these remains are not the first of their kind to be discovered. My predecessor, before he left, spoke of once having chanced upon many such remains, all misshapen and all in the same general area. What he told me was vague in the extreme and the details were unhelpful. It seems that at some time in the past an extraordinary calamity occurred, though what agency, human or otherwise, could produce such hideous results, I am at a loss to understand.

I should dearly like to investigate the matter further, but, alas, I cannot. There is a Celtic legend attached to that whole region that seems to have affected even my hard-bitten legionaries. They will not venture near the place, and I dare not force them for fear of adding mutiny to my already considerable burden. To be honest, I can hardly blame them. The whole area is blighted and exudes an air of menace that is hard to define.

But there is some compensation. More interesting by far than the skeleton are the documents that were found on its person. They were written on crudely fashioned strips of parchment and appeared to be part of a larger manuscript. The author does not seem to have been terribly pleased with his handiwork. Whole pages have been violently scored through and even partially torn. I do not think that the creature we found was the author—for one thing, his hands were too badly deformed to even hold a pen, let alone write with one. My surmise is that the bones are those of an associate or perhaps even a thief who was attempting to bury or steal the documents when tragedy overcame him—perhaps once inside the hole where we found him, he found himself unable to climb out—he cannot have been a very agile fellow.

Nor is that all. A further search of the area re-

vealed the rest of the manuscript of which these
pages appear simply to be an inferior part. Though
not complete, it is nearly so and represents a real find
and if authentic—as I believe it is—contains conclusive proof that there once existed on this island a
civilization almost as sophisticated as our own!

For the most part the documents treat of a king—
Arthur—who ruled about a century before Claudius
landed. It is a name that seems to strike a faint chord
in my memory. Was there not an Arthur among the
enemies of the Republic? I should be grateful if you
could enlighten me on this point, for none of the
material I have studied, even your own excellent bi-
ography of your father-in-law, Agricola, in which you
treat in some detail of the early history of the Britons,
makes mention of such a figure. Certainly, the writer
of these documents makes several astonishing claims
concerning the achievements of his protagonist, which
do not accord well with the historical record as I
know it.

As for that smaller manuscript, those chapters which
our poor misshapen friend was found clutching in his
bony claws, this, too, is quite remarkable. Though it
is clearly in the same hand and deals with the same
period and subject matter, yet the style is markedly
different. I cannot help forming the impression that
the author, while clearly dissatisfied with this extract, could not find it in his heart to destroy it
completely and concealed it instead. Is it not puzzling
the lengths some writers will go to? But even this
corrupt manuscript makes fascinating reading and I
find myself deeply envious of the mind that fashioned such a work.

Anyway, my dear friend, all this you must judge
for yourself. The bulk of the manuscript, and to my
mind the most authentic part, I am sending to you,
together with this missive, by special courier. I have
every confidence that it will reach you safely, insur-

gent tribesmen and Mediterranean pirates notwith-
standing. In case it does not, I am retaining that
single chapter that is so strangely out of keeping with
the rest.

I await with interest your views on this singular
matter. It may be that some of our history may have
to be rewritten—how odd that these insignificant Britons should be the cause of that!

Regards,
Fabius